To Meg
From David

I went to a talk
by the author. I was
impressed by his passion
that the story of the
Haitian people

A Slippery Land

by
RICK CONTI

Copyright © 2016 by Rick Conti

Printing version 1.1

While many of the events in "A Slippery Land" were inspired by actual events witnessed by or related to the author, this book is a work of fiction. Most of the names used herein are the names of actual people the author knows or is acquainted with. While a few characters might resemble their namesakes in some manner, *most do not*. In particular, *none of the malicious characters herein resemble or were inspired in any way by anyone I know.*

DESIGN BY TAYLOR DUEKER
http://www.taylordueker.com/

For Jane

And for all the Fanias, Roses, and Granmès of Haiti:
May your future be as bright as your smiles.

Lavi se tè glise

"Life is a slippery land" - Haitian proverb

Chapter 1

January 12, 2010 – 4:45 PM

FANIA LIVED IN HELL.

Not that she was aware of it any more than the fish in nearby Baie de Port-au-Prince knew they lived in water. It was only to outside observers, none of whom Fania had ever met, that Haiti resembled a place of unending suffering and torment. They saw only crime, poverty, hunger, and homelessness in a recurring cycle of tumult. To them, it was an abyss of despair where nothing changed except the players in a tragic theater of misery.

To Fania, it was home.

Like those fish in the bay, however, Fania forever struggled against an irresistible tide that, with every step she took, pushed her back two. Even as she stood on the roof of her home, leaning toward the school that sat only a few dozen meters away and where most of her friends spent their days, she felt that tide's force.

Her dreams were simple for a fifteen-year-old girl. An education. Reading and writing. Humble dreams, more remote than the far off peaks of the Massif de la Selle that served as a backdrop to her neighborhood in the Village Solidarité section of Port-au-Prince. Just as she couldn't imagine climbing those forbidding hills, she couldn't conceive of being in a school, reading books, or writing letters.

This was the day when all that could change. The news her father carried would determine whether those mountains would be brought within her reach or, if his news was bad, she would continue to dream of distant peaks.

"Fania!"

Her mother's voice abruptly shook Fania from her musing and sent her scrabbling down the concrete walls of the house. Her unfinished chores held more urgency than her unfulfilled dreams.

* * *

Inside, anticipation hung like the fine particles of dust that filled the air. The family had long since grown accustomed to seeing the air they breathed; the constant presence of the dust made it disappear. When something is everywhere, it ceases to exist.

But apprehension, anticipation's malicious twin, followed like a rabid dog nipping at its heels. Good fortune never walked alone in Haiti. Hopeful elections carried with them violence and turmoil. A cool, refreshing rain inevitably brought streams of filth running through the tiny hovel that was the Dieusel family home. It had reached the point where they dreaded good news for the trouble it promised.

"Fania, stop daydreaming and finish cleaning those bowls." Although Roselyn was a patient and kindly person, she was often frustrated by her daughter's tendency to be distracted by the slightest thought. To Roselyn, this was such an occasion as Fania washed the same bowl for the fourth time.

"Sorry, *Manman*. When do you think Papa will be back?"

Roselyn went to her daughter and gently cupped the girl's face in her hands. "The time will go faster if you concentrate more on your chores, *cheri*." She punctuated her statement with a kiss on Fania's forehead, something she did often to bring her back to reality, as bleak as it might be.

To anyone who saw the pair together, it was obvious they were mother and daughter. As Fania's beauty was ages beyond her youth, so her mother's was not diminished by her 35 careworn years. When they strolled side by side along their rutted, muddy street with oversized burdens balanced securely

5

on their heads, men of every age, lounging by the road playing dominoes or listening to radios blaring hip-hop, would stare with pleasure and without shame. The grace and allure of the mother and child were in complete contrast to the drab surroundings of the slum where they lived.

Fania returned to scrubbing the few plastic bowls and cups they owned, along with the bent utensils and chipped plates that rounded out their entire collection of dinnerware. They were never completely clean, though, because the water itself had already been used to wash some of their clothing and was of uncertain origin to begin with. Clean enough had to be clean enough.

Once she finished with the washing, Fania splashed the dishwater into the street where it joined the neighborhood's waste and ran down the road, cutting an ever deeper furrow along its length.

She placed the cleaned items on the wobbly table that held most of the family's belongings and also served as dinner table and work space. The table sat in the center of their one room concrete house, only one step from each of its four walls, walls that were often flecked with seven or eight lizards flattened against the concrete to avoid detection.

The stained mattress that served as the family bed leaned against the wall during daylight hours. When it was needed, it swapped places with the table. The three plastic chairs they owned, one of which had no back, were stacked on top of the table.

A small book rested optimistically in the middle of the table. Fania picked it up, flipped through its pages, and stared at the letters. They meant nothing to her as a means of communication, but in them she saw cryptic clues that would lead her to a new beginning, a treasure map of sorts. As she perused the book, the already dim dwelling became suddenly darker. Fania wheeled around to see her father in the doorway, silhouetted by the bright Haitian sun.

"Papa!" She ran and squeezed him in excitement. He didn't return the embrace. His face revealed nothing.

"Enoch," her mother said, "don't keep us waiting."

Enoch's expression went instantly from empty to elated. "I got the job!"

His pronouncement set in motion a celebration that echoed off the concrete walls and invaded the surrounding homes. Roselyn shrieked, Fania danced and clapped, and Enoch kissed them both.

When they had all calmed down and Enoch had a chance to recover, he told them, "It's not much, just taking care of the school's security and doing some janitorial work, but it's a real job. And..." He looked at Fania who held her breath and looked as though she might burst. "...free tuition for family members!"

, Fania leapt higher than she thought possible. She could have floated there forever, levitated by nothing but joy. "When can I start?"

"After waiting all these years, you're in such a hurry, *ti moun?*" He knew his daughter didn't like being called a child, but he also knew nothing would dampen her spirits today.

"*Wi*, Papa! When?"

"Any time after I start. As soon as Monday; six days from now. The Christmas break ended yesterday, so classes have just begun for the semester. You'll have missed next to nothing."

Fania hugged her father once more. Roselyn enveloped them both in her arms. Enoch, usually the most restrained member of the family, nevertheless had tears filling his eyes as he said, "We need to celebrate." He separated himself from the others. "Fania, go to the bakery and buy a loaf of bread."

Fania and her mother exchanged glances of amazement. Roselyn's expression contained traces of worry as well. "Are you sure? Can we afford it?"

"We can now," he responded with a confidence in his voice his wife hadn't heard for many years. Enoch retrieved a small rusty can from behind a handmade straw broom that leaned against the wall. (Against all odds, Roselyn kept her home as tidy as was possible in Haiti.) He overturned the can and several coins tumbled into his open palm. "Take this to the baker. Get a fresh loaf, baked today."

He handed the coins to Fania who gawked at them as if they were solid gold rather than brass-plated steel, tarnished almost beyond recognition. Only the size and shape distinguished one from another.

"After today, everything changes for you, *ti moun*."

"I'm not a child anymore, Papa."

"You will always be my *ti moun*, Fania." He looked into

her eyes and kissed her cheek.

"You heard your father, girl, get going." Roselyn picked up the broom and, wearing a broad smile, swatted Fania on the bottom.

"*Dakò!*" she complied as she charged into the street. With a dexterity that came from years of practice, she navigated the boulders, trash, and pools of filth that filled the roadway. In her preoccupation, she missed the cheerful greetings of her friends as well as the bothersome catcalls of admiring men.

She arrived at the bakery panting for breath. Except for the large gap in the front wall through which the baked goods were dispensed, the bakery was indistinguishable from most of the other buildings on the street. Fania couldn't read the word "*boulanjri*" written above the opening, but she had no problem recognizing the crudely painted pictures of bread, rolls, and pastries that decorated the wall around it. There were, in fact, no pastries for sale—simple loaves of white bread were about the only things ever available there—but the old woman who owned the place thought the drawings would attract customers. They also made her feel better about her otherwise shabby shop.

The owner was at the window as she always was, vainly trying to drive flies away from her wares. The few loaves outnumbered the woman's teeth. Her permanently affixed squint made her look a bit frightening to the young girl, but Fania's resolve was unshaken.

With her breath still labored, Fania told the woman, "One freshly baked loaf of bread, *souple*."

Her polite request didn't impress the old baker. "Fresh?" the woman protested, her eyes almost growing round at the affront, "Do you think I sell anything else?"

"Sorry. My father insisted."

"You tell your father my bread is always fresh." With a hand scalded many times over from her baking, she swatted a fly that had alighted on one of her loaves. "Do you have money?"

Fania displayed her coins with pride. The woman opened one of her eyes fully to inspect the cash. The lack of a squint did nothing to enhance her appearance in Fania's estimation. At last, the woman took one scrawny loaf and held it out through the window.

Before Fania could complain about the size of the loaf, the entire building before her began to shake. She realized she was shaking as well. The roof of the bakery fell on the old woman, leaving her extended hand reaching from the wreckage, still clutching the bread for a brief moment before it was loosed from her lifeless grip and tumbled to Fania's feet, frozen where they stood.

Fania staggered as she watched her entire world disintegrate before her eyes. Her mind was unable to process the unprecedented sights. Sturdy looking houses collapsed on themselves, their concrete walls snapping like dried bread. Violent cracks were followed by the thuds of falling slabs and the sound of stone grinding against stone, which forever after was the sound Fania identified with the poverty in which she lived.

The low rumble of the quaking earth filled her ears, weirdly offsetting the high-pitched screams of the men, women, and children who ran panicking in the streets.

One of the starving street dogs that had been scampering around the bakery hoping for castoffs trembled so violently it looked as if he might shake off the ragged skin that hung loosely from his skeletal frame. Bewildered, he wanted to escape, but his feet, like Fania's, felt rooted in the ground.

A square cast iron window grate thrown from the second story of a fallen building rolled down the street like a confused wheel.

Huge clouds of cement dust billowed to the sky creating a choking fog as more buildings toppled and disappeared. Fania began to gag as the haze enshrouded her.

The whole event lasted less than a minute, but while it happened, Fania's entire being was consumed with trying to remain upright. She was momentarily unsure of where, when, or who she was.

After the earth stopped shaking, she continued to do so for several seconds. Even then she was transfixed, unable to comprehend the catastrophe she'd experienced. Her soul seemed to have temporarily abandoned her to seek safety elsewhere, forcing her to await its return before she could resume her existence.

When her senses returned, she took in her surroundings. Her village was gone. In its place was a wasteland of shattered buildings and people. The few structures that weren't completely destroyed appeared to have frozen during a process she feared could resume at any moment. The one power line that served a few dwellings on the street lay on the ground like a serpent spitting sparks from its forked tongue.

The old woman's hand reached out to her from the ruin of the bakery. The loaf of bread still sat at Fania's feet. A loaf of bread to celebrate.

"*Manman*! Papa!", she screamed as she flew back down the street.

It was without thinking and barely looking that she found her way back home. Her mind was in as much upheaval as the earth had been seconds ago. It would have been no use going by landmarks; most of them were gone, the rest unrecognizable. Her life had been without significant change for the past fifteen years. How could her entire world have altered in a few seconds?

When she stopped, she found herself before a pile of rubble where her house should have been. She was more confused than frightened or distressed. *How can this be?* she thought. *How could anything destroy the joy this day had promised?* Nothing made sense. The image of her parents, still jubilant from her father's news, was etched in her mind.

Reality returned to her as suddenly as the quake had hit. Although she had been outside when the shaking began, the catastrophe hit her with such violence, she might as well have been in one of the fallen buildings. The roof of her life had collapsed on her, crushing her, even as the foundation disappeared from beneath her feet.

She leapt on the concrete heap. Tossing aside one piece of rock after another, she wailed continuously. "*Manman*! Papa!" Tears flowed from her eyes. Blood oozed from the cuts and scrapes emerging on her hands and knees, but she didn't notice. Everything disappeared from her mind and senses except her need to find her parents.

In her hysteria, Fania lost her balance and tumbled off the pile. She lay on the ground next to a massive slab that was no longer identifiable as part of her home. Her body heaved with silent sobs. She pressed her hands to her eyes, unconsciously hoping she could keep her tears in and reality out. She tried to force herself to believe her first sight upon uncovering her eyes would be an intact world where a loaf of bread was held out to her and her parents awaited her arrival to begin a celebration.

When she finally dredged up the courage to look, no such sight greeted her. Instead, the first thing she saw was half of her father's bloodied, lifeless face. Its expression looked like one of disappointment that she had taken too long to return from her errand.

She knew it didn't matter, but Fania felt compelled to release her father from his concrete tomb. She tugged on the slab that had crushed him until her muscles screamed as loudly as her cries of grief. Nothing moved.

Chapter 2

"SHOES SHINED, five *gourdes*. Get your shoes shined for church."

No one in the poor neighborhood of Cité Militaire needed a watch or a clock, even if they could afford one. The call of the elderly shoeshine as he hobbled down the alley ringing his tinny bell informed everyone the day had begun. The crowing of the roosters was no help; they squawked all night long.

The shoeshine's rounds brought him by the Victory Orphanage, its walls adorned with brightly (if clumsily) painted images of angels, butterflies, and rainbows. Surrounded as it was by the same makeshift tents that had populated the area in the year since the earthquake, the perky figures never ceased to bewilder the shoeshine. They did no more to cheer the families in the tents than they did to improve the lives of the children living behind the walls.

The old man didn't expect to conduct any business there. The children's shoes were cleaned by the caregivers who served them. The caregivers didn't make enough money to pay to have their shoes shined. Occasionally, teams of Americans would visit the orphanage, doing their good deeds to ease the guilt they felt about their affluence. They always had many shoes and paid well. There was no team at the facility, so the shoeshine moved on, ringing his bell and pitching his services. Other than from the chickens who scattered from his path, he attracted little attention.

An imposing wall, topped with razor wire and embedded shards of glass, surrounded the orphanage compound. It was never clear, neither to those who passed by nor to the children who called the place home, whether the barricade was intended to keep trespassers out or residents in.

Inside the fortified structure, the sounds of an approaching storm built to a deafening peak. The feet of running children slapping against the tile floors competed with the enthusiastic trill of their voices moving like cascading water through the halls. The commotion filled every corridor, room, and crack in the walls, some left unpatched since the earthquake. Thirty-five girls and boys of all ages streamed into the dining area and grabbed their customary seats at an expansive table, from the adolescents at one end, to toddlers at the other. A few of the oldest girls cradled infants too young to sit on their own.

Once they had all settled in, one seat remained empty.

The children waited patiently as two older women placed before them bowls of the traditional Sunday breakfast of squash soup. Some of them didn't care for the spicy concoction, but none turned it down. Most were from homes where they prayed for daily bread but were never certain those prayers would be answered. They took nothing for granted.

Given the squalor in which they lived, the happiness spread liberally across all the children's faces was totally unexpected. A more likely reaction to such need and loss would be bitterness and spite. The little ones didn't understand that equation, but the slack was more than taken up by the headmistress of Victory Orphanage, a prematurely grizzled woman named Nadine Veilleux.

Nadine wasn't content with being miserable herself, she felt the need to spread her particular brand of gloom to everyone in her vicinity. She lorded over her staff without mercy. The children too were objects of her wrath and excessive discipline. Their resilience and mutual support kept them afloat.

"Quiet, children. You'll be late for church if you don't hurry up," Nadine barked. They all fell silent under her grim gaze. She surveyed the room, her fists clenched and her eyes growing wider each second. "Where... is... Fania?" She forced the words out from her throat one at a time as if each were a laborious birth.

A nervous charge shot through the dining area. Being late for meals was one of the worst transgressions against Nadine's routine. The children all feared for Fania, Nadine's primary object of derision on any given day. A sin such as this would unleash her fury with more venom than usual. She tapped her foot on the tile floor. The sound echoed ominously through the room.

Summoning up all his courage, a boy of about ten, who wore a T-shirt advertising a yacht club on Long Island, spoke up.

"We haven't seen her all morning."

A subdued murmur of agreement spread over the length of the table.

"She was still in her bed when I left the room," chimed in a petite girl in a blue denim jumper embroidered with a bright red apple, many of its stitches undone. The jumper showed the excessive wear it had endured as it was passed down along a chain of seven different girls in America until it reached the point of deterioration at which it could be freely discarded. Haiti was the final destination for many such castoffs.

"We'll see about that," Nadine said as she grabbed the discipline rod that hung on the dining room wall. It was conspicuously displayed there so every child could see what fate awaited them for the slightest act of noncompliance. It was a branch from a prickly bush. Most of the thorns had been removed, but it was jagged enough to inflict severe pain and leave a nasty mark.

Before storming up the crooked concrete stairway that led to the dormitory style bedrooms, Nadine stopped and screeched back over her shoulder. "Carlene, say grace. You have two minutes to finish breakfast and be ready for church."

The children looked at each other, dreading the horrible fate that awaited their favorite resident of the home.

Fania was oblivious to the approaching peril. She rolled back and forth in her creaking cot, sweating and nauseated. The thought of being the next victim of Haiti's horrific cholera epidemic was in the back of her mind, but she knew the real cause of her affliction. In some ways, it was worse than cholera.

The spacious room in which she writhed contained wall-to-wall cots exactly like hers, but all the rest were empty with sheets tucked tidily in. There were no other furnishings. At one end was a doorway (but no door) that led to a hall. At the other, a sheet hanging from a tension rod separated the sleeping area from the bathroom. To spare the inadequate septic system, the toilet had the unwritten restriction of being flushed only for "substantial" reasons. As such, the entire bedroom usually reeked of urine.

Even in her feeble state, Fania's beauty was unaffected and unmistakable. Sickness could do nothing to disguise her haunting dark eyes, perfectly sculpted face, or delicate lips. Somehow, she had become even more radiant since arriving at the orphanage a year before, as if in death her mother had bequeathed her loveliness to enhance her daughter's.

Groaning softly in her bed, she was still agitated by the recurring nightmare that visited her again the previous night. In the vivid dream, she always stood in the middle of a dirt road holding a loaf of bread. Vehicles sped down the road toward her, swerving at the last second, barely missing her on either side. Her mother and father came running to help her, but her feet were sunk, immovable, in the muck that made up the roadway.

Before her parents could reach her, cinder blocks started to rain down on them from the sky. They tried desperately to avoid the blocks, but they were always struck and knocked to the ground, crushed. The blocks fell until Fania could no longer see her parents.

Then the blocks fell over Fania. She was afraid because she couldn't move to avoid them. Instead of falling on her, they fell in a circle around her, piling up until she was enclosed on all sides by a circular wall of blocks, reaching as far as she could see. Once they climbed to the vanishing point, the wall began to shake violently. She always awoke just as the walls were about to collapse on her.

Frightened, exhausted, and queasy, she stayed in bed hoping the sickness and the memories would release her or at least loosen their grip. They didn't. Another nightmare was on its way.

At first, the sick girl didn't see Nadine standing by her bed. It wasn't until the indignant woman did her signature toe-tap that Fania became aware of her presence. She didn't even bother to turn. She knew what to expect next, but she was too ill to care.

Nadine gave her one swift, solid lash with the rod across the thigh, leaving a distinct red mark with the ironic shape of a smile just above the girl's knee. Fania winced in pain. "What do you think you're doing? Am I supposed to control all those little beasts on my own?"

Fania rolled to face her. The cot squeaked a complaint. "I'm sorry, *Madanm*. I'm not feeling well this morning."

"Not well? Ha! Do you think I feel well this morning?"

Fania struggled to get upright, a hard enough process on that flimsy platform even when she was healthy. "I wouldn't know, *Madanm*, but..."

Nadine had no interest in what Fania knew or how she felt. She hung over the girl, her eyes ignited with spite.

"You think you're so special, don't you? You aren't, you know. You're just another wretched orphan beyond adoption age. No one wanted you before and no one wants you now. Pastor can put you out any time he wants now that you're sixteen. I'm surprised he let you stay this long."

"I'm sure he has his reasons," was the girl's troubled reply, infected with a hint of resentment. It was half counterattack, half surrender.

Nadine answered first with the rod, turning the previous smile-wound into a grimace. She followed up with the angry retort, "Don't talk back to me. If the children are late for church, it will be your fault. Pastor will give you another whipping and I want to be there to see it. Now, get going!"

Fania knew it was impossible to be late for church. The services started at whatever time all the preparations were finished, usually an hour or so after people arrived. She had no desire, however, to be subjected to any more of Nadine's or the Pastor's discipline. She rose uneasily to her feet and made her way to the bathroom, steadying herself against the wall all the way.

Downstairs, the children were finishing up their breakfast, dutifully returning their empty bowls to the kitchen where the plump, cheerful cook, Melande, greeted them each by name. Although she tried, Melande couldn't offset the toxic atmosphere Nadine created.

Eventually, one child was left at the table. Six-year-old Marie-Fleur, with her bulging eyes and crooked teeth, was not what anyone would consider a pretty girl. While most of the children at Victory Orphanage looked sufficiently robust, for Haitian children anyway, Marie-Fleur never appeared to be entirely healthy. That unfortunate tendency was accentuated further on this morning by tears and reddened eyes.

Those eyes were currently engaged in monitoring the stairway, anxiously waiting for Fania to appear. Fania was her best friend and honorary sister in the orphanage. She was also the only person who could tolerate the little girl's painful stutter. After all others gave up and walked away in frustration whenever the little girl tried to finish the simplest sentence, Fania never wavered in her attention. With her patience, Fania had earned Marie-Fleur's undying love and loyalty. The frail child would not give up on her friend and ally now. She doubted Nadine would actually kill one of the children, but the possibility was not beyond her imagination.

When Fania's polished white shoes appeared on the top step, Marie-Fleur leapt to her feet and met her before she could reach the bottom. She clung to Fania as if the older girl would fly away had she not anchored her there.

"I s-s-saved s-s-some s-s-soup for you, F-f-fania." She pointed back to the single bowl left on the otherwise cleared table. Marie-Fleur had sacrificed her own breakfast. The void she felt in her stomach was nothing compared to the void she felt whenever her *gwo sè* was absent.

"*Mèsi*, Marie-Fleur, but I don't think I'll have time for it this morning. I'm so late."

"H-how are you f-f-feeling?"

"I'm okay. You'd better move along or you'll be in trouble with Nadine, too."

Both girls giggled until Nadine and her incessant scowl darkened the kitchen door. When Melande imitated her expression behind her back, the girls tried but failed to suppress another fit of snickers. When Nadine turned to see what they were laughing at, they took advantage of the distraction and disappeared outside.

Shuttling the kids to and from Victory Baptist Church was Ben's favorite job. Still in his teens, he fancied himself prematurely sophisticated. He could do without the noisy and overactive little ones; they made him nervous, sometimes angry. It was a small price to pay, however, to be near Fania.

He sat in his *tap-tap* with its engine idling loudly, backfiring from time to time, shocking the chickens. Sometimes they fluttered their feathers so violently they became airborne, which shocked them even further. The *tap-tap* was nothing more than a long bed pickup with a multicolored cap but Ben was justifiably proud to have it at his command. The man he drove for let him take it every Sunday because it was the only one he owned that could hold all thirty-six residents of the orphanage.

Some of the slogans and images painted on the *tap-tap's* cap were appropriate for the church: "*Mèsi Jezi*" was emblazoned on one side. Others were less suitable: "I feel so good" was across the windshield. There was a crucifix somewhere in the mix, but it was lost in a jumble of *futbols*, Nike Swooshes, and other icons of American and Haitian culture. The color scheme defied description.

When Ben heard the children's voices, he checked his appearance in his rearview mirror. The harder job was adjusting his personality to something he thought would appeal to the girl he dreamed about all week, waiting, counting the days until Sunday. She had rebuffed his attempts at charm, ridiculed his gangsta styling, and rejected his romantic advances. She might go for a religious pose, but he couldn't even fake that.

The kids fairly flew from the front steps of the orphanage, through the gate, and into the back of the *tap-tap*, shepherded by

Fania whose hand Marie-Fleur clenched. As the pair headed for the back of the vehicle with the others, Ben hopped out and bowed to Fania, blocking her way.

"*Bonjou, Madmwazèl* Fania," he said. "Your limousine awaits."

The smile that came to Fania's face was half sincere, half mocking. "Some limousine," she said as she stepped toward the bed of the taxi.

Ben took her free hand and looked in her eyes. "You'll be more comfortable in front with me, Fania. So will I."

"I need to be with the children, Ben." Fania tried to dismiss him with as little cruelty as possible.

Ben was undeterred. "Don't you get tired of being with little children? Wouldn't you rather be with a grown man?" He ran his finger across his wisp of a mustache to draw her attention to the one feature he felt validated his manhood.

"Certainly," she replied. "Do you know where I can find one?"

Stung, the humbled driver slunk back to his seat, already considering plans for his next encounter with the beauty.

The entire bumpy ride to the church was filled with the non-stop clamor of children singing, laughing, and shouting, accompanied by no shortage of good-natured jostling. Fania was a willing participant in these antics, but she became somber at the same point in the ride every week. It had become such a fixture in their routine, the rest of the group hushed along with her. She looked down the road that led to where her family's home had been. It was still a graveyard of leveled homes.

"I w-w-wish I knew your *m-m-manman* and p-p-p...", she stopped to calm herself, "papa, Fania. D-d-do you think th-they would have l-l-l-l..." Struggling once more, Marie-Fleur paused and took a deep breath as Fania, who knew exactly what the girl was trying to say, waited patiently. "...liked m-me?"

Gazing at the girl through moistened eyes, Fania answered, "They would have loved you, *ti sè*." Although neither girl would ever have a sister, their shared experiences made them as close as siblings. Both knew what it meant to be lonely. A gentle hug followed Fania's fond assurance, "Just like I do."

The rumpus in the back of the *tap-tap* continued until they reached the massive iron gate of the church. Chalked scrawls indicating support for political candidates from elections going back more than a decade covered its surface. It was always kept closed until an authorized vehicle needed to enter the courtyard outside the church. The congregation entered through a smaller adjacent doorway. Ben gave a couple of blasts of the truck's horn and an armed guard appeared. He and Ben saluted one another and, with tremendous effort, the guard edged open the gate barely wide enough for the truck to squeeze through.

The way the children bounded from the truck's bed, one might have thought it had suddenly become scalding hot. From there, they formed a nearly solid line that snaked up the stairs to the giant sanctuary on the second floor of the impressive complex.

Inside the main hall, dozens of rows of crude wooden benches wobbled in uneven rows from the raised pulpit in front, receding into the shadows at the far end of the church's expanse. Gaping holes in the walls allowed what little air that moved to pass languidly through the space, giving the seven hundred or so attendees precious little relief from the blistering heat.

A corrugated metal roof more than twenty meters above the floor trapped the medley of sounds that bounced around the concrete shell: feedback from the sound system as it was tested, musical instruments being tuned, and the constant rumble of hundreds of conversations going on simultaneously.

Every man in the hall was dressed impeccably. Bleached and starched white shirts, perfectly pressed dark suits, appropriately pious ties, and black shoes polished until they gave off a glow of their own. (The shoeshine did well this morning.)

As if to compensate for the conservative attire of the men, the ladies wore dresses of every design and hue imaginable. Gathered together, they resembled the heaps of sweet, multicolored *bonbons* women often hawked from wooden boxes on the street outside the church. The styles of the dresses varied as widely as the shapes of the women themselves.

Head coverings were common among the women, especially the older ones, and ranged from simple scraps of white cloth to hats so elaborate they only maintained their precarious perches because of the many years those ladies spent balancing countless equally ungainly, though far more practical, burdens on their heads.

When the children entered the sanctuary, most of the adults watched their parade with elevated hearts. In those innocents—their bright faces, easy laughs, and smiling eyes—they saw the future of their church and their country. It brought them hope. They also saw their own pasts, which brought a heaviness approaching despair. They couldn't reconcile the two. It tainted even their worship.

Each week, the front row was reserved for the residents of Victory Orphanage. They settled in, girls at one end, boys at the other. Marie-Fleur, of course, was snuggled tightly against Fania. In their prominent location, the harder the children tried to behave—and they tried with all their strength—the greater the chance of calamity. Tripping and slipping, hiccups and burps were so common in church they might as well have been part of the liturgy. No one in the congregation was even mildly troubled by their conduct. More often, it incited suppressed laughter and solace lacking in any other area of their lives.

The atmosphere changed immediately and dramatically upon the solemn entrance of the church leadership. Six gray- and no-haired elders walked to six of the seven chairs that ran along the back of the platform where the pulpit stood. They were followed by two huge men whose sole purpose was intimidation. Those two took their places at the front corners of the platform and crossed their arms. One had a jagged scar that ran from his ear to his neck. It inspired nightmares in the children who saw it each week.

A long pause and a reverent silence preceded the entrance of Pastor Eli. The imperious aura he cast about the sanctuary and over its occupants had nothing to do with his physical appearance. Slightly chubby, he was shorter than anyone with him at the front of the church and, indeed, most of the adults (and a few of the children) in the entire room. Neither his receding hairline nor his narrow glasses, which looked to have been designed to bestow a perpetual glower on their wearer, contributed to his mystique. It was there nonetheless. It couldn't have been more tangible if it lived and breathed on its own. He cherished and cultivated it.

He settled into a chair that resembled a great throne, inadvertently emphasizing his lack of stature. Sitting in the middle of the line of taller elders with his toes brushing the platform, he could have passed for a child.

Yet he still exuded power and dominance, so much so it was a wonder there was any room for God in the place. The distinction was lost on some of his flock.

More than any of the others in the room, the children from the orphanage were in awe of him. They knew he was the master of each of their fates because he owned and operated their home. Although they rarely interacted with him personally, Nadine represented him as his dogged enforcer. She was as close as they wanted to get to him. On Eli's appearance, Marie-Fleur pulled herself even closer to Fania, so close she felt the shiver that shook Fania's body.

The 7:00 AM service began promptly at 7:45, give or take

half an hour. (The second service would be delayed by more than an hour, as it usually was.) It followed the same order of service every week: Several songs were sung by the congregation, then a procession of singing groups tramped across the front of the church. They varied widely in age, appearance, and quality, but their enthusiasm was uniformly extravagant.

After a half hour prayer by the eldest elder, the portion of the service that tested the endurance of the children more than any other, Pastor Eli stepped to the lectern. His face was stern. It was always stern, but today it bordered on grave. The congregation felt oppressed by it. They feared they were in for a sermon that would shake them as they hadn't been shaken since the previous year's earthquake that forever undermined their lives.

His opening prayer was the dark cloud that foretold the storm to come.

"Lord, we have gathered in thy presence to hear thy voice. Fill me with thy Holy Spirit, that I may speak unto my sheep with prophetic authority. Let them be warned of the consequences of transgressing thy commands. Amen and amen."

Opening his eyes, he scanned the crowd like a buyer appraising cattle for slaughter.

"The Psalmist says 'Search me, O God, and know my heart: try me, and know my thoughts: And see if there be any wicked way in me.' He's talking about sin, brothers and sisters."

The congregation responded with a chorus of, "Amen."

"God hates sin."

"Amen."

"He cannot abide its presence."

"Amen"

"Neither should His people."

"Amen! Amen!" A few stood at this, hands raised, palms upheld.

As he often did when he was caught up in the spirit and wanted his people to be as well, Eli removed his jacket, descended from his lofty position, and approached his audience. Sweat drenched his shirt.

"All have sinned and fall short of the glory of God," he ranted. He pointed randomly at people in the church as he said, "You have sinned, you have sinned, and you have sinned." The accusations didn't diminish the responses of approval. "Man is conceived in sin." More amen's. "Sometimes he is conceived *by* sin." Amen. "I'm talking about fornication."

With that, the amen's were fewer and less fervent. Some of the parents glanced nervously at their children, who squirmed more than usual. A few teens perked up for the first time in months. Eli was not moved by any of their reactions. He had a message and it would be heard.

"We need to follow the example of the Psalmist. Wickedness must be exposed and rooted out, no matter where it is."

"Amen!" His followers were once again caught up in his zeal.

Here he walked up to the seats where his young charges sat and placed his open hand on the head of a three-year-old girl whose hair hung in braids decorated with beads of a dozen different colors. The little girl flinched at his touch.

"And where is sin more dangerous than in the midst of the least of these? Jesus loves the little children and he wants to protect them from sin."

"Amen." The people all adored the children, so their response was exceptionally heartfelt.

"Jesus says 'It were better for him that a millstone were hanged about his neck, and he cast into the sea, than that he should offend one of these little ones.'"

"Amen!"

"Woe to the one who would cause one of these little ones to stumble."

"Amen!"

"Woe to you, Fania Dieusel!"

Silence. Only a few street sounds and the trailing echo of Eli's words remained in the congregation's ears.

His pudgy finger singled Fania out of the line of children. Their backs stiffened as one before they all turned to gawk at her. Fania trembled so violently her mind flashed back to the quake that took away her parents.

The entire congregation went silent. Some wanted to withdraw the amen's they had so willingly volunteered mere seconds ago. They looked at Eli. They looked at the petrified children. They bore their eyes into Fania.

"Stand, sinner," he barked at Fania. She obeyed mechanically. "Girl, can you deny that you are with child?"

"*W-wi*... I mean no, I didn't... but how can you..." Even if she were able to utter a meaningful response, Eli was not about to relinquish control.

"We need hear no more. Your own lips declare your guilt. You have sinned and set an evil example for the other orphans. You are expelled from the orphanage and this fellowship immediately."

Under the spell of Eli's accusing gaze, Fania hadn't noticed the two monstrous men from the front of the church who had sidled up to her. They were so close, each of her shoulders rubbed up against them.

With Eli's pronouncement, the two men seized Fania by the arms. They lifted her, frozen in fear, off the ground.

Outside in the courtyard with the people who were either late for the first service or early for the second, Ben had heard every word of the sermon. His hands gripped the wheel of his *tap-tap* with a tension he'd never felt before. All at once he felt anger, pity, love, frustration, compassion, and resentment. But he wasn't sure who many of those feelings were targeted at.

A gap opened up in the mass of people gathered at the bottom of the stairs descending from the sanctuary. Fania appeared, driven along by two men who, had it not been for their formal clothes, could have been taken for the gang leaders who maintained a reign of violence in many of the Haitian slums. The resemblance was not a coincidence.

Fania broke free of their grasp and rushed to Ben. She leaned into the *tap-tap* window. "Help me, Ben. It's not how it sounds. I didn't..." Her plea was cut off as she was yanked away by the man with the scar. Ben moved to get out of his truck to assist her, but the other man shoved his door closed, pushing Ben back, slamming his head against the opposite door.

Fania was thrust through the gate and into the street where she fell to her knees, crying. She looked up at the church to see Marie-Fleur leaning out of an opening high up in the wall, wailing and calling out. "F-f-f-f-" Before she could even get the name out, a hand pulled her back into the building.

In a fog of pain and anguish so real she was blinded by it, Fania tore down the road away from the church.

Chapter 3

BY THE TIME she collapsed at the base of the wall, Fania's tears had long since dried up, leaving tracks on her face like the bare riverbeds that scarred the Haitian countryside during a typical summer drought. Leaning against the wall, she sat on a patch of dirt facing a bay that led to an ocean she knew was pristine and beautiful somewhere far beyond her pain. The thought came to her that if she threw herself into the water, her body might eventually wash up on a distant shore that was not filled with filth, where fish swam rather than floated lifeless in the scum that coated the surface. One way or another, all her problems would be behind her.

* * *

After she was chased from Victory Baptist Church, Fania wandered the streets in search of a friendly face. There were none to be found. Many of the people she had known were killed in the earthquake along with her parents. Others had fled Port-au-Prince for the countryside. Those who were still in the area had somehow already heard about her plight and wouldn't even meet her pleading gaze.

"I have children of my own," one of her mother's old friends informed her. "I can't even feed them. How would I care for you and your little mistake? Why would I?"

Out of desperation, she had even gone back to the orphanage. When Nadine met her at the compound gate, blocking her way, Fania couldn't remember seeing her so cheerful. In fact, she had never seen the woman smile. It took the misfortune of others, especially Fania, to dislodge the scowl from her face.

"What do you expect me to say, princess?" She put on her best sarcastic tone, one she exercised often. "I'm so sorry for you, my child. It's a shame that such a terrible thing should happen to such a sweet girl." At that, she broke into a laugh so bitter, the shriveled dogs that picked the street for scraps yelped and skittered away.

"I have nowhere else to go," Fania begged.

"You'll have to think of something. The Pastor sent word that you are not to be allowed back in here."

"What about my things?"

Another cackle. "What things? You came here with nothing and you leave with nothing. You're lucky I let you keep the clothes you're wearing." She lowered her voice to a threatening growl. "Go away, whore."

She disappeared, slamming the gate in Fania's tear-streaked face, leaving her stunned and enraged. In hopeless frustration, Fania slammed her fists against the iron barrier and screamed, "Witch! I hate you! Everyone hates you!" The painful truth of her condemnation didn't reach Nadine's ears. Nor did the expressions of anger stay the girl's tears. They streamed all the way down to her shoes, badly scuffed from roaming the harsh streets.

Sixteen. Pregnant. Homeless. Her mind wasn't even clear enough to realize the hopelessness of her circumstances. She walked. She ran. She lurched. She cried. She prayed. Where does one go when there's nowhere to go?

She passed through tent encampments that still grew wild like weeds all over the capital. Nearly every square meter of open space had been usurped for temporary living quarters by the homeless population.

Stumbling through the sprawling tent cities, lost in their mazes, she wondered how she might find a place to stay, if only for the night. Among the thousands of milling people, Fania momentarily felt she might not be alone. But she knew she was.

It was no use looking for refuge among the tents. The denizens of those improvised communities were as desperate as she was. Spending a night there was an invitation to more trouble. The danger to lone women in the tent cities was known to all.

That's how it came to be that, as the sun went down, Fania found herself at the water's edge. Behind the wall that supported her slumping body, a shipping facility packed with dozens of freight containers was not enough to separate her from the past she wanted so badly to wipe away. Before her, a hazy full moon lit Baie de Port-au-Prince where a handful of decrepit fishing boats bobbed on the gentle surf along with countless pieces of trash. She couldn't see them, but even more boats, older and forgotten, slowly rotted beneath the surface.

Eyes drooping with fatigue, Fania considered the possibility that this dismal yet peaceful spot would be as good a place as any to spend the night while she considered possible plans for the near future. For the first time that day, there was the slightest sliver of hopefulness awakening in her heart. That's when she felt the hand clamp over her mouth.

Renaud Lacroix lived on the frayed edges of a society whose edges were ill-defined to begin with. Had there been credible law enforcement in Port-au-Prince, he would have spent most of his thirty-odd years on the wrong side of it. On the few occasions he found himself aligned with the forces of authority, they were illegitimate and he was their muscle.

Seven years before, he'd left behind a family in Gonaïves,

even as he himself had been left behind. So much flooding and destruction had visited the small city, he wasn't sure if his wife and children were still alive or if they had been swept out to sea with so much else of Gonaïves. Even if they were still there, he was certain they had moved on with their lives. He had.

His own father had left for America when Renaud was a small child. He retained little memory of the man who promised to send for his brothers, sisters, and their mother as soon as he earned enough to pay for their passage. He'd sent money, letters, and gifts for a few years, but his communications decreased in frequency as time passed. Eventually, all contact ended and his name never again came up in conversation. There were rumors among distant relatives that he had a new family in New York.

Recently, Renaud found himself bouncing from crime to crime and job to job, meeting his needs wherever and however he could. One of those needs rose within him when he saw the beautiful girl in the dress that looked more appropriate for an elegant party than a nighttime stroll along a muddy beach.

He leered at Fania as she nestled into a corner formed by the retaining wall around the shipping facility. Her eyelids sank along with the sun. She was alone, unaware, and in the dark. The area was always deserted at that time of night. She was easy prey.

Creeping along the wall behind Fania, he made no sound at all. It was a talent he had used often to get into places where he was not wanted. She never noticed his presence until he covered her mouth with his large, calloused hand.

Since she was half asleep when Renaud grabbed her, Fania had no idea what was happening. She was too surprised and confused to even struggle at first. So much had happened to her in the previous twelve hours, this felt like the next logical chapter of her nightmare.

When she finally became aware of the danger she was in, she tried to scream. As she did, the man's hand squeezed her face harder, his other hand tightening on her throat.

"Shh! Quiet, little girl. There's no one to hear you this time of night," she heard the gravelly voice say. "We can both enjoy this, or you can fight me. Then only I will have a good time. Which will it be?"

It was then, when Renaud's hunger was about to be satiated and Fania's glimmer of hope about to be extinguished utterly, that a blade as long as his forearm and as sharp as his intentions pressed against his neck.

"May I suggest a third choice?"

The voice was frail but urgent. On its strength alone, Renaud might not have relented. The blade was sufficiently persuasive. He let go of Fania. Not trusting her legs, the girl rolled away across the muddy ground and turned to catch a glimpse of her rescuer. What she saw made no sense to her and she wondered if it were a dream. She shook her head, squinted and looked again, more intently.

Cautiously, Renaud rose and turned. The blade remained a few centimeters from his neck. Gripping the handle of the imposing knife was a woman he guessed to be about 70 years old. Her gray hair was pulled back in a tight bun and there were several gaps in her gritted teeth.

A reflexive laugh escaped Renaud's mouth.

"Old woman, do you have any idea what you're getting into?"

She responded by flipping the knife deftly in her hands and saying, "Do you?"

Renaud was growing frustrated. "This doesn't concern you."

Her hand and her gaze were steady. "Oh, but it does. It concerns every woman in Haiti. Leave her alone. Now!"

The enraged man made a lunge for her. More quickly than a woman her age had any right to move, she stepped aside and swung the blade at his extended hand. He shrieked and fell to the ground, clutching his right hand. The tip of his index finger was missing.

"You're crazy!" the man howled, his face contorted into a cross of pain and confusion.

"You're crazy if you try that again. Next time, the cut will be between your legs. That would put a quick end to your fun once and for all."

Renaud held his bleeding hand and looked at her in disbelief. His skepticism couldn't support sufficient courage to risk more body parts. He bounded to his feet and flew into the night. The old woman watched him until he disappeared, then waited a moment longer. Satisfied, she strode to the water and washed off her blade, completing the job by wiping it on her threadbare dress.

She turned to Fania, who was still shuddering on the ground. "Come with me, young lady. He might be back with friends."

The two women ambled along, each absorbed in her own silent contemplation. Fania's mind was unable to capture a rational thought, dizzy as it was from the twisted path her life had taken in that single day. The old woman was more clearheaded. She even dared to entertain a hope that thus far in her life had been a stranger to her.

"What's your name, child?"

"Fania. Fania Dieusel," the girl replied, not looking up.

"I'm happy to meet you Fania. I'm Mimose, but everyone calls me Granmè. I've been like a grandmother to my village for as long as most of them can remember. And longer than I can." She chuckled at her own joke. "You're fortunate there's a full moon tonight. That's when I take my walk by the bay. It's the only time I dare."

"From what I saw, you can take care of yourself."

"Skill is good; wisdom is better. What were you doing out there? If I hadn't come by when I did, you'd be in trouble."

"I'm already in trouble," Fania noted, emotionless.

"Then why did you come here? This is a place to find trouble, not to run away from it."

Fania stopped. Until that moment, she'd been walking blindly, allowing the old woman to lead. What she saw when she finally took in her surroundings was a slum not unlike others she had been to. There were no lights in the area. Only the full moon made it visible. No moon at all would have improved its appearance. It was probably not much better before the earthquake. There were equal numbers of concrete boxes similar to the one she'd grown up in, corrugated steel lean-tos, and tents. Heaps of crushed concrete randomly dotted the area.

About a hundred meters to their right, stark in the moonlight, an imposing building dominated the humble skyline, looming over the ramshackle dwellings that surrounded it. The small structures looked as if they had huddled around the larger one for protection. The enormous box didn't give off the sense of a protective presence, however. It was more that of a bully who had bludgeoned them all into submission. Fania had no idea what the building was, but it frightened her.

"Where am I? I lost my way."

"La Saline." The name made Fania's already tentative steps stutter slightly. The old woman noticed. "You've been here?"

"No. My mother always told me to stay away."

"Your mother is wise. Why aren't you with her now?"

She choked on the words as she answered, "My parents died in the earthquake."

There was a long, understanding pause in their conversation before the aged woman spoke up, compassion softening her voice. "We all lost something. No matter how much we rebuild, that wound will never completely heal."

The silence resumed. This time, Fania broke it. "Can I ask

you another question?"

"Of course."

"Where are we going?" Fania asked not out of fear, but as one simply seeking information. The girl wasn't sure the old woman could be trusted, having just met her and recalling the intimidating way she wielded her knife, but her options were limited. In fact, Granmè was her sole option. She knew she could do worse than to put herself in the care of such an able protector.

"That depends on you. Either a temporary shelter or, if my impression of you is correct, home. Do you have someplace to go?"

Fania didn't have the will to answer.

"I didn't think so. I'd like you to stay with me until you know what you're going to do next. How do you feel about that?"

The smile that came to Fania's lips, though slight, was more genuine than any she had worn in the past year. At the orphanage, she was compelled to smile constantly. Anything else might bring the rod from Nadine or Eli. She had no idea what she was walking into, but it felt like her future.

Chapter 4

FANIA AWOKE in dim filtered light imagining she was engulfed in a rare Haitian fog. From somewhere beyond her murky confines came the spirited sounds of children at play. She sustained a collision of emotions as she momentarily thought she was back among her beloved children in the loathsome institution.

It took a few moments for her to recall where she was and how she had arrived there. She was alone under a light gray plastic tarp. Although she couldn't read them, the letters "USAID" were visible backwards through the translucent material.

Alone in the tent, her senses recovered, she worried that the woman who called herself Granmè had stolen her belongings and left her. Then she remembered she had no belongings. All she had were the clothes she was wearing, and they were bedraggled and torn. Her shoes *were* missing, though.

Seeds of relief already sprouted in her heart because she'd slept without dreams, which, in her recent history, meant without nightmares.

The light that peeked in through gaps in the tent indicated it was mid-morning. In spite of the conditions, sleeping on a single blanket with a rolled up flannel shirt for a pillow, she had slept later than she ever had back at the orphanage.

The events of the previous day had worn her out physically and emotionally. Although she couldn't consciously identify it, her mind and body were experiencing respite at being away from the orphanage where she felt the sting of Nadine's rod any time she stayed in bed a minute too late. Her body understood instinctively it needed sleep and for once it had the opportunity to get enough of it.

The nausea she'd been feeling for a few weeks was still with her. It revived the memory of her dilemma, which made her heartsick as well. She was anxious about her new setting but curious nonetheless. Pulling aside the flap that served as the tent's door, she poked her head outside and immediately threw up what little was left in her stomach.

Granmè sat beside the opening, sharpening her knife on a

rock. In spite of the stench from the vomit that pooled next to her, she smiled.

"*Bonjou* to you, too. Should I get used to this unusual greeting?"

"I'm sorry, but I ..."

Granmè didn't let her continue. She picked up a pile of dirt, dropped it on the fetid mess, then scraped it off to one side. "How far along are you?"

"I don't know," Fania confided.

"Don't worry. I'll find a doctor to see you. Meanwhile, if you're feeling better, come out here. We need some time to get acquainted."

Fania did feel better, although she was hungry. The orphanage was not a pleasant place to live, but at least she was usually served three meals a day there. With some effort, she dragged herself out of the tent. Granmè gave her a small piece of bread. "See if you can keep that down." The girl devoured the fragment.

Next, Granmè handed her a stack of clothes. "That dress you're in is fine for church, but you'll need some things for every day. These belonged to a neighbor who owes me a favor. They should be the right size for you. Oh, and here..."

Granmè leaned over and picked up Fania's shoes from the ground. They were shined to a perfect gloss. "A friend of mine shined them. I didn't want to wake you, so I took them off while you slept. You were sleeping so soundly, I wondered if you were still alive."

Fania wore her amazement on her face. "You get food and clothes, have shoes shined, find doctors. How?"

"As the oldest person in the neighborhood, I suppose I've earned a few privileges."

"They're probably afraid of your blade," Fania added.

"If that's my cup, I'm not ashamed to drink from it. Now get that filthy dress off and change into one of these. Later in the week we'll go down to the river to do laundry. For now, rest. We can get to know each other."

That's exactly what they did. Settling on two stones Granmè had rolled to either side of the tent opening, the two talked. For the most part, Fania talked. Each cathartic word she spoke brought fresh healing. She didn't know what it was about Granmè, but she wanted to tell her everything on her mind and everything in her heart.

Fania's voice cracked with pain as she spoke of the earthquake that had shut the door on her past life of love and hope, opening a new one that had led to suffering and grief.

She painted Granmè a bleak picture of her cheerless year at the orphanage but stopped short of giving her any details of her pregnancy or her expulsion from the church. Memories of the children in the orphanage were the only words that came from smiling lips. Fania adored the children she served and shared the previous year with. Each was a shining star illuminating that dark season of her life. She loved to tell their stories.

There was *Ti* Jean (not to be confused with *Gwo* Jean, also in the orphanage), a three-year-old boy who regarded anything on the floor as a *futbol*, and shouted, "Goal!" as he kicked the object, whether box or spoon or shoe or, on rare occasions, ball. Fania laughed aloud as she reminisced about Emilie, a girl of six who had cunningly amassed a collection of cockroaches in a discarded oatmeal container. Nadine's reaction when she opened it unawares brought laughter behind the woman's back for weeks afterward. Fania's voice turned wistful at the tale of Davidson, a four-year-old boy who almost suffocated when he hid in the luggage of a teenager staying at the orphanage on a youth mission trip. The fantasies some of the children clung to about escaping to the States quickly fizzled at the near tragedy.

The two women, more than fifty years separating them but quickly growing as close as yesterday and today, shared their deepest emotions as freely as the wind threaded the streets and alleys of La Saline.

Granmè listened silently and compassionately. She had long ago given up the possibility of offering comfort to a daughter. Now, each conversation with Fania was like a balm on a heart that had been shattered more times than she could count. Until she met this dejected young woman, she thought she was beyond healing. Now she harbored hope for a final chance.

In her wounded heart, Granmè felt a consolation that could only have come from the God she knew had sent Fania to her in her final years. How differently would she have felt if she knew it was a church's indifference to Fania's plight that had driven the castaway into her life?

By the time the sun had sunk to a dim, swollen red ball,

both were more tired than if they had spent the day braving a hectic market. Even when they finally reclined for the night, sleep was delayed as they continued sharing their hearts, hopes, and dreams.

Their mutual restoration established a bond each could sense. It was a bond of trust and love that might have been premature in any other setting, but it was as natural as the sun between these two children of Haiti.

Within a few days and without knowing exactly how it had happened, Fania realized she'd been adopted by this woman she hadn't even known a week before. She was staying in her cramped tent and wearing clothes she'd provided. The concept of home had been lost to Fania in the last year. Thanks to Granmè's care and hospitality, its meaning, with all the comfort and security it implied, was being restored within her.

Fania wanted to believe her life had turned a corner for the better but, based on her brief experience, she remained skeptical.

Most mornings, the scene by the river in La Saline was the same. The community, mostly the women, gathered to bathe, clean clothes, and exchange the latest news. Usually, there wasn't much news to share. Life was at its best when there was nothing new. Change was more often than not for the worse. Now and then, something positive happened, but that was rare and disappointment usually followed in its wake, as the good turned sour or failed completely like a bad crop.

Such was the mindset of the average citizen of not only

La Saline, but Port-au-Prince and Haiti in general. They knew life was different elsewhere. Letters from relatives who had settled overseas in places such as Miami and New York, told tales of opportunity and riches that became the foundation of dreams for so many Haitians.

Even though the majority of people had no television, most had seen them either in shops or, if they had the audacity to wander into one of Port-au-Prince's few affluent neighborhoods, through windows of wealthy citizens' homes. There they would catch glimpses of what they felt they had missed out on because, through no fault of their own, they had lost out in the birthplace lottery.

More than most, Fania was aware of this disparity. In his bedroom, Pastor Eli had a television that was taller than most of the children in his care. Although she couldn't know for sure, Fania believed the man's wife Paulette spent most of her days indiscriminately viewing whatever appeared on the immense screen. She would emerge for some meals (most were served to her in her room) and Sunday church services.

Paulette was an obese woman for whom most activities, except eating, were battles whose outcomes were anything but certain. Fania knew she should feel pity for the woman, but she couldn't generate the compassion.

At the river's edge, there was no obesity—no excess flesh at all, in fact. The women's bodies reflected their lives. They had less than they needed, but managed to survive all the same.

On this day, there was news to convey among those who

arrived, clothes balanced on heads and babies on hips. Even though it was beyond her hearing, Fania could tell what the tidings concerned, or rather *who* they concerned. The ladies' sidelong glances and occasional frowns let her know she would be the topic of conversation on most lips today and for a long time to come.

"How do they know?" She asked Granmè, rightly assuming her new guardian was aware of what was being passed around the way a stalk of sugarcane was passed among ravenous children. The sweetness of both lingered on the tongue and though they did more damage than good, it was a pleasure to savor each for a time.

"No one knows anything, but they have good imaginations. It brings them satisfaction to think they've figured something out. We'll betray nothing to them."

With that, they joined dozens of others kneeling by the water scrubbing clothes. Granmè worked with a tiny bar of lye soap, the same piece she had extended for months of use through great economy.

The etiquette for use of the river was well understood by all. Downstream from the clothes washers, bathers cleaned themselves and their children. Farther down, others were free to relieve themselves. It all worked well until someone neglected the unwritten rules. No one gave any thought to the end result that accumulated in the harbor. Today's necessity forbade any thoughts of the long term consequences.

Granmè purposely chose a spot away from everyone else

so they could talk freely. "Now, Fania, do you know who the father is?"

The abruptness with which Granmè broached the topic was unsettling for a moment, but the young girl was learning more and more to see an ally in the old woman, so she confided in her. "There was only one man."

"That's good. Will he help you?"

"He wants nothing to do with me."

Granmè gave the blouse she was holding an extra forceful twist, causing water to gush from it. "I'm not surprised." After a moment's hesitation, she added, "God help us." Her exclamation began as a sincere lament for the state of her society, but ended as a plea for mercy.

The reason for the appeal was the sudden appearance of the middle-aged woman who settled on the bank beside them. Wilmina Paul-Louis was known to all as the primary source of gossip in La Saline. The currency of her conversation was rumor and scandal. If it was in short supply, she was not above counterfeiting some.

Despite her younger age, Wilmina's unkempt nest of hair showed as much gray as Granmè's and her face had more wrinkles than the clothing she dropped on the rock between herself and the other two women.

"Good morning, Granmè. Who is this?"

"It's none of your business, Wilmina, but I'll tell you so you're less likely to make something up. Her name is Fania and she's come to stay with me for a while." Granmè could barely suppress her contempt for the woman. She didn't make much of an attempt.

"Is it true what everyone is saying, Fania?"

Out of pity and for the girl's protection, Granmè answered, "Everyone is repeating the rumor you started, no doubt."

"Granmè, I'm concerned for the girl."

Granmè clucked her tongue at her. "*Pa mete pye nan tout soulye*", she said, quoting one her favorite Haitian proverbs, one that was particularly fitting for Wilmina: "Don't put your foot in every shoe."

Never one to be influenced by common courtesy, Wilmina addressed Fania directly again. "The *houngan* can help you with your problem. He's helped many other women here."

"I don't think we'll be needing your witch doctor, Wilmina." Granmè picked up the damp clothes and stood. "We should be getting back. The water isn't the only thing that stinks here."

Fania gathered the rest of the clothes and followed Granmè off. Wilmina called after them. "Fania, you can make up your own mind."

Granmè was grumbling and Fania was thoughtful as they walked away.

"What was that woman talking about?" Given the future she was facing, Fania was more than curious about anything that could be done to improve her lot.

Granmè responded with an uncharacteristic edge in her

voice. "Don't listen to her. She's a superstitious fool. She lets that *houngan* run her life."

Fania grew defensive. "The truth is I don't think I should have this baby. If he's helped others, maybe..."

"*Wi*, helped others to an early grave." Granmè's biting tone continued, making Fania nervous.

"What else can I do? How could I possibly raise a child?"

Granmè stopped and took one of Fania's hands in hers. "I'm sorry to sound so harsh. Wilmina brings out the worst in me. I have to believe there's a better way. You told me you helped care for all the children at the orphanage."

"I can't do it on my own, though. Do you think you could find someone who could help me get out of my..." she searched her mind for a euphemism before settling on, "...my situation?"

"For enough money, you can buy the devil himself. Is that what you really want?"

"I don't know. It seems like the easiest way."

Granmè challenged Fania with another of the wise proverbs she was partial to. "The mango that falls at your feet is rarely fit to eat."

Children played *futbol* in the street while Granmè and Fania laid out their damp clothes over the tent to dry in the sun. The ball the children used was made of wadded up strips of cloth they had scavenged from the streets, streams, and inattentive people of the village.

"Are you feeling better about your life now, Fania?"

"Should I?"

"You're no longer alone. At least, I hope you feel that way."

"I do and I appreciate it, Granmè, but beyond that mountain are many more mountains."

"We can only climb one mountain at a time. It takes patience to raise the sun."

The *futbol* game was growing increasingly competitive. The ball, such as it was, took a severe beating. Finally, the game came to a halt as screams of accusation replaced more typical noises of a match. The ball was unraveled to the point of uselessness, just a loose clump of rags, and a nine-year-old boy named Robinson was taking the brunt of the blame from the rest of the players.

As the other, older boys heaped abuse on him, Robinson had no choice but to stand there, head hung in shame, and endure their outrage. Granmè had heard enough, however. She beckoned to the boy, "Robinson, bring me the ball."

Relieved to be called away from his tormentors, he approached Granmè with the ragged ball in his outstretched hands. "Granmè, they said I broke the ball." The other players continued to tease and jeer at the boy from behind his back.

"Don't worry, Robinson, we can fix this. They're jealous because you're so strong. They wish they could kick hard enough to break the ball." Little Robinson, the scrawniest player on the barely functional field, stood straighter and held his head high at Granmè's encouragement.

The other kids watched as she worked her magic. Occasionally asking Robinson to hold a scrap of cloth in place, her hands flew around the mutilated *futbol*, tucking and tying until it once more resembled something that could take the place of a real ball. She winked at the boy then tossed the globe up in front of her and kneed it to him. Taking the pass in the air, the little boy headed it out toward his astounded playmates and grinned ecstatically back at his rescuer.

"Is there anything you can't do?" asked an astonished Fania as they returned to laying out their washing.

"I can't make your problems go away," Granmè answered.

"Perhaps I can," came a voice as a shadow fell across the two women. The shadow seemed unusually dark. They turned to see Claude, the *houngan*, a severe-looking man somewhere in his late fifties. He had obscure—and to Fania, fearsome—designs tattooed down his arms and on his chest, which was exposed behind an open leather vest. He wore brand new jeans. A small leather sack hung from one hand.

Granmè's face revealed the disdain she held for the man and his *vodou* practices. She turned her back on him before saying, "We have no need of your tricks, witch doctor."

He was undaunted by her rebuke. "You speak with great disrespect of my life's work."

"All your work has done is keep this village in fear and poverty while you grow rich. Go away."

The *houngan* went on the attack. "It isn't in your best interests to anger the *loa*."

The old woman's voice was as quick as her blade and twice as sharp. "I've survived these seventy years without the help of your *loa*. I'll take my chances."

"Are you afraid to let the girl speak for herself?" A tense silence descended over them as Granmè turned to Fania. Claude spoke directly to her for the first time. "Young lady?"

Fania glanced back and forth at the combative pair. She took a deep breath and, without looking into the *houngan's* eyes, said, "No *mèsi*, sir."

"A respectful response, though unwise. The power of the *loa* can be a great blessing or a dangerous curse."

"You have her answer, priest. Now leave us alone."

At that, the *houngan* bowed piously, shook his leather sack in their direction, causing Fania to flinch, then strode away. His shadow left with him, but Fania felt as though its darkness lingered. She didn't know what to make of the man but she was aware of two things: She trusted Granmè and the *houngan* gave her a chill deep inside her being, even though the sun was blazing overhead.

"Let's go for a walk. His presence has made this place uncomfortable for now. I'll show you around the village and you can meet some of my more pleasant neighbors." They walked off in the opposite direction from that which the *houngan* took.

The two women strolled arm in arm down a dirt path among tents and rubble. Fania had lived her entire life in Haitian slums, but La Saline looked and felt different. The hunger here was more prevalent and more acute. Distended bellies protruding beneath skeletal ribs were not uncommon, nor was the sparse reddish hair that marked severe malnutrition.

Granmè greeted a young mother who cradled an emaciated baby in her arms. The infant busied himself by fondling his umbilical hernia, which was about the size of a light bulb. The mother smiled back but it was an empty expression; there was no joy in it.

Beyond isolated tufts of brown grass, widely spread clumps of withering weeds, and thorn bushes whose spikes approached the length of Granmè's dagger, there was no vegetation. Concrete, rocks, and refuse were the only crops that thrived there.

At a crossroads of narrow alleys created by one intact and three crushed houses, Fania saw something at her feet. It was a puppy, no more than a few weeks old as far as she could tell. It stretched on its side on the ground, gasping for breath. Its feeble body heaved with the effort of inhalation, each wheeze weaker than the last, each taking more time and effort. Fania knew that, if she ever walked this way again, even as little as an hour later, the dog would be dead, doubtless picked apart by other desperate animals.

They walked on, Fania trying to forget the image of the puppy. She never did.

Farther along, a man smoked a pipe as he sat on the front stoop of his tiny home intently carving a piece of wood. Although he was fully engrossed in his work, he looked up when

Granmè passed and beamed a genuine, if toothless, grin. He wore a T-shirt advertising a Haitian bank. On the back of the shirt read the unlikely message, "In spite of all my problems, I'm proud to be Haitian."

Passing a shanty created from sheets of corrugated steel leaning precariously against each other, Fania waved to a little girl who was peering out from behind one of its teetering walls. Fania thought the girl adorable, with her beaded, braided bangs partially concealing her shining eyes. The waif sucked on her lower lip and looked surprised at the attention Fania showed her.

At one point, Fania had to help her elderly companion over a deep drainage ditch. It was easy for Fania to forget how old Granmè was because of her strength and vitality, but she was still an old woman, ancient by Haitian standards. She was capable of summoning up youthful energy at will when she required it, but afterward she would be weakened that much more by the exertion. Fania had no idea how long she could keep it up. She never admitted it, but Granmè wondered the same thing.

"The *houngan* frightens me," Fania confessed.

"That's his job. He takes money from people who fear his power. Make no mistake, Fania. He has real power, but it's not for anyone's good but his own. We're best to have no dealings with him."

"That's fine with me. I've had enough of religion, no matter what kind."

"You've had a bad experience?"

Granmè wore the look of compassion Fania found so calming and inviting. She felt comfortable answering even such an uncomfortable question. "*Wi*, in church."

"Don't give up so easily, Fania. God is good, even if some who claim His name are not."

Fania was in no state to be consoled on the subject. "Those are sweet words, but after what I've been through, they're hard to swallow."

They turned down a cramped alley between two long concrete walls that weren't part of any buildings. A barb from an overgrown thorn bush jabbed Fania's ankle.

"Let me take you to my church here in La Saline. Maybe you'll change your mind."

"I don't know if I could go to a church anymore." Fania shook her head, trying in vain to shake off her memories.

"There was a time I felt the same way, after I lost my last child."

"Last child?"

"In my life, I've given birth to three girls and a boy. Three of them never saw their first birthday. The fourth, my youngest daughter, didn't survive much longer. My anger at God was so hot, I was feverish all the time."

They both walked in silence as each fought memories of pain and anguish.

"I'm sorry," Fania told her.

"No, I'm the one who should be sorry for bringing up such

things with you here carrying a child."

As she finished speaking, they stepped out of the alley into a wide open courtyard. In the center of the space stood the overbearing building Fania had seen under the full moon on the night of her arrival in La Saline. On seeing it, she shivered again, as she had when speaking to the *houngan*.

Granmè noticed a change in her demeanor. "You're troubled, Fania?"

"What is this place?" She stood still, unable to breathe as she asked her question. She felt that the building might devour her if she moved or spoke in a way contrary to its will. She wondered how a building could have a will of its own, but that this one did was undeniable.

"Fort Dimanche. The Dungeon of Death. This is where the Duvaliers dealt with their enemies. That was long before your time. I wasn't much older than you are now when it started. For many years, the sounds of the inmates' screams as they were tortured kept me awake. I didn't sleep until I heard a shot that brought the silence of death. Sleep comes slowly to me even to this day. That's why I was out walking the night we met."

Both stood still in silence. Fania had vague recollections of horror stories told in furtive whispers about the men called "Papa Doc" and "Baby Doc" Duvalier who imposed a thirty-year reign of terror on Haiti. She'd heard about people, even a few close relatives, who had been dragged away in the middle of the night by their henchmen, the notorious black-clad *tonton macoutes,* for reasons no one was ever sure of. Now she knew where they had ended up and it was right in her backyard.

"I could give up on humanity after those years, as you have given up on God. I've found the good, too. I found you."

"I'm thankful you did."

"No one will force you to go to church. God will come to you in His own time, and yours."

Granmè kept her word and never pressured Fania to attend church services with her. Granmè went on her own but never ceased praying for her young charge. As time passed and the pregnancy dragged on, she grew increasingly distressed for Fania and prayed all that more fervently. If the girl was to recover from whatever damage had been done to her, God would have to do the healing. In spite of all her talents and influence, Granmè knew such a feat was beyond her.

Every other waking minute of every other day, however, found the two inseparable. The shared time was invaluable to Fania, whose knowledge of the ways of the slum was nonexistent. She scrupulously observed every move of the old woman. Neither voiced the thought, but both knew Granmè would not always be there to shepherd Fania and her unborn child. She would need the skills she absorbed to improve the chances of survival for her and the new life she carried. They might even serve to make life more than just a burden.

The only other time the two were separated was late at night, after Fania had gone to sleep. Granmè didn't require much sleep; a few hours a night gave her body all the rest it needed.

Her spirit could have used far more. At times, the sleepless hours were agonizing and interminable. She spent those hours walking at the seaside, as she had the night she met Fania, or staring at the slumbering young lady, praying and dreaming all the while.

With the odds of dying during childbirth astronomically high compared to developed countries, pregnancy in Haiti was a challenge, treated more like an illness to be cured than an event to be celebrated. Add to that the mortality rate of Haitian babies in their first years—a fact painfully evident to Granmè—and it was clear to all that giving birth wasn't something to be taken lightly. As Fania's due date drew nearer, she and Granmè grew increasingly tense.

They did all they could to prepare for the arrival of the new baby, but there were limits even to Granmè's abilities.

Chapter 5

FANIA ALWAYS LOVED early morning. The heat of day had not yet reached its full, oppressive power. Shadows, in rare supply most of the day, were long, deep, and cool. There was a lull before the cloaked serenity of night succumbed to the uproar of daily life. Other than the welcome familiar sounds of a few chickens, roosters, the shoeshine, and the egg seller, the streets were empty and quiet.

Later, when the sun pounded on heads as trucks and *tap-taps* rumbled by at speeds completely out of proportion to the quality of the roadways, peace was as distant a memory as the Haitian rain forests.

This morning, her concentration was on the pain she felt in her lower back. Somehow, Granmè had conjured up a gaunt mattress for her to sleep on. Being not much more substantial than a plantain peel, it did little to relieve the pang. She was thankful, of course, for the mattress and everything her adopted grandmother had done for her, but it was hard to feel anything but the stabbing sensation that was her bedmate. She wondered if she'd inadvertently fallen asleep on Granmè's dagger.

When she tried to roll over, her swollen belly prevented her from getting any farther than her side. She knew the baby was the real cause of the pain she felt, a pain that not only afflicted her back, but also her mind as she pondered the future she could offer a child in that setting.

Yet she had to admit to herself that her life had been blessed in the months since she had come to live with Granmè. The old girl was the most resourceful person Fania had ever met and one of the most loving. Yes, they were hungry from time to time, but they always found something to eat before they became desperate.

Still, she was living in a tent. And Granmè was getting older.

As on every Sunday morning, even on those when the pain wasn't keeping her awake, the sounds of music, singing, and shouting roused her. Church was in its full fervor and Granmè would be there as she was every week, getting caught up in the Spirit along with the rest of the congregation.

Fania had still not overcome the resistance she felt toward attending the service but she understood from Granmè's sweaty face each week, it must be a dynamic experience. As soon as she returned, she would lay her gray head on the ground in her tent and sleep for three hours, almost as long as the service had lasted. Haitians, for all they lacked, knew how to worship God. It was the one time when their cups ran to overflowing.

Feeling more revived and unable to sleep, Fania rose for the day. She emerged from the tent and stretched. The music sounded more appealing than usual, more hopeful. For the first time, and for a reason she couldn't frame her thoughts around, she felt drawn to it. At first her steps were tentative, but the extravagantly festive singing drew her, made her more confident as she edged closer to its source. Before she knew it, she was standing at the door of the little hall.

In a book many years ago, Fania had seen pictures of churches around the world. Some looked as if they were set in heaven itself, soaring steeples with bold crosses striving for the sky. Even Pastor Eli's church, while anything but gaudy, was impressive in its size.

Nothing about the La Saline church—she didn't know its name, or even if it had one—was impressive. It was another tiny concrete box, so small that people were forced to cram together, stand in the aisles, and sit on the floor. The looks on the faces of the worshipers, however, did make an impression on her. There was something less forced, more open and inviting than she had known at Victory Baptist Church. The church might have lacked a name, but it had no shortage of passion.

Granmè's attention rarely strayed from the elements of the service, especially the songs. Movement near the door distracted her this morning. She looked over to see Fania, hands resting on her bulging belly. She stopped singing, leapt from her spot on the end of a long wooden bench, and hugged the bewildered girl. Taking Fania's hand, she sat back down and, at the expense of the family next to her, made space on the bench for both of them.

Although the rest of the congregation continued to sing, Granmè couldn't stop glancing at Fania. The woman's ancient, dancing eyes displayed as much delight as the entire crowd singing. Fania was still uncomfortable in the environment. Not knowing what else to do, she brought Granmè's hand, which had never let go of hers, to her belly.

The song came to an abrupt end at precisely the same time that Fania's baby gave a swift kick to the wall of its womb. In the sudden silence, Granmè cried out in delight. Everyone in the humble sanctuary turned to gawk at her, but she was unfazed. She held onto Fania and smiled with a joy she'd experienced only four times before. Each of those times, the joy, like the children that brought it, was short-lived.

The two sat holding hands for the remainder of the service. By its end, Fania was even softly singing some of the songs she recalled. Visions of her ejection from Eli's church, for so long an unwelcome resident of her mind, began the slow process of vacating her memory. The relief she felt was as real as the hand that clutched hers.

After the service, Henri Antoine, the church's minister, a tall, robust man of thirty-two, greeted his flock as they flowed out. Seeing Granmè with Fania, his face broke into an effusive smile.

"So this is the mystery girl Granmè brags about. *Bonjou*, Fania. It's a great pleasure to meet you at last," he said as he reached out his hand to her.

Fania scarcely lifted her hand to meet his; she didn't raise her eyes at all. Henri was young, but he had seen the effects of abuse more than he cared to consider. He recognized and understood the girl's restraint. He grasped her hand in both of his and held it warmly.

Under her breath, Fania replied, "*Mèsi*."

"You're welcome back anytime, although I hope your Granmè can control herself in the future." He and Granmè laughed and Fania allowed herself a shy grin.

The two women walked off as Henri continued shaking the hands of the parishioners. Granmè resisted asking Fania why she had decided to come to church. Had she inquired, she wouldn't have received a definitive answer. Fania was still trying to work it out for herself.

Fania was about to offer her thoughts, but a pain in her abdomen interrupted her. She had an idea what was happening, but didn't want to acknowledge it. When she slowed her steps in response to the ache, Granmè noticed.

"Let's get you back home."

Everyone called him "*Doktè* Georges", but he was a medical student. He had grown up in La Saline and was the medical practitioner of choice for all those in the village who knew him. Through the church, he had found a benefactor in the US who was willing to finance his education through primary school and university.

He worked diligently through his thirteen years of school and four at university knowing any further education depended on good scores at every level. As a result, he found himself in his second year of medical school at *Université Notre Dame d'Haiti.*

Through his regular visits to his old neighborhood, Georges had acquired more medical experience than some doctors could expect in a lifetime. What he lacked in modern medical equipment, he more than compensated for with creativity and tenderness. Fania experienced both during her long delivery.

Georges could offer no medication to lessen the agony of childbirth. If there had been a complication, he would first have had to procure suitable transportation, then find a hospital that would take a nonpaying patient.

Fortunately, other than the usual painful rigors of labor, Fania's delivery went smoothly. Georges examined the infant as he spoke, "Granmè could have delivered this little girl without my help. She's birthed more children in this village than any doctor."

"We are grateful for your help just the same, *Doktè*," Fania said.

"Not a doctor yet, young lady. Fortunately, babies don't care about degrees. They come when and how they want." Georges completed his examination of the newborn and wrapped her tightly in a blanket he had brought with him. He placed the bundle into the arms of the exhausted and disheveled mother. At last he announced, "Congratulations, your daughter is strong and healthy."

"And beautiful, like her mother," Granmè added.

"She'll probably be beautiful all her life, but she'll need nutrition if she's to retain her good health." Georges spoke to Fania, but the warning was for them both. "Will you be alright?"

Fania was in no condition to respond to any of this as tears rolled down her cheeks while she stared at her new daughter in near disbelief. The old woman answered, "You know me, Georges."

Georges let out a laugh so unrestrained and joyous, it might have billowed out the walls of the tent. He continued to chuckle as he packed the few instruments he carried into a worn leather satchel he'd inherited from his mentor, a retired doctor. "If anyone can take care of things, you can, Granmè. I'd love to stay and visit, but I have to get back to my classwork. I'll check in on you later in the week. Meanwhile, come see me any time. As long as I'm not in class." He laughed again then slipped out through the tent flap.

Mother and guardian remained reverently silent as they stared at the sleeping newborn. As they watched, the infant's face contorted into something resembling a cross between a smile, a grimace, and a wink at the surreal setting she was born into. The women reacted with laughter that rang bell-like and merely added to their worshipful mood.

"She's beautiful, isn't she?" Fania asked mostly to herself. Her heart was so full it made her voice tremble.

She wanted to be strong for her young charge, but Granmè was crying, too. "She's a vision of beauty. What will you name her?"

"Since she's so beautiful, I'll call her Rose in honor of my mother."

"A wonderful choice, and you will be a wonderful mother."

"I feel better about it with you here to help me."

"I'll be with you as long as I can, *ti manman*." She silently wondered how long that would be. Leaning over, she kissed Rose on the cheek then Fania on her sweat-covered brow, matted with a web of hair as intricate and entangled as their lives had become in the instant of the child's birth.

As the mother and daughter slipped into a deep slumber, Granmè thanked God for her life. The peaceful scene before her was more than Granmè had ever dared dream, even back when she was known simply as Mimose and her dreams were great indeed. The words of her father, never an encouraging influence in her life, echoed in her ears even after all these years, "In Haiti only crazy people start dreaming." Today, at an age well beyond what any Haitian had a right to expect to see and having buried four children, her dreams had been realized and her life as well as her heart were full.

She gazed on the holy sight and shed grateful tears.

Chapter 6

A FEW MONTHS after Rose's birth, a Canadian missions group set up a food distribution program at the La Saline church to help feed the families of the village. Meeting baby Rose's nutritional needs became easier overnight. There was no guarantee the program would be around for long. Foreign groups were forever establishing new services only to close up shop a few months later due to compassion fatigue or dried up funding or both.

For the time being at least, the food program had brought a merciful end to the mud pie businesses that had thrived in the slum for years. With no other food available, some resourceful women mixed mud with a little oil and salt to make the bland, pale gray disks that were then baked in the sun. People bought them for one *gourde* each to feed their children when their hunger pangs made them cry out in pain. No one missed the mud pies except the ones for whom they provided work. To compensate for the loss of local income, the mission hired citizens of the village to help administer the food distribution.

As so often happened in the food line, Fania, holding one-year-old Rose in her arms, found herself standing near Wilmina. She tried to avoid the woman as much as possible, but it wasn't worth passing up the meals.

At first, Wilmina assumed a cordial facade as usual. "Where is Granmè this morning?"

Fania didn't want to answer, knowing that the old gossip would twist whatever she said and spread her version around the whole village in the most malicious form imaginable. "She was tired. I said I'd bring her back something."

"Aren't you afraid the missionaries might deny you an extra meal? Or are you willing to beg?" Wilmina always had a way of making even the worst situations more trying. After observing Granmè for the past eighteen months, Fania had learned how to most effectively respond to her cynicism.

"Aren't you afraid your *houngan* will curse you for taking food from the Christians?"

"He'll have to live with it until he can conjure up food for me and my daughter."

Wilmina's disclosure caught Fania completely by surprise. "Daughter? I didn't know you had any children."

"I brought my little girl to the orphanage when her father left because I couldn't care for her. She was sent back to me yesterday because the orphanage is full and she lost her sponsor."

Fania squeezed Rose tighter as she asked, "How could you give up your daughter?" She didn't intend it to sound like an accusation. Had she been able to soften the message, Wilmina still would have taken offense. As such, her reply was even more caustic than usual.

"Don't be so smug. You might have to do the same some day."

"I could never..."

Fania was prevented from worsening an already disagreeable conversation when a little girl flew by shouting, "*M-m-manman*!" She clutched Wilmina's legs. "I d-d-didn't know w-w-where you w-w-were. I w-was afraid you'd l-l-left m-me!"

Fania recognized Marie-Fleur immediately, but the little girl didn't see her. When Wilmina reached down and wrenched her daughter from her legs, Marie-Fleur caught sight of Fania for the first time. She was so shocked, she couldn't get Fania's name out.

"F-f-f-f-f..." Her hands went to her mouth as if she wanted to pull the cherished name from her own lips.

"*Ti sè!*" Fania said as she stooped down to hug her. The embrace they shared was so tight that Marie-Fleur could hardly breath, even if the surprise hadn't already knocked the air from her lungs.

"W-w-here did you g-g-go, Fania? W-w-why d-d-did you l-l-leave us?" It was then that she noticed Rose settled snugly on Fania's hip. Marie-Fleur's eyes shone as brightly as a newly minted fifty-*gourde* coin, and grew almost as wide. "W-w-who's th-that?"

Fania held Rose out to her and answered, "This is my little girl. Her name is Rose. Rose, I want you to meet my very special friend, Marie-Fleur." Instinctively, Rose felt her mother's pleasure at meeting the other girl. She opened and closed her hand in a sign of greeting.

After a deep breath and a long gulp, with no stammer other than a slightly elongated "R", Marie-Fleur uttered, "*Bonjou,* Rose."

Rose returned a giggle. Marie-Fleur was captivated, not realizing that Fania had tickled the baby to get the reaction.

Wilmina's annoyance with the attention Marie-Fleur was lavishing on Fania and Rose came out as a series of guttural noises. When the two failed to heed her less-than-subtle cues, Wilmina yanked her daughter away.

"How do you two know each other?"

Both tried to answer at the same time, causing them to laugh in unison, almost musically.

Fania obliged, "We were together in the orphanage."

"F-f-fania was my b-b-b-big s-sister in that terrible p-p-place. I m-m-missed you s-s-so m-much."

"We're neighbors now. You can visit Rose and me any time you want."

"Yay!" the girl cheered, clapping.

"Enough. Go back home and wait for me, girl."

"B-b-but we..."

"Do as you're told!"

Marie-Fleur dragged herself off, but looked back at Fania with each step, fearing it had all been a dream and Fania would once again vanish if she took her eyes off her *gwo sè* for more than a second. After turning a final corner out of sight, Marie-Fleur peeked back around and blew a kiss to Fania, who returned it.

"She's such a sweet little girl."

Without acknowledging the comment, Wilmina turned her attention back to the line and ignored Fania for the remainder of their time together.

The woman's behavior might have hurt and discouraged someone else, but Fania was used to an oppressive presence when she and Marie-Fleur were together. Wilmina was just another Nadine. Such bitter dispositions carried their own punishment. Unfortunately, Marie-Fleur undeservedly shared their consequences.

Carrying a bag of food in one hand and Rose in the other, Fania strolled back to the tent. From a distance she could see that a storm was brewing and without a doubt Granmè was in the center of it. A crowd, mingling and murmuring, had gathered around their humble dwelling.

The entire area was buzzing with activity. Two workmen held about twenty meters of string along the side of the road, cutting right across Granmè's tent entrance. A third man looked ready to tear the tent down at any moment.

The fourth man was Lamosier, the leader of the little work crew. He was a short, middle-aged man with a lean, powerful body that was nothing but muscle and sinew. His demeanor and the deference the others showed him made it clear to any who observed the scene that he was in control. The other workers and most everyone else who ever interacted with him called him "Boss Man."

No one was working now, however. Everyone's attention was fixed on a confrontation that promised to be more entertaining than one of the cock fights that were sometimes held in the shadowy corners of La Saline.

Standing nose to nose were Granmè and Lamosier, neither ready to yield a single millimeter.

"You're doing a good thing, but you don't need to destroy our homes in the process." Her tone would have intimidated most people, but in Lamosier, she had finally met her match.

"What homes? All I see is rubble and a few tents."

"I see the only place I have to lay my head." As she saw Fania come into view, Granmè added, "Not to mention this young mother and her child."

Confused and concerned, Fania called to Granmè, "What's going on?"

Refusing to take her eyes off Lamosier for an instant lest he raze her home while she glanced away, she answered, "He says they're building a new school."

"All this land has been granted to an American group to build a school for the children of La Saline," Lamosier declared as he waved his hand over Granmè's house and the surrounding land and homes. At that, the grumbling grew louder, but there was a smattering of cheers among it as well.

The news brought excitement to Fania's face and voice. "That's wonderful."

Granmè pushed ahead. "Not if they have to throw people out of their homes to do it." She finally dared to look away from Boss Lamosier and turned to the gathered throng. "Your homes will be next. What good is an education here if your children have no place to live? I want this school as much as anyone, but there's no need to displace families to build it."

Conflicting shouts came from the crowd. Most of them were enjoying the battle of wills. A few side bets were being placed on the outcome. They knew Granmè's determination, but the Boss Man appeared to be a worthy opponent. Plus, he had the power of America behind him. That power, they had learned painfully from their nation's history, was not to be denied.

"There's space in the field behind here. Put your school there."

"There's not enough room," Lamosier countered.

"Then build up. The air is free."

With a conviction even Granmè had to admire, Lamosier answered, "The Americans want it built here." To assert his claim, he placed a stake on the ground in front of her and, with one powerful stroke of his hammer, pounded it thirty centimeters into the ground.

Granmè was unimpressed. With a grunt—and a gasp from the onlookers—she yanked the stake from the ground and handed it to the astonished Boss Man. "Tell your *blan* friends they'll have to build around us because we're not moving." With that, Granmè entered the tent, followed by a less assured Fania.

Inside the quiet, shaded tent, Fania watched Granmè rearrange the few belongings in their home. It was her preferred activity when she was feeling particularly agitated. Fearing the answer, Fania asked her, "Do you think we'll have to move?"

"Squatters have rights in Haiti. Besides, no foreign group will want to be responsible for putting an old woman and a baby out on the streets."

"Are you sure?"

"No," Granmè answered with resignation as she plopped to the ground, exhausted by her showdown with the Boss Man.

The American group driving the project, an offshoot of a denominational missions organization, had been working in Haiti for decades, yet nothing appeared to change. They had no idea why. After the earthquake, they increased their efforts but with nothing more to show for it. They meant well, but at best they were doing things *for* the people rather than with them. At worst, they were doing things *to* them.

They didn't want any harm done through their work, but they also weren't as sensitive to Haitian culture as they should have been. As a result, harm *was* done, partially due to their insistence on doing everything the "American way" and partially because some unscrupulous Haitians saw the deep pockets of the Americans as fair and easy prey.

This time, as it turned out, Granmè's perception of the predicament was exactly correct. When Lamosier brought the construction stalemate to the attention of the building committee from the American group, who were all staying at a recently constructed upscale hotel downtown, they feared ejecting people from their homes would result in bad publicity and they relented. They told Lamosier to perform the construction in such a way as to disrupt as few families as possible.

All the negotiations and maneuvering ended up affecting only one home: Granmè's. The few other families whose homes were in the path of construction found other places to stay, either with nearby family members or in the countryside where they felt safer anyway. Few people held a strong devotion to La Saline. Moving was no hardship for them.

But Granmè remained, along with Fania and Rose.

Chapter 7

THERE MAY HAVE been times when Granmè regretted staying in her tent, but she never expressed it to Fania or anyone else. In her mind, the principle outweighed the inconvenience of being part of a major construction project. Three-story walls went up on two sides of her home leaving the tent in shadows all but a few hours of the day.

Workers constantly scurried about carrying buckets of sand, water, rocks, and concrete mix. Massive trucks, barely able to navigate the narrow roadways, shook the ground as they shuttled fresh supplies of materials several times a day. The pair went about their daily business as though nothing had changed. By most measures, nothing had.

The two women, always with little Rose in tow, went about their daily routine with the consistency of the phases of the moon. Trips to the river to wash clothes or bathe also offered the chance to gather with neighbors and catch up on each others' mostly uneventful lives. Wilmina kept Fania at arm's length but others in the village found mother and daughter a delightful addition to their squalid community.

Gradually and not without emotional trauma, church became a part of Fania's life again. At first, she was little more than Granmè's shadow, rarely emerging from her protective presence. Fania feared rejection in spite of Pastor Henri's consistent encouragement and unconditional acceptance. The presence of the *vodou* priest Claude, who always seemed to be lurking nearby, leering at her, drove Fania closer to her God and to Granmè. Over time, her faith became her own once more.

Rose needed no such adjustment. In keeping with her initial *in utero* disruption of the church service, she was invariably the most demonstrative worshiper. As she grew, her unbounded enthusiasm and apparently unlimited energy did more to lift the spirits of the congregation than did any of Henri's sermons. He never complained; he found her revels every bit as refreshing as the rest of his flock did.

The feeding program at the church made life easier, but the need to earn money never ceased. Granmè was a master at making something from nothing, or close to it. It didn't hurt that she knew someone everywhere. Using her blade for more benign purposes, she scaled and cut fish for a friend at the fish market. The warehouse manager who distributed the sickly sweet yellow "fruit champagne" soda would sell her a case at a discount from time to time, which she would resell wherever crowds gathered.

Gangs weren't uncommon in the slum, but they were neither as visible nor as oppressive as those in, say, Cité Soleil, the most notorious of all Haitian slums. Political activity didn't reach its slimy tendrils into La Saline as often as it did in other neighborhoods. In that way at least, the village's insignificance was a blessing more than a curse.

The other saving grace was that Granmè's reputation as both a pillar of the community and its staunchest defender caused the gang members to leave her, and by association Fania and Rose, undisturbed.

Fania wasn't left completely alone by everyone, however. The men of La Saline, and more than a few who simply passed through, always had their eyes on her. The presence of a child in her life frightened some away. Others were well aware of Granmè's blade and her willingness to use it in defense of her adopted family. The few who made it through those barriers were put off by Fania herself. Her faith in God may have been restored after her ordeal at Victory Baptist Church, but her distrust of men hadn't waned in the slightest.

Rose wasn't affected by her mother's aversion to the opposite sex. In fact, everyone and everything were objects of the little girl's affection and curiosity. She constantly amazed Fania and Granmè with wisdom and love beyond her tender years. She showered extravagant love on everyone she met, but saved her greatest devotion for her mother.

Those feelings didn't go unrequited. Fania adored Rose in a way she wouldn't have believed possible before the little girl entered her life. Some nights, watching her daughter sleep, she thought of her own past and wondered if her mother had felt the same emotions as she watched over Fania as a small child. Those musings created a fresh bond with the mother she'd lost half a decade earlier.

Fania wondered, *Does love die along with its giver?*

For as long as Rose could remember, which was not long at all, Granmè had been promising to take her and her mother to the Mache Fè, the Iron Market, for her third birthday. The destination had grown in her imagination to a mythical state that reality had little hope of equaling. Yet, once she got there, it was greater still.

Little Rose had never seen such a majestic sight. The towers on either side of the gateway through which they passed seemed to her to reach up to heaven. As she gaped, she thought she saw a cloud catch on one of the pinnacles and stop skidding across the sky for the briefest moment before loosing itself and continuing its course to the horizon.

Once inside, the child tried to take in the immensity of the space. She was used to being dwarfed by her surroundings, but the Mache Fè dwarfed everything and everyone in or near it. She was sure that her entire village of La Saline would fit inside it.

Granmè told Rose she could pick three gifts, one for each year of her life. "How will I choose?" the child asked with tears welling up in her eyes as she contemplated such a crucial decision. Sheer happiness might also have contributed to her state.

Fania knelt down at her side and comforted her. "Take your time, Rose. There's no hurry."

Hand in hand in hand, the three generations walked by stall after stall, each selling modest wares. Rose was captivated by a vendor selling a colorful collection of *bonbons*. She dipped her hand into the heap of sweets then looked over her shoulder to check with her mother that it was all real.

Next to the candy vendor was a booth selling books. Fania picked one up and stared blankly at it as she flipped through its pages.

Granmè noticed a touch of sadness on Fania's face, something that always changed her mood as well. "Would you like a gift, too, *ti manman*?"

"I'd like to have a book." Her voice was as dispirited as her expression.

"Then we'll get you one."

Fania shook her head. "If only it was that simple. I also want to be able to read it."

Granmè drew close to her. "You don't know how to read?"

"No. My parents could never afford to send me to school. At the orphanage..." Her voice trailed off with a desolation that seared Granmè's heart. "I've tried to hide it from you all this time, but with Rose getting older, I'd love to be able to read and write."

"Then let me teach you. Pick out a book that looks interesting and we'll read it together. Then find a candle so we can read while Rose sleeps. Night will be our classroom."

Her spirits soaring above the market roof at the thought of fulfilling her long held ambition, Fania singled out the book whose cover most enticed her. It bore a photo of a mother cuddling a newborn. When Fania handed it to her to complete the transaction, Granmè didn't need to ask why she had chosen that particular book. With the book in hand, Granmè launched into her bargaining with the same skill and intensity with which she wielded her knife. The book vendor didn't stand a chance.

John wore a polo shirt with a Playboy bunny logo affixed to the left chest, though neither he nor his customers had any idea of its significance. When he became embroiled in negotiations for one of his books, he adopted whatever guise suited the circumstances. Correctly judging Granmè to be a ruthless adversary, he assumed the persona of a poor, exploited widower.

When Granmè first offered one *gourde* for the book, John scoffed. "Since my dear wife Jessyka died, I'm forced to sell her precious books to feed our twin babies," he moaned. "I must get all I can. Ten *gourdes*."

"Twin babies at your age?" Granmè rightly appraised his age in the mid-sixties. "That's a fine tale."

"I'm a most virile man for my age." There was a twinkle in his eye, but it was aimed at Fania. "Nine."

Pointing at another book in his pile, she pushed on, "Your late wife read books about tractor maintenance?"

"Eight *gourdes*," John conceded, "but I'm losing money on it."

"The cover is torn on ours. I'll give you two *gourdes* because you're a bad liar and I feel sorry for you."

"Seven *gourdes* is the best I can do."

Granmè stared at him with a look that withered his will. She turned to Fania, "I think I saw better books in a stall on the other side."

John's facade was crumbling and he sensed it. "Did I say seven? That one is six, but it's the last book of its kind in all of Haiti."

The old girl was homing in on her victim. "No more than three. I don't want to spoil your twins." She flashed him a knowing grin.

John knew the battle was lost, but he shot one last salvo. "Four. They need supper."

"Let's go, Fania. This man doesn't want to sell us anything today." Granmè took Fania's hand and turned to leave. Not recognizing this was all part of a tried-and-true strategy, Fania's heart sunk.

It only took one step for John to surrender. "*Dakò*, three, but my babies will go to bed hungry."

"Sold," Granmè declared in triumph.

As she claimed the well-deserved spoils of her victory and handed the book to Fania, Granmè took a deep breath and closed her eyes.

"Are you all right, Granmè?" Fania held her arm.

As always, she responded with a smile, saying, "Just tired. I can't bargain the way I used to. It takes a lot out of an old woman. Plus, I'm always trying to keep up with you two. I'll find a place to sit down near the entrance gate. Look for me there on your way out."

Watching Granmè hobble away, Fania realized once more how frail she looked. The image of the mighty guardian with the threatening dagger was slowly but relentlessly giving way to that of an old woman weakened by age and sorrow.

Mother and child emerged from the gates of the market looking as if they'd plundered *Sogebank* for all its holdings. The book in Fania's hand was to her no different than a treasure chest unearthed from a pirate's cache on Latòti. With Granmè's instruction, she looked forward to unlocking its riches.

Rose toddled out fully laden. In her left hand was a giraffe carved out of wood that was all too rare in Haiti, although that problem was beyond her understanding. Her right hand gripped another wooden toy, a tiny red boat with a scrap of soiled cloth for a sail. She couldn't wait for the next time her mother did their laundry so she could test it in the river. Her final gift was half gone already as she alternated between chewing and sucking on the bright red *bonbon* that first caught her eye.

Between the distraction of their acquisitions and the general bedlam of the market, they didn't notice Granmè sitting on the curb by the road. A shrill whistle captured their attention, one immediately recognizable as Granmè's. Two fingers in her mouth and a few missing teeth endowed her with the ability to generate a piercing whistle that overpowered any competing commotion.

When they looked up, they could see her pointing to an idling *tap-tap.* She called to them, "Come along, ladies. This driver is going toward La Saline. He's leaving any second." Fania and Rose rushed to join her behind the packed vehicle. As all three prepared to clamber into the truck, a confusion of shouts and crashes resounded from behind them.

David had suffered many epileptic seizures in his twenty-five years. Living in Cité Soleil, where nothing shocked the inhabitants, the bizarre episodes went practically unnoticed. Some neighbors even thought they were a good sign that the *loa* had temporarily taken up residence in him.

With a few adjustments and a considerable amount of denial, David had learned to live with the spells. It didn't occur to him, never able to afford medical treatment or education regarding his illness, that driving a truck wasn't a reasonable vocation for someone in his condition. It was a job in a place where employment was scarce. That was all he knew.

When he blacked out behind the wheel of a dump truck overflowing with sand while careening down Boulevard Jean-Jacques Dessalines, he never saw the crowds scattering or heard the screams of terrified parents pulling their children from its path. Nor did he hear the crunching of the bones of the woman standing behind the tap-tap he ran into.

Before Fania realized what was happening, she found herself on the sidewalk with Rose. Granmè had pushed them aside just before the out-of-control truck slammed into the rear of the *tap-tap*. Her reflexive actions had saved the two girls at the cost of her own life. Fania sat stunned as a crowd gathered around the accident scene. Although pinned and crushed, Granmè gave the only daughter she could save one last smile before she slumped onto the street.

Chapter 8

"SHE DIED THE WAY she lived: sacrificially." Those were the only words Fania heard from Pastor Henri's impassioned eulogy at Granmè's funeral.

No one could remember such a well attended funeral for a resident of La Saline. But then no one could remember a person like Granmè. Even those who had had their differences with her —Wilmina, for example—recognized and came to mourn her loss to the village.

Fania could in no way have afforded any kind of ceremony

to honor her adoptive grandmother. A coffin and plot cost money she didn't have. The village demonstrated its respect further by contributing toward the cost of the funeral through a collection Pastor Henri initiated. The amount was sufficient to purchase a simple wooden box and a plot in the corner of a burial area populated mostly by shrines more elaborate than the houses the dead had occupied during their time among the living.

Henri shared some memories of and tributes to his favorite church member. People listened and made comments of agreement as he spoke of Granmè's importance to him, his church, and the community as a whole. He made special mention of her great love for Fania and Rose and how they had so enriched the last few years of her life. He told the gathered crowd that her love was in her deeds, as the greatest loves always are.

Fania needed no reminder of Granmè's sacrificial and unconditional love. It was with her still. That it would follow her all through her life, she was confident.

Wilmina truly would miss Granmè. Despite their differences, the old woman had never held back a helping hand when Wilmina was in need. Even so, she couldn't resist a petty taunt at Fania's expense as she left the graveyard. She didn't care that Rose and Marie-Fleur could hear her when she asked, "What will you do now, squatter? You don't look so sure of yourself with your protector gone."

The vicious comment was wasted on Fania. Nothing could cut more deeply than the pain she endured at the loss of Granmè.

First the parents who raised her and now the woman who saved her were all gone. The grief was multiplied by the vulnerability she felt at being suddenly thrust onto the front line of life. She was the head of the Dieusel family, yet she still felt like a child herself.

For some reason, her mind wandered back to Granmè's promise to teach her to read. She would never have that chance. What could Fania teach Rose?

In the days after Granmè's death, Fania didn't move from a spot in the corner of the tent. She never wanted to move again. She was afraid of the world. Rose was all she had left. Her sense was, if she abandoned her corner and attempted to face the world again, it would take Rose, too.

Friends and neighbors stopped by to share food and drink with them. Otherwise, they might have wasted away. Fania knew their consideration was at least as much out of respect for Granmè as it was for the safety of her and little Rose.

Rose stayed by her mother's side for as long as she was able, but the mourning period for a child of three is brief compared to that of adults. Rose had an intuitive sense of the temporal nature of life, so death didn't shake her as it did her mother. Furthermore, she possessed a childlike faith beyond that of most prelates that death itself had only a precarious grip on life. On the third day following the funeral, almost by instinct, she leapt from Fania's side and ran out into the road. People come and go, but a child still has to play.

It took Fania a minute to react to her daughter's absence, enveloped as she was in her den of grief. "Rose!" she cried as she stumbled out of the tent.

The sun assaulted her eyes and temporarily blinded her. Once her eyes adjusted, she saw Rose playing with two other children, a girl in a florescent green tank top several sizes too large and a boy wearing an unlikely long-sleeved flannel shirt and nothing else. The trio was engaged in a game that involved a rusty piece of metal and a fraying segment of rope. She couldn't divine the rules of the game merely through observation. She wasn't sure the kids themselves were aware of them, but the underlying message of the game was clear. Life goes on. Those left behind carry on.

A slumbering spark of solace she thought had been extinguished flickered within Fania as she watched the kids skip, swing, and bounce to the rhythm of the unknown sport. She sat on the stone Granmè used to occupy so often as together they watched the neighborhood go through its daily cycle of waking, performing the chores that kept life going, then slowing to a sleepy end.

Even small children run out of energy eventually, especially when their fuel supply is limited. It was an exhausted Rose who settled on the other stone, the one on which Fania used to sit. The significance of the positions was not lost on the young mother. She was burdened now with responsibilities for which she felt totally unprepared. She felt as though those two stones weighed down her shoulders as she contemplated her new place in an upended world.

Late that night, as Rose slept peacefully beside her, Fania found breathing difficult; she felt the tent closing in on her. Sleep being out of the question in her state, she stepped out and looked up at the starlight slipping in and out of clouds, filtered as it always was by the haze that hung permanently over La Saline. She dipped her hand into the small pail of water she kept by the tent entrance and wiped it across her hot brow. It dripped refreshing rivulets down her face, neck, and chest.

The moon was the same one under which Granmè had found her so long ago—full, silver, and as high as God Himself. She wished she could take a walk by the water's edge as Granmè had that night, but she realized she didn't need to travel anywhere to find someone who needed her help. That one was sleeping in the tent behind her. As a child living in La Saline with a single mother, Rose was as vulnerable and needy as she herself had ever been.

At the mere thought of Rose, Fania's breathing grew more free. She smiled at the moon and ducked back into the tent. Sliding her blanket across the floor of the tent, her toe struck something sharp. Looking down, she saw a sliver of moonlight seeping through the tent flap, glinting off burnished metal at her feet. She lifted Granmè's knife into the full light.

Unlike everything else in the tent, the blade was cool to her touch. She gripped the handle, alternately squeezing and releasing it. Without thinking, she flipped the knife in her hand, maneuvering it as skillfully as Granmè once had. She had no idea where that ability came from.

As it spun, the blade scattered specks of reflected moonlight throughout the tent. One shard of light sparkled playfully on Rose's cheek. When the allure of the splintered light finally faded, Fania slipped the knife under the wad of cloth that served as her pillow and she curled up to sleep. Her anxieties had dissipated, a mellow calm taking their place. Sleep swept over her as gently as a gull riding the thermals above Île de la Gonâve.

The morning was brighter than Fania had known in some time. The light strengthened her sufficiently to allow her to settle once more into the routine she'd learned from Granmè: taking the wash to the river, getting food from the church, and walking around the neighborhood with Rose.

At the end of a day's work and play that saw her adapting to a new level of existence—or at least taking a significant step in that direction—Fania settled contentedly outside her home with Rose at her side. Her home. As she meditated on the many shades of meaning those words had lately taken on for her, Henri came by holding a wooden box about the size of a cinder block.

"I've been waiting until you had adjusted some to your loss. Nothing will ever be the same, I know, but I'm glad to see you and Rose are moving on with your lives," the young pastor consoled as he held the box out to her. "This is yours. Granmè asked me to hold it for you. She knew she wouldn't be with you forever, although I wasn't always so sure." His comment made a smile twitch at the corners of Fania's mouth. "It's not a treasure, just a few of her keepsakes."

Fania hesitated. To her, receiving this token would be one more gesture toward releasing Granmè forever. She wasn't ready for that step, but she took comfort from the reassurance in Henri's eyes. Her courage restored, she reached out in a way that reminded her of the moment she first took the newborn Rose. His gift delivered, Henri made a move to leave, then stopped and turned back with a smile. "Then again, maybe it is a treasure." He smiled once more and left the little family.

It was all she could do to restrain herself from investigating the mysterious chest as soon as it touched her hands. Unsure of the emotions the unveiling would press upon her, Fania waited until she had privacy. After singing Rose off to sleep, she lit the candle Granmè had bought her at the Mache Fè. It was the first time Fania dared to ignite it. To her eyes, its glow shone brighter than such a small candle should have cast. The extra illumination was welcome because the moon, shrouded in clouds, offered no light.

She'd never seen such a box, made from pure mahogany so deep and dark, it seemed to absorb the candlelight. It was polished to a luster that reminded her of the children's shoes at the orphanage on a Sunday morning. The rich wood brought her back to the stories her parents had told her, stories that had been passed down from their parents, of how majestic trees once covered a lush Haiti, only to be eroded into dirt and despair.

She rubbed her hands over the surface of the box as if her caress could awaken some spirit contained in the wood, maybe even touch Granmè. Her fingers traced the elaborate designs carved into its lid, images of a Haitian countryside that no longer existed: flourishing forests and deep pools of clear water fed by waterfalls electric with hissing foam, fruit falling abundantly and freely from overburdened mango and coconut trees. She opened the hinged cover with a caution she didn't understand.

The contents were of little value by the rest of the world's standards, but anything that made Granmè's memory more vivid was a treasure to Fania. A small linen sack held some bills and coins, no more than a few hundred *gourdes*. She knew she needed the money and it would go to good use, but the rest of the box was of far greater interest.

A notebook with handwriting that was obviously Granmè's brought frustrating memories to Fania's mind and heart. How she would love to read those words, but they might as well have been scratch marks made by the chickens who scurried around in the dust of La Saline hoping no one would claim ownership of them. She wanted to read those words with a passion that tore at her. The possibility of having someone else read it to her, coming between her and Granmè, she dismissed without a second thought.

Some pencils and pens, once more reminding her of her illiteracy, were tossed in among some baubles. She slipped on a bracelet of black beads but put it back in the box when its click-clack sound caused Rose to stir. A box of matches might be helpful if they still lit. She caressed a glimmering white hair clip made from a single translucent shell, wondering if it was intended for one of Granmè's lost daughters.

The most intriguing find was a bundle of papers tied up in twine. The paper was like nothing she'd ever seen before, darker, with a heavier texture than she'd ever felt, yet brittle. A round impression had been made into a few of the pages. She ran her fingers over the raised letters wishing she could read by touch where sight failed her. She was particularly taken by something that resembled a faded gold coin, but bigger and as thin as a corn leaf, that was stuck to one of the papers.

All this, like much of her new life, was foreign and frightening to her. She put everything back into the box as close as possible to the way Granmè had stowed it. She blew out the candle and lay down to sleep, one hand still touching the chest.

Two disturbing sounds woke Fania the following morning. The first was a loud, wet thud that came from above. She might have ignored it along with the rest of the usual din of early morning had it not been for another, barely audible sound. A whimper of pain from Rose's lips shocked Fania into full maternal alertness. Even in the shady tent, Fania could see Rose was trying to brush something off her arm. She picked up the child and carried her into the light as another thump sounded on the tent's roof.

Fania splashed water onto her daughter's arm, which was speckled with a wet gray substance. The spots were red and raw where the blob of muck had been. Rubbing her wounds had caused Rose's hand to be covered and it started to burn as well. Fania dipped the girl's entire hand into the water and wiped it clean. She held her daughter close until the tears stopped.

With Rose cared for, Fania took in all that was happening. Large globs of wet cement were falling from high up on the school's wall where men were working. By now the tent's roof was laden with the mess and it was drooping to within centimeters of the ground. She realized a small wad of the fresh mixture, which contained skin-searing lime, had found its way through a tear in the roof and landed on Rose.

Looking up at the source of the destructive mess, she saw two men standing at the edge of the wall, holding shovels. Both were grinning down at her. Although it had been almost four years since she last encountered him, she recognized one of the men as Renaud. She still had nightmares about his attempted attack on her the night she stumbled into La Saline.

"There's more where that came from," Renaud shouted with a laugh. The other man continued to smile, but didn't share his co-worker's level of amusement. A reprimand from the Boss Man diverted their attention and both returned to work.

The tent that had been Fania's home for so long, the home that Granmè's determination had spared from demolition during the construction of the school, was now destroyed by that very construction just the same. As Fania stared at the tent's slouching roof, Granmè's spirit, which was always most potent in the face of such adversity, seized Fania's soul, feet, and hands. She set Rose on her hip and stormed off.

*   *   *

In Haiti, nothing goes away. If something can be reused, scavengers will find it and it will continue in another life. If not, it tends to pile up somewhere unless and until it's forgotten and becomes a permanent part of the landscape. In this way, the houses that had been destroyed during the school's construction still existed in bits and pieces in piles of refuse where a road left La Saline and faded into a field of mud, low brush, and trash closer to the harbor. That's where Fania found herself among the scavengers, piling broken cinder blocks, stones, and scraps of wood onto a sheet of discarded corrugated steel.

When the steel could hold no more, she dragged it (with a semblance of help from Rose) the quarter kilometer back to her home, now just a tarp plastered to the ground by about fifty kilograms of wet concrete. Since cement was still falling, though in smaller amounts, Fania made another trip to the junk pile, returning with more bricks on another steel sheet. This time, Rose gave up any pretense of assistance and hitched a ride on the steel sedan.

By the time Fania completed her second trip, the workers had moved on to another part of the construction. After considering how to proceed, Fania headed off to Wilmina's house, Rose scuffling along beside her.

Most days, especially when her mother was struck with one of her chronic, disabling headaches that would leave her without sight for hours at a time, Marie-Fleur could be found playing alone in front of Wilmina's tiny concrete hovel. Even in a slum where there was so much want, children found cruelty in plentiful supply. The little girl's stutter was fair game, especially for the older kids. Solitude became her greatest ally and most frequent companion.

Rose, however, shared Fania's unreserved love for the girl. They would play continuously until Wilmina's headache cleared. Then, aware that her daughter was off enjoying the company of the family she had painted as the enemy, Wilmina would drag the poor girl back into the house. Marie-Fleur was saddened each time she was parted from Fania and Rose, but the joy of their company lingered longer than her heartbreak. She was gifted with a grateful heart that was able to banish disappointment while retaining a sense of appreciation for the pleasure long after it passed.

When Fania arrived at Wilmina's house, Marie-Fleur was playing alone outside once more. She was overjoyed to see Fania and Rose, but greeted them quietly. Fania realized the girl was being careful about upsetting her mother, but she had no qualms about doing so herself. She slapped her open palm on the house's concrete lintel.

"Wilmina! Are you in there?" Fania could have looked past the sheet that served as a door to the one-room box and seen all there was to see, but she waited, hearing some rustling before a hoarse voice croaked back.

"What do you want, squatter?"

Annoyed by Wilmina's address and tone, Fania jerked the

door covering aside, flooding the space with light that was not a welcome guest to its occupant. Wilmina, who had been holding her head in her hands, covered her eyes. "I want Marie-Fleur to come to my house and play with Rose for a while."

"C-c-can I, *Manman*?" the little girl peeked in and pleaded.

Wilmina didn't even hesitate. "Take her," she said before shoving the little girl back into the light and pulling the door flap closed. Marie-Fleur didn't need the push. She grabbed Fania's hand as she would a lifeline rescuing her from a raging river. The three left Wilmina to suffer alone, which was all the woman wanted anyway.

As they always did when given the chance, Rose and Marie-Fleur passed the time in play with a freedom and joy reserved for children who have nothing but each other. Even the seven year gap in their ages, accentuated by their youth, did nothing to lessen their harmony. In their short time together, Fania had conveyed to Marie-Fleur the attitude and conduct needed to entertain and be entertained by a much younger child.

The fact that Rose didn't notice or care about her playmate's stutter made it all the more enjoyable for both.

Adult supervision would have been unnecessary, so completely were they absorbed in their activity. That was the point for Fania, who began her efforts by tugging the tent, laden with wet cement, off her tiny squatter's lot.

As Fania stacked bricks and rocks where the sides of her tent had been, then reinforced them with the fallen cement, still wet from her constant stirring and adding of water, the girls were engaged in a game involving holding hands and spinning in circles.

The two walls forming the entryway were complete by the time the playmates became too dizzy to continue and thus moved on to a rock-throwing competition. Soon, a tickle-fest was in full swing, so the two little girls didn't hear the racket Fania made as she hoisted the wobbling sheet metal roof in place.

Exhausted from their hijinks, Rose and Marie-Fleur sat on the ground drawing pictures in the dirt. Even more fatigued, Fania sat dividing her attention between the young artists and the unpretentious new home she had built for her family of two.

The timing was perfect. The headache that had lowered Wilmina's defenses was gone around the same time that the children's energy and imagination were spent. She stormed onto the scene and yanked Marie-Fleur to her feet. She shrieked, "My daughter is not your slave. What do you think you..." It wasn't a sound, but a sight that interrupted her tirade. Seeing Fania resting before a house as real as her own and more solid than many, she was caught completely by surprise.

"Wha-wha- h-h-how d-d-did..." She couldn't continue, especially after her daughter looked up at her and smiled at their temporarily shared speech disorder. The irony somehow eluded Wilmina.

"Go home!" she shouted as she swatted her daughter's bottom in an act of pure frustration. Wilmina gave Fania one last parting glare that might have lowered the temperature in La Saline a few degrees. "You're still just a squatter," she muttered, and she was gone.

Only then did Rose notice that a solid house had appeared where her flimsy tent of a home had been. In her young mind, all sorts of scenarios circled. Some involved tiny men with equally tiny tools. Others were the products of darker corners of her imagination bound up with spirits or demons. Her confusion was understandable. She had never seen a house materialize where there had been none.

All her fantasies disappeared when she looked at her weary mother, recovering on her usual stone seat. The cement burns on every centimeter of bare skin, the cuts and scrapes all over her arms and legs were testaments to her sacrificial love, something Rose had been the recipient of since birth. In her own childlike way, she was well aware that her mother was capable of making a home for her. Now it was clear she could make a house as well.

Chapter 9

Dust flowed freely through gaps in the walls of the newly constructed house. Over time, mother and child would find and collect stones to plug the holes, turning their house into a life-size jigsaw puzzle.

On windy nights, the steel roof, attached more by hope than anything else, rattled above their sleeping heads, but Fania and Rose never slept better. The door was only a breach in one wall, covered by a scrap of the old tent vinyl, but they couldn't have felt more secure.

The sturdiness of the house was aided by the fact that two of its walls were three stories high, shared with the school, which was nearing completion. So near, in fact, that the morning after the little Dieusel family began occupying their new dwelling, children were already streaming into the school's courtyard, squealing with excitement.

Fania stepped out of her house and stopped one of the kids to ask, "Where's everyone going?"

Out of breath, the boy, barefoot and empty-handed, slowed slightly to answer, "They're starting to sign up students at the school." He quickened his pace again and was off. Fania was caught up in the boy's energy when she briskly woke Rose and dressed her in her best dress, pink, with white lace around the neck and hem.

"Are we going to church, *Manman*? Is it Sunday already?" She was still rubbing sleep from her eyes.

"No, *cheri*. We're going to school."

Standing in the courtyard surrounded by the ongoing construction, Fania and Rose looked up at the walls of classrooms that towered all around them. Mourning Granmè's death and building her own home had so occupied Fania's time and mind, she didn't realize how close the school was to opening. On a long white banner spanning the space, red and blue letters spelled out, "*Lekòl Lespwa*." If Fania could have understood what was written there, she would have appreciated the appropriateness of the name: "School of Hope."

That hope was displayed even in the construction itself. Although the school was about to be occupied, rebar tentacles reached high above the last completed floor, a sign of optimism that there could be a future in Haiti and it could reach the sky.

So overwhelmed were they by the structure surrounding them and the crowds swarming around them, they both stood frozen. Rose thought perhaps some giant had dropped the Mache Fè behind her house or maybe her new house had been built next to the market.

Fania's mind was more focused. More than anything, she wanted to give Rose the education she had never received. Her excitement was subdued, however, because of her history of disappointment. Life had conditioned her to maintain low expectations.

A careening kid stirred them from their thoughts when he almost knocked them off their feet. At last, Fania could detect a central point to the vortex of people. Several adults sat at a long table. Each had a stack of papers and long lines before them. Holding Rose's hand, Fania took her place at the end of what appeared to be the shortest queue.

When she reached the table, she was no more sure of herself than when she wandered into the confusion in the first place. The woman at the table flashed a compulsory smile and looked at the two of them. "Are you both going to school?"

Fania wanted to say yes, but instead responded, "No, only my daughter Rose."

"How old is she?"

"Three."

"In that case, you need to register her for preschool over in the first line." With that, she pointed to the most distant line and redirected her attention to the person behind Fania. "Next."

Fania shuffled over to the location the woman had indicated, starting at the end of the line once more. With so many new sights to take in, Rose was perfectly content to wait. At registration, some of the children had been given colorful, bulky backpacks, which they hung over their shoulders. The packs were so large she wondered how the smaller children stayed upright.

At last, Fania reached a middle-aged man who never even looked up from his papers. "Name?"

Fania took a look around to see if he were speaking to someone else. When she felt certain she was the object of his inattention, she asked, "Whose name?"

The man finally looked up and over the glasses perched at the end of his nose. "The student's name."

"Rose Dieusel."

"How is that spelled?"

Fania thought she might cry. "I don't know."

"Do you both live in La Saline?"

"*Wi.*"

"Fine," was the man's response as he scribbled something on his sheet. He tore off a piece of paper and handed it to an increasingly bewildered Fania. "Take this to the table over there." Again without lifting his gaze from the table, he pointed over Fania's shoulder.

As instructed, Fania dutifully carried the strip of paper, the contents of which were a complete mystery to her, to another line at another table. For all she knew, she would be permanently turning Rose over to the school. Or maybe, she mused, it was a love note from an official at one table to someone at the other.

She began to envy Rose's opportunity to master language, to be able to understand the messages that were scrawled on concrete walls or plastered on billboards. That would surely take several years, but now she sensed it was within reach. She started to feel excited for her child.

The excitement lasted only as long as the new line she found herself in. When she got to the front, she handed her slip to a kindly, round-faced gentlemen in a suit and tie. The man, whose name was Basile, was headmaster of the school. He asked, "Do you have your sponsorship papers?"

"I'm sorry?" was all Fania could think to say.

"Does the child have a sponsor?"

"I don't know what that means."

"The sponsor pays for her education. If she doesn't have one, you have to pay the cost."

Something hopeful in her had failed to consider the fact that an education wouldn't be free. That was why she had never had one.

"How much?" she asked with futility tainting her voice.

"One hundred per semester."

"One hundred *gourdes*?" The question was simply a way to

delay the inevitable. She had the few *gourdes* Granmè had left her in the box, but knew without question it wouldn't be enough.

At that, Basile stared intently at Fania. His eyes revealed a tension between an official detached distance required for his administrative role and a sympathy that the humanity in him wouldn't allow him to deny. Based on what he heard in the voice of the young woman standing before him, he knew he was about to break a heart.

"Dollars," he finally uttered before adding the stake in the heart of her hopes, "American dollars." He saw her throat tighten and tears well up in her eyes.

"I'm sorry to have wasted your time, sir." Fania turned to leave. If nothing else, the years of disappointment her life had already known dulled the pain of moments like this.

Basile motioned to a petite woman of about thirty who was standing nearby. "Monite, can you take over for me here, *souple*?" The woman was the picture of efficiency and professionalism. Basile depended on her for more things than he would admit to his superiors or even to her. He stood up and took Fania aside as Monite sat at the table and assisted the next family in line.

Basile explained to Fania the way the school tuition worked. Aware that none of the families in La Saline would be able to afford the tuition on their own, the American group funding the school project had lined up American sponsors for the students. It had happened soon after Granmè's death. In her mourning, Fania had missed it. All the sponsors were taken.

Basile tried to console the young mother who, being close to the age of his own daughter, raised in him a compassion he didn't have the luxury of extending to every family. "We can take her picture and put her on a waiting list for a sponsor. The sponsor pays for tuition, materials, and a uniform." He smiled at Rose and continued, "She's a lovely girl." Rose smiled back at the man, lowering her head slightly at the compliment. "She shouldn't have a problem attracting a sponsor. The Americans always choose the most attractive children first."

"How long would that take?" Fania asked, the hope returning to her voice against her will.

"Assuming she gets a sponsor in time, she could begin next year." Basile noted that, although she smiled, there was disappointment in her eyes. "Of course, there are other possibilities. How important is this to you?"

His question was ominous even if his tone wasn't. She'd experienced enough of the darkness in men's hearts that she hesitated to be completely honest with this man about whom she knew nothing. It was her determination to provide a future for Rose that decisively banished the chilling thoughts his question formed in her mind.

"It's everything."

"I thought so. Come with me, ladies."

As he marched across the chaotic courtyard, children scattered from his path the way the chickens moved out of the way when anyone walked down a street in La Saline. For some reason, the alarm in Fania's heart about his intentions diminished with each step they took.

When they stopped before what looked like a cave entrance in the corner of the building, Basile called into it, "Theodore, are you in there?" A man who was at least half a meter taller than Fania emerged from the passageway. His clothes were filthy, his eyes were intense, and a bushy mustache covered his upper lip. "How are things looking in there?" Basile queried the tall man.

"About what you'd expect. Marta drove another girl out," Theodore replied.

"Then I might have exactly what you need." He turned to Fania. "Are you willing to work for your daughter's education?"

Basile welcomed a certain degree of indignation in her voice when she replied, "I expect nothing less."

Theodore joined the conversation. As he spoke, his expression softened. "I think what Basile is offering you is a job in the cafeteria. You'd work while your daughter is in school. The pay would cover your child's tuition."

Basile added, "With a little left over." He stared at Fania who stood unresponsive for a moment. "Is this so hard a decision?"

"No, it's hard to believe," she said as a tentative smile formed on her lips.

"Then you agree?" asked Basile.

"*Wi*! *Men wi*, I'd love to do it." She found herself bouncing on her toes like a child about to receive an unexpected and undeserved gift.

Theodore leaned toward her and hissed, "But you haven't

met Marta." He wheeled and dissolved back into the dark passageway.

Basile extended the caution, "Are you sure you can work for a difficult personality?"

Thinking of her nemesis Nadine, Fania replied, "Difficult is not such a big problem once you've handled impossible."

Basile erupted into laughter. "I had a feeling about you. Report to the kitchen next Monday at 10 AM."

"What about Rose?"

"She doesn't get off so easy." Basile knelt down before the little girl who wore a quizzical look. "You must be in class at eight!"

Rose looked up at her mother. "What's class?"

Fania answered with laughter in her voice, "You're going to school, *ti flè-m!*" She picked up her "little flower" and swung her completely around.

Basile waved the piece of paper he had taken from her earlier. "I'll complete your registration. Come by at the end of the week to get a uniform."

Everything she had observed at *Lekòl Lespwa* conspired to bewilder little Rose. She didn't know what school meant except that it was a monstrous building off of which her house hung like an unripe plantain. She didn't know who all those people were or what they were doing. She wasn't sure she wanted to wear a uniform. Would it have medals and badges like the officials she'd seen on the streets? Her comfort was that her mother was excited. *If Manman likes school*, her simple and trusting mind thought, *then I want to go.*

Fania's excitement kept her awake that night. She envisioned a day many years in their future when Rose would come home from school laden with books to study. Fania wasn't so proud that she couldn't submit herself to her own daughter's tutelage. It was, if anything, an appealing idea.

As Fania contemplated the various pleasant paths that for the first time she could actually imagine stretching into their future, Rose slept silently on the blanket beside her. The contented *manman* leaned over and kissed her forehead, wishing Rose all the things she had missed in her life.

"Sleep well, my precious girl. The sun is shining on your future."

Chapter 10

"I DON'T LIKE this color, *Manman*", Rose complained as Fania fastidiously smoothed and straightened the girl's uniform. Fania shared her daughter's dislike for the bright orange material the outfit was made of, but what it represented pushed aside any aesthetic qualms she may have held.

A school uniform. How many times as a child had Fania watched her uniformed friends and neighbors parade proudly up muddy roads with notebooks in hand and oversized packs slung over their shoulders wishing all the time she could be among their number? Now it was her daughter who would fulfill that dream. For the first time in her life, she understood the frustration and sadness her own mother must have endured at not being able to do the same for her. Sadness, delight, regret, thrill, fear, and joy all fought for territory in her heart. The battle that ensued kept her on edge the entire day. In the end, they all managed to win.

Fania and Rose joined the river of orange that flowed into the courtyard on the first day of school. Although school had officially begun, workers carrying shovels, buckets, and cinder blocks could still be seen atop the building. Fania shivered at the thought of Renaud looking down at her. She didn't dare look up for fear of catching his leer.

In the middle of what looked to Fania to be total anarchy, she wasn't able to recognize whatever system was in place for classroom assignments. She surveyed the area seeking a gathering of children Rose's age. There were signs directing parents and students, but they might as well have been invisible for all the good they did Fania. That fact only served to increase the feelings of inadequacy gnawing at Fania's soul.

She caught sight of one little boy who looked to be about Rose's age. She followed him, dragging a more and more fearful Rose along behind. The boy entered a classroom on the ground floor. Fania was glad of that. The thought of little Rose scaling the uneven, debris-strewn, concrete steps winding their way to the upper floors alarmed her.

When they reached the doorway of the classroom, Rose stood on the threshold, unable to move. Fania couldn't leave her there as she was but Rose showed no indication of taking the next step on her own. The anxious mother tried to find words of comfort. "You're going to be fine. You'll have lots of fun playing with all the other children. I'll be home, right on the other side of the wall." It was hard to convince Rose when she herself, in spite of all her prior optimism, was so unsure.

Her hopes for an uneventful first day were fading when a smiling woman with short hair and the tiniest waist Fania had ever seen approached them with her arms extended.

"Who is this lovely young lady?" She knelt down and looked in Rose's apprehensive eyes.

Rose's answer was no louder than a whisper, "My name is Rose."

"A beautiful name for a beautiful girl. I should have guessed that. Do you like guessing games, Rose?"

"I guess so," she answered, not appreciating the irony.

"Good, because I'm going to guess some things about you." She closed her eyes, assuming an expression of intense concentration. "I guess that you are... three years old." On hearing her hunch, Rose's eyes widened in wonderment. "And I guess that this is your first day in school."

Rose audibly gasped at this. She looked at her mother with an amazement only a three-year-old is capable of experiencing. Fania looked back at her and shrugged her shoulders.

"I have something over here I want to show you, Rose,"

the teacher said as she took Rose's willing hand and led her away. The teacher glanced back and winked. Fania watched, wishing there was someone who could give her the same reassurance the teacher had given Rose.

As if in response to her silent request, another teacher approached her and said, "She'll be fine. She'll be having so much fun, she won't even notice you're gone."

Fania's smile was a sad one. "That's what I'm most afraid of."

Back in her home, Fania thought she'd suffered enough anxiety for one day, but her day was just beginning. A new job working for the infamous Marta loomed in her immediate future. Although she feigned courage to Basile, she dreaded being at the mercy of another tyrant. Her imagination had two hours in which to nurture the unknown into a major crisis.

Her anxiety-inducing speculation was suspended when she heard a faint voice coming from somewhere nearby. She looked around and even peeked outside but still couldn't determine its source. Turning her head slowly, she realized the voice was coming through the wall. By pressing her ear against the concrete, she could hear the voice more clearly as she picked it up midsentence.

"...and welcome to Creole class at *Lekòl Lespwa*. I'm *Pwofesè* Simeon. Our study will start with the basics, but since you are a class of older students, I'll be moving quickly. If you have trouble, you can always come to me after class for help.

Now, take out the workbooks you were given at registration."

Excited, Fania looked around the room, half expecting a workbook to be miraculously at hand. She returned to reality and to the wall and pressed against it once more.

"...will be due at the start of each class. Remember, your workbook is your lifeline in this course. If you forget it..." There was silence followed by laughter. Fania guessed the teacher had made some gesture of doom that amused his students.

Fania remained listening at the wall until the class ended. The side of her face was sore from being pressed against the rough surface and some pieces of loose concrete still clung to her ear and cheek. She noticed neither. Her mind was swimming with possibilities, but she had no time to meditate on them. She had barely enough time to make it to the cafeteria for her first shift.

Marta was everything Theodore had warned and Fania had feared. She ruled the kitchen with an iron ladle, both figuratively and literally. She was not above smacking a stray hand with the worn, dented implement she always carried. It didn't matter to Fania. She was determined to steel herself against any fate to ensure Rose could stay in school.

Lunch at *Lekòl Lespwa* consisted of small bowls of rice or noodles, usually mixed with whatever morsels became available —beans or scraps of meat. The women in the feeding line handed bowls to the endless parade of uniformed children, who received each bowl with a gratitude more suited to a person being served a gourmet meal. As they worked, Marta marched back and forth behind the women, shouting every time she noted the slightest variance from the strict, arbitrary routine she dictated to them at the start of their work day.

"Use your right hand!" She screamed at an unfortunate left-handed server, who also received a ladle in the posterior for her error.

"Spread out more! You two are too close together." She swung the ladle like an ax between a pair of workers, one of whom had inadvertently shuffled a few centimeters in the wrong direction.

Once they settled into a smooth rhythm, the crew had an easier time of it. Such efficiency did nothing to soothe Marta. She moved into the kitchen to terrorize the cooks. That left the women in the line free to complain about her as consolation for their pains.

By the time the children had all passed through, the entire staff looked and felt as though they'd spent a month in the sugarcane fields. "I thought that line would never end," said Fania as she tried to sit down.

"Don't get comfortable," Marta barked. "We're not done yet. Here come the teachers. Try to get things right this time, ladies."

On cue, several adults lined up to be served. One handsome young man, exceptionally dark-skinned with high cheekbones and lively, piercing eyes, stood first in line, maintaining a conversation with an associate behind him. Both looked sharp in long-sleeved white shirts and dark ties.

"I warned them I'd be moving quickly. They're an older class, so I'm sure they have the capacity to keep up. It depends on how much it means to them. I'll try to make myself available to help them whenever I can."

"It could be a long semester for you, Simeon." The men laughed then turned their attention to the service line.

Fania was in no state to serve, however. Recognizing the first teacher by voice and name, she gawked at him with her mouth hanging open. Simeon stood directly in front of her for several seconds, watching her expectantly.

The truth was, he didn't at all mind a chance to stare at her. Despite the sweaty kerchief pulled over her forehead and the stained apron covering most of her form, Fania was an alluring sight.

"Do I have to say a secret word?" he asked her with a wide, natural smile on his face. His smile, which Fania thought was as warm as the Haitian sun and twice as bright, shook her from her reverie.

She nervously returned his smile, though a more restrained version, as she handed him a bowl. Simeon thanked her and moved on more slowly than he should have. He was as mesmerized by her as she was by him. Although still distracted, Fania continued her distribution.

The exchange was not lost on Marta. "You're going to have to work faster than that if you expect to keep this job. You're here because Theodore brought you. That doesn't mean I have to keep you." Her threat had teeth. Fania picked up the pace, but her mind was still on the attractive man with whom she had locked eyes and on whom, without his knowledge, she had placed the burden of a dream.

Fania, still carrying her apron and kerchief, was exhausted from her day in the cafeteria as she waited outside Rose's classroom with a group of parents. They all looked as impatient as Fania felt. An ear-piercing bell chimed, then was quickly drowned out by the sounds of excited children storming the yard. Desperation distorted Fania's face as she searched the mass of juvenile humanity for her daughter. After what felt to her like an unending vigil, she spied Rose waiting at the doorway of her classroom. The instant their eyes met, they dashed for one another.

Fania picked up Rose and clung to her. After a long, tender embrace, she put her down and knelt before her. Looking into her eyes, she said, "I've missed you so much. How did you like school?"

"It was fun. Can I go again?"

Fania burst into laughter and tears at the same time, "You can go every day. For as long as you want!" With her tears glowing on her cheeks, she pulled her daughter into another embrace. They lingered that way for so long that most of the other families had gone their ways by the time they separated.

"Why are you crying, *Manman*? Are you sad?"

"No, *ti flè-m*, not sad at all." A sly look suddenly came

upon the young mother's face as she spoke to the little girl. "Rose, would you like to go exploring?"

"Yeah!" was the girl's enthusiastic response.

"Come with me."

Scanning the area all the while, Fania led Rose past a series of empty classrooms, some with the dust still swirling from the hasty exit of students. At each door, she peeked in then moved on. Finally, she came upon a room that she estimated was the one adjoining her home.

Fania placed Rose in the doorway and said to her in a conspiratorial whisper, "You wait here and keep watch while I look to see if it's safe inside." Rose complied while Fania crept in and scrutinized the entire room for something she couldn't describe but hoped she'd recognize when she saw it. She wasn't even sure it would be there.

Thinking this was all a fun game, Rose yelled, "Look out, *Manman*!" Fania jumped. When she turned and saw the girl's mischievous smile and wave, she smiled back and returned to her quest. Her face lit up when she spotted some papers under a bench. She grabbed a small notebook from the pile, dashed for the door, and grabbed Rose. Fania raced across the courtyard, feeling very much like the petty thief she'd become. Rose didn't know what they'd done, but she enjoyed the childlike tickle of guilt.

That night, Fania stroked Rose's hair as she slept and hummed one of the songs they'd learned in church. Somehow, her hum harmonized with the sleeping child's soft, gentle snoring. This activity assuaged (but didn't eliminate altogether) the guilt she felt about taking the workbook from Simeon's classroom.

In an instant, her expression turned from tender to fiercely determined. She turned to face the wall her home shared with the classroom and stared at it with an intensity that might have bored a hole through it. It couldn't, so she did what to her mind was the next best thing. She pulled Granmè's knife out from under her blanket and started hacking away at the cement between two of the cinder blocks at eye level from her vantage point where she sat in her house. After a few seconds of effort, she stopped and looked over at Rose. The child dozed away peacefully, undisturbed by the sounds of her mother's labors.

Fania returned her full attention to the wall. She scraped away at the cement until there was an open gap between the two blocks. She blew into the space, clearing it of debris, then peered through the crack. The space was about a centimeter high and twenty wide, but she knew the world would pass through that opening if her plans worked out. It was with a deep sense of satisfaction and no small thrill of hope that she rested her head that night.

Chapter 11

ROSE LEFT FANIA BEHIND as she ran to school for her second day. There was no dawdling outside the classroom this time, only an excited, "*Ovwa, Manman,*" tossed over her shoulder as she passed into the room, already bustling with activity.

Fania didn't have time to feel slighted by her daughter's carefree farewell. She was preoccupied with her own thoughts. Once Rose was out of sight, Fania dashed out of the school and raced home. Dirt and small pebbles kicked up as she sped along. Her hurried pace caused her feet to nearly slide out from under her as she made the turn into her home.

Once inside, she rifled through Granmè's box. With fevered excitement, she pulled out a pencil. She then retrieved the stolen workbook before leaning against the gap she'd made in the wall the night before. Simeon's voice came through so clearly that in her heart and mind, if not her body, she was sitting in the middle of his class.

His tone today was scolding but not overly harsh. "...very difficult time without your workbooks, kids. Many of your friends and family don't have the advantage of attending a school like this. I can't replace them every time you lose one."

Her curiosity driving her, Fania pulled away and peeked through the hole. Simeon, whom she recognized from the cafeteria line, stood before the room full of students waving a workbook through the air. The room, appropriate to its location, was simplicity itself—necessities only. The twenty or so students looked to be in their late teens, not much younger than Fania herself. They sat at long, crude wooden benches with attached writing surfaces. Most of the kids were paying attention.

"Please show your appreciation to your families and sponsors by showing up ready for class," his lecture continued. At that point, he handed the workbook to a boy who was missing his right leg from the knee down. "Any questions before we start?" A couple of hands shot up.

Fania could taste her guilt. She'd taken the workbook of a poor boy who was already at enough of a disadvantage. Her penance, she resolved, would be to work that much harder on her studies. Alternately looking and listening through the hole, she flipped through the workbook with an enthusiasm few of the other students demonstrated.

Later, in the cafeteria after the line of students wound down, the ladies in the feeding crew caught their collective breath knowing the break wouldn't last anywhere near long enough. Fania could see on some of the other women's faces that the pace and the pressure Marta exerted on them all was taking its toll. Having a job was a luxury not to be taken for granted, though. For some of them, their day-to-day survival depended on the money they earned there. They would endure.

For Fania, the stakes were higher. True, she needed the money less than most. In her years with Granmè, she had learned the skills of survival in the slum. A few *gourdes* could buy bottles of soda or bags of water she could sell for a profit elsewhere. Those extra *gourdes* could be made to go a long way. No, it was Rose's education that kept her going. She would sacrifice everything, including her own life, to make Rose's life easier and more fulfilling than her own had been. She wanted Rose to dream great things as she had, but she wanted her daughter to see those dreams realized.

With the fire of that vow burning within her, Fania's time of rest came to an abrupt end. For some reason, the teachers behavior was as disorderly today as the children's. When Simeon stood before her, Fania's lips tightened, making her genuine smile appear forced.

"No games today?" Simeon joked with her. The man in line behind him laughed, making Fania feel foolish. She handed him a bowl and looked away. Once he walked down the line, though, she stared after him.

Fania could feel the cold steel of Marta's ladle a centimeter from her ear. "If you'd rather stare at the teachers than work, young lady, I can give you plenty of free time to do so." Fania returned to her duties with a fury driven by a vision of Rose as a teen attending university.

The sunny courtyard was like a furnace on most days but it felt cool after a few hours of laboring in the cafeteria. As she waited for Rose to finish her class, a gentle breeze carried Fania's imagination away to a lush countryside of hopes and desires she had never dared entertain before. It was a place of color, more than the gray she always seemed to be wrapped in, bright luminous shades foreign to her eyes. It was Rose's rainbow she envisioned.

As Fania made her way across the hectic yard, distracted by her rapture, she was intercepted by Renaud stepping into her path. "Remember me?" In his presence, Fania froze and shook at the same time. "At first I didn't recognize you from high up on that wall. I've thought about you for a long time. They tell me there is no old woman to protect you now."

"I can take care of myself," Fania replied with more confidence than she felt.

With his semi-finger pointing straight up, the thug

promised, "Just in case, I'll be watching over you."

Fania was still trembling as she strolled back to her home with orange-clad Rose chattering away beside her. Her daughter's voice, though rambling and breathless, was no less soothing. She wanted the girl to go on and on until some semblance of peace returned to her.

"I like coloring." She handed Fania one of her works of art without breaking verbal stride. "I like lunch. We have a spinning ride. I like that. I like playing with the toys. I don't like fights. Samuel and Kinson fight. Why do they fight, *Manman*?"

"I don't know. Sometimes boys misbehave. Now go inside and change out of your uniform." As Rose disappeared into the house, Fania started at a shrill voice coming from behind her.

"You look quite pleased with yourself." Fania spun around to see Wilmina and Marie-Fleur standing there. "Your waters may be clear now, but they will be muddied."

"Save your proverbs for someone as witless as yourself, woman," replied Fania, hoping her slight would send the woman away or at least silence her.

"It's fate. The *houngan* says the *loa* are displeased with you."

Before Fania could think of a reply that would adequately communicate her disregard for the opinions of Wilmina or her *loa*, she saw Marie-Fleur standing by wearing the same sweet, untainted smile that always adorned her face. The little girl showed no interest in her mother's venom. "Hi, F-f-fania. W-w-where's Rose?" At the sound of the girl's voice, Rose peeked her beaming face out of the doorway. Wilmina would have none of her daughter's cheerful mood.

"Shush, girl. We're going home." They walked away.

Under other circumstances, Wilmina's rudeness might have annoyed Fania. Between the near miss with Renaud and her excitement at her and Rose's improving prospects, she found she had no patience for it today. Twenty years living in Haiti had accustomed her to expect resistance and disappointment, but it had also instilled in her the capacity to rise above and overcome them. She had finally experienced her first taste of formal education. No cranky neighbor or threatening bully would distract her from what she now saw as her life mission.

Her routine over the next few months was consistent but never boring: Drop Rose off at her classroom, return home to eavesdrop on Simeon's class, then rush off to her job, trying to steer clear of Marta's ire, something at which she was not always successful.

When she wasn't listening in on the class, she kept the hole in her wall blocked with a scrap of paper that had once been part of a cement sack. Those scraps were often used by the cement workers to plug leaks in the makeshift wooden forms they improvised during their cement pours. Paper remnants would forever be poking out of random locations in the walls. One more would never be noticed.

The evenings found Fania doing schoolwork while Rose

slept.

Although the students inside the classroom struggled from time to time, Fania felt born for this work. Each day, the tasks became easier, her understanding growing deeper.

One day, when she was feeling insecure about her work, she snuck into Simeon's class and left a completed assignment on his desk. The next morning, the teacher asked his class about it.

"Who left this paper on my desk?" He was met by silence, most students assuming from his tone that it involved a transgression of some sort. Simeon scrutinized his students' faces for signs of recognition but found none. "Too bad," he continued, "the work here is perfect."

A boy flung his hand up. "That's mine, *pwofesè.*" The boy's shirt touted the virtues of an American beer brand. He was also missing part of his left ear.

"Nice try, Jameson, but this has neat penmanship," Simeon said as he held the paper up for display. "I'd recognize your chicken scratches anywhere." The entire class laughed, including Jameson. The noise was well timed. If the classroom had been silent, they would have heard the sounds of a restrained celebration through a small hole in the back wall.

Halfway through the first semester, Fania was able to decipher some of the messages in Granmè's notebook. Many of Granmè's thoughts were recorded there, as were her favorite proverbs.

There is always an easy way but I must press on for a

better way. Pi bon pwason naje fon anpil.

The principle was not new to Fania. "The best fish swim deep," Granmè always advised. The old woman had lived her words every day of her life. Now, though, Fania could read it for herself. These weren't just words on a page. Granmè was speaking to her.

Fania's ambition to read had been with her since she was five years old. An older friend had read her a story about a little girl's first ride in a *tap-tap*. She was entranced by her friend's ability to create a fragment of life out of nothing but what were to her random marks on a page. It wasn't until this moment, though, looking at a message from *lòt bò dlo*, across the water, beyond life, that Fania grasped the power of the written word.

In some strange way, Granmè was alive, but not like some benumbed *zonbi*, without a will of its own. Her words revealed the living heart of the woman. In a way Fania never thought possible, Granmè was with her, guiding her as she always had.

Chapter 12

As the semester progressed, empty seats began to appear in Simeon's class. Through no fault of his own, students drifted into other spheres of life. The draw of the streets of Port-au-Prince took some. For others, the demands of the immediate swamped the promise of the future as they returned to help their families survive another day.

Simeon's dedication was such that he would have taught if only one student sat in his classroom. Or on the other side of the wall, if he'd been aware of his hidden student and her commitment to his lessons.

When his final class of the semester ended, Simeon scanned his empty room with little regret. He collected his belongings, then took one final sweep through the room looking for items that had been left behind. That was when he noticed the crack in the wall. Fania had forgotten to stuff her paper into it on this day. Simeon stepped out into the courtyard and called off. "Boss Lamosier?"

Lamosier was always ready for any needs he hadn't already anticipated, which were few. "Something I can help you with, *pwofesè*?" he replied as he came running. He never wasted an instant of time nor a drop of energy.

"Can you come in here and take a look at this?"

Lamosier followed Simeon to the hole. It was about half a meter from the room's floor. Under it, they saw a small pile of sand and debris.

"What do you make of this? Do you think it's safe?"

"How long has it been like this?" asked the concerned Boss Man.

"I don't know, but this is the first time I've noticed it."

"I doubt it's a problem," Lamosier reassured him. "Probably happened during settling. I'll patch it up before school resumes."

"*Mèsi*, sir," he said as he extended his hand to the Boss Man. Where some in the teacher's position looked down on him as a laborer, Lamosier was the object of tremendous respect, even admiration, from Simeon. His skills were exceptional and his work ethic impeccable. And the high regard in which the other workers held him was awe-inspiring. Simeon wished he commanded such deference from his students.

True to his word, Lamosier himself plugged the hole in Simeon's wall before the next semester began. Upon seeing the change, Fania was undeterred. In anticipation of the upcoming semester, she once more scraped away at the same spot until she had a clear view of her future.

The brief break in the school schedule was no less filled with activity. Boss Lamosier took advantage of the fact that there were no children around to inhibit progress by moving construction along more efficiently than ever. Marta no doubt was off devising new ways of tormenting her charges in order to drain every drop of energy from their already frail bodies.

Along with the other teachers and school administrators, Simeon met with the American group who funded the school. They discussed ways to improve the effectiveness of the school's methods, including training programs to be offered during the summer break. The possibility intrigued Simeon, who loved learning almost as much as he did teaching.

Fania and Rose made the most of each day they spent together. Christmas and the New Year held the prospect of gifts and new possibilities the young mother never before had the courage or means to consider. Even Haitian Independence Day on the first of January promised a freedom neither she nor her country had ever known.

For Christmas, they took a trip to one of the nearby markets to select a modest gift for Rose. (Fania still didn't have the nerve to visit the Mache Fè since Granmè's death.) As the two perused tables filled with goods they couldn't afford, Fania came upon a pile of books. She was now able to look beyond their multicolored covers. Their contents were no longer mysterious marks etched on the pages. She could read many of the words! Using a few *gourdes* she couldn't spare, she selected a brightly colored picture book with a drawing of a young girl looking out over the ocean at a small red boat as rain fell on her face.

That night, Rose went to sleep wearing her prize: a straw hat with a feather. She dreamt that a magical macaw had given its feather to the hat maker and whoever wore the hat would grow to be wise and beautiful. Fania occupied that and the following nights with practicing her writing and reading her new book, hoping one day soon to read it to Rose.

The morning of the first class of the new year, Fania was once more sitting by her wall diligently writing in her workbook. Through the gap in the wall, she could see there were even fewer students than there had been at the end of the previous semester.

She scribbled in her workbook until the school bell clanged.

"Time's up," Simeon announced. "Leave your papers at your places and I'll pick them up after you leave."

Fania looked at her work. She was proud of what she had accomplished in so short a time, but confused about what to do next. Since the start of her clandestine education, she had lived moment to moment, not anticipating what her next steps might be. She looked through the hole and saw Simeon pace along the rows picking up the completed papers. At the back of the room, he saw the hole had mysteriously reappeared. He knelt down and studied the opening, running his finger along the gap.

On an inexplicable impulse, Fania took a step into unexplored terrain from which she would never be able to retreat. If she'd taken more time to contemplate the possible consequences of her action, she might never have proceeded. She spoke cautiously into the hole, "*Bonjou, pwofesè.*"

The voice was as delicate and unexpected as a flower in La Saline, but the effect was so intense, it knocked Simeon to the floor. When he regained his composure, he moved back to the wall and uttered the most obvious of questions, "Who's there?"

"One of your students." Fania wasn't sure what she was doing. She followed the lead of the teacher and her heart.

"The shyest one in Haiti, I'd say. Where are you, in a closet?"

Silence.

Beyond curious, Simeon wanted to keep the dialog going. "Are you the one who made this hole?" he asked as he slid his finger back and forth in the breach.

"*Wi*. Please don't fill it again. My blade is getting dull."

Blade? Fearsome images raced through his brain. "Why are you doing this?"

"I want to learn to read and write."

The pleading tone of the voice was apparent and it moved the teacher in Simeon. "You've come to the right place. Or near it at least. Why don't you come to class?"

"I'm not a registered student."

Simeon's curiosity compelled him to kneel and peer through the hole. Hearing him shuffling, Fania leaned to the side to evade his gaze. The teacher tipped his head back and forth in an attempt to see something on the other side. All he got for his efforts was a view of a dim grayness. "Your voice sounds familiar. Do I know you?"

"No." Fania answered tersely, fearing an extra syllable could give away her identity.

"How long have you been listening in?"

"Since your first class."

Knowing his next statement would likely put a devastating end to the girl's plans, whatever they might be, Simeon spoke with reluctance. "I'm sorry to tell you that you won't be able to eavesdrop on us much longer."

"Are you going to report me to the school?" The resignation in Fania's voice traveled through the hole with more volume than did her words.

"Oh, no. They're planning to move my class soon. You'll be getting history lessons in this room."

"Why?"

"Some new classrooms were completed on the second floor. School administration thinks these older kids should be up there. I'm not happy about it either."

"What about that boy who's missing his leg?"

There was a long pause as her question drilled its way into Simeon's heart. Why hadn't that problem occurred to him already? Was he growing insensitive to his class's needs? He was forced to ask himself, *Who's really behind a wall?* "Schneider? You're right, getting up those stairs would be a hardship for him. I'll talk to Basile. They'll have to change their minds." He let out a sigh of relief, but didn't know why. "Congratulations. Your compassion may have salvaged your education."

Fania smiled as she sat with the workbook in her hands. "I hope so. I've learned so much already."

"How are you coming along with the work?"

Fania wanted to be bold, but her voice cracked as she said, "Grade my paper and I'll know."

A curled up piece of paper came sliding through the opening. Simeon took it and unrolled it as slowly as he might a fragile scroll that held the answer to some ancient riddle.

"I guess I can do that for so determined a student. Few of these kids go to such lengths to learn." Glancing at the page, he recognized the handwriting. "You're the one who left that paper on my desk last semester?"

"Yes. And *pwofesè*?"

"There's more?"

141

"I'm sorry about the workbook."

He looked at the paper more closely and let out a whistle. "So that's where it went. I owe Schneider an apology. You should be punished for taking it..." His long pause was torturous as Fania awaited his judgment. "...but as long as it's being put to good use it's hard for me to find fault. How will I return your paper?" Simeon waited for a reply but none came. Fania had already hustled out to her job.

On returning from the cafeteria that day, Fania found a surprise awaiting her. A piece of paper was protruding from the hole in her wall. She clutched at it and scanned the markings anxiously. It wasn't all comprehensible, but she got the essence. Each problem was accompanied by a check mark. At the top, under a couple of stars that told Fania all she needed to know about the results, it read, "Excellent work, mystery student." Her spontaneous squeal of delight took Rose, who was changing out of her uniform, by surprise.

"*Manman*, are you all right?"

"Oh, *wi*." To underscore her happiness, she lifted Rose and nuzzled the little girl's neck. She rejoiced not only in her own learning but in what she might one day pass on to her daughter.

At the river several days later, Rose floated her toy boat while her mother wrung out some clothes. When Fania turned her head, Claude, the *houngan*, materialized beside her as if he had risen silently from the depths of the earth. "How are you managing without Granmè, young lady?" he asked without a trace of emotion.

"We miss her, but we're getting by," was Fania's equally cold reply.

"I'm glad to hear it. I hope your good fortune lasts, " the witch doctor lied.

Fania turned to face him full on, something she'd never dared do before. "What do you really want?"

His voice was warmer, but it was so forced it chilled Fania's blood. "There are many ways I can be of service to you. I'm afraid the old woman poisoned your attitude toward me."

"I have my own mind."

"You have enemies in the spirit world." Claude reached out and touched her exposed knee. "I could counsel you."

Fania had heard and felt more than enough. She grabbed all the wet clothes around her and rose to her feet. Turning her back on the leering man, she called, "Rose, we're going." She strode into the river, took her daughter's hand, and pulled her away as the *houngan* watched, vexed and frustrated.

As she always did, Rose gazed with love and admiration on her mother as they strolled casually side by side, Fania balancing a generous basket of wet clothes on her head with utmost poise. After thinking as deeply as a three-year-old is capable of, Rose gathered all her courage and asked, "*Manman*, can I carry some of the clothes on my head?"

The question made Fania stop so abruptly, Rose thought

she'd walked into an invisible wall. Although the little girl was never less than precocious, Fania was still taken aback by her request, which indicated a level of confidence and a sense of responsibility she didn't know her daughter had attained.

Part of her wanted to refuse the request because it would make the chore that much more difficult. When she considered it in terms of nurturing her daughter rather than simply completing a task, there was no choice to make.

Fania removed everything but one dress and a rag from the basket. She wrapped a moist towel around Rose's head to increase the surface area for the basket to rest upon. Holding most of the clothes under her own arm, she gently settled the basket on Rose's head.

Merely standing there, before taking a single step, Rose's glee was immeasurable. She extended her arms out to the side and slid her foot ahead slightly. No movement from the basket. Two more steps. The basket wobbled, but Rose was able to keep her load intact.

It was the most protracted walk Fania had ever made from the river to her home, but it was also the most satisfying. Except for a couple of instances when Fania stealthily kept the basket from tumbling, Rose completed the trip successfully on her own. The girl had an extraordinary ability to compensate for the shifts of the load by adjusting her walk and her posture. Fania knew it was a talent Rose would always need for life in Haiti, balancing burdens far more vital than a dress and a rag.

*   *   *

The next day in class, Simeon's voice echoed uncharacteristically loudly off the concrete walls of the room, ringing in the ears of his students. "The test will be next Tuesday. Please be on time and be prepared."

Schneider, the fifteen-year-old boy who was missing one leg, was an especially bright student. Wearing a T-shirt promoting a half marathon run in Michigan in 1991, he raised his hand and spoke up at the same time. "*Pwofesè*, why are you shouting?"

Simeon looked perplexed. "Was I? Perhaps I was. Sorry. I wanted to make sure everyone..." He shouted the word "everyone", jarring some of his students. "...understood how important this test is. Class dismissed."

One person knew the answer to Schneider's question. In her cramped home, Fania sat chuckling to herself as the classroom emptied.

The sound of scuffling shoes faded from Fania's hearing. Soon after, a single set of footsteps approached the wall and stopped a few centimeters from her shoulder.

"I have good news for you," announced Simeon's voice through the wall. "The administration changed their minds. We're staying right here, thanks to your insight."

"*Mèsi Bondye!*"

"How are your studies coming?"

"You should be the one telling me, *pwofesè*."

Simeon smiled. "You have me at a disadvantage. You can see me, but I can't see you."

He could hear the smile in her voice as she responded, "Maybe we'll meet at graduation."

Simeon crouched by the hole and tried peeking again to no avail. "That might be a while. In the meantime, do you need extra help with anything?"

"The exam frightens me."

"You're obviously a bright woman and you work hard. You'll do fine."

"I wish I had your confidence," was Fania's sincere response.

"You can come by my desk after class like any other student." He waited hopefully but with little expectation for a positive answer. He knew in his heart she wasn't like any other student. With resignation, he added, "I tried. I'll come by here after class whenever I can to see if you need help."

"*Mèsi anpil.*"

"It's my pleasure. In fact, I was thinking..."

Without warning, Fania jumped up and cried out, "*Bondye!*"

"What's wrong?" Simeon's concern surprised himself.

"I have to go." She stuffed the piece of paper into the gap and, with a rustle of activity, she disappeared.

Rushing to make it to the cafeteria before her shift began, Fania was still putting on her apron as she emerged from her house. Her progress was halted by a voice from above, which made her feel as if the ground was once more shifting beneath her feet.

"Do you need any help with that?" Fania glanced up to see Renaud smirking at her from atop the wall. "Or any other piece of clothing I can help you with?"

She was relieved when she heard the voice of Boss Lamosier bark out, "Renaud! You're not being paid to flirt." Renaud cringed and disappeared from view, but Fania still felt his gaze. It burned like the wet cement on her skin, but she couldn't wash it off this time.

The progress of the serpentine lunch line was already well along when Fania rushed into the cafeteria. She hoped Marta would be distracted, but the master of the kitchen rarely missed a detail. That was the reason she was kept on in spite of her ruthless treatment of the staff. Not a moment nor a *gourde* was wasted under her watch, and no one went hungry.

Extreme hunger was something Marta had experienced firsthand. She'd also witnessed its causes. In a previous job, she'd watched the wealthy foreign organizers of a feeding program siphon off donated goods and sell them. The rich got richer and the children wasted away.

While others saw heartlessness in her manner, they never understood her motivation. Children should never have to deal with hunger and want; that was her philosophy. She would do anything to prevent it, including giving her adult workers nervous breakdowns.

Marta looked at Fania but said nothing. The flustered mother found her place and began distributing bowls of a rice dish flecked with meager pieces of chicken. Marta's silence was more unnerving than a swat from the ladle. When Marta finally addressed her, it was in an ominous whisper. "Do you have any idea what some people in this village would give to have your job?"

"I'm sorry. I was busy with some work at home. I promise it won't happen again."

Her voice rising with each word, culminating in a shout, Marta said, "If it does, save yourself the trouble and don't bother coming in at all."

Fania shuddered, nearly dropping the bowl she was filling.

While Fania sweated out the kitchen heat and Marta's unrelenting glare, Simeon leaned against the wall at the back of his classroom. From there, he took deliberate, measured steps along the wall. When he reached the corner, he scooted out of the room and resumed his path from the outside corner of his room to the courtyard exit.

Passersby must have been curious to hear Simeon counting out loud as he finished his purposeful walk along the exterior wall of the school. "Three, two, one, zero." When he stopped, he was directly in front of Fania's doorway. Seeing the hovel, entry covered with a torn sheet of vinyl, he thought of the voice he'd come to know. He tiptoed to the door and inhaled sharply, about to call out. Something stopped him.

It was a defining moment for Simeon. With an impulse that sprang from a dark place inside him he didn't even know existed, he longed to tear away the flap that covered the door and invade the woman's sanctuary. He wanted... No, he felt entitled to know this woman who had captured his thoughts, maybe even his heart. That urge battled with a more virtuous desire to respect the privacy she so obviously and zealously guarded. Restraint ruled and, after a few seconds of further indecision, he retreated as quietly as he had approached.

Chapter 13

SIMEON WAS STRAIGHTENING out the rows of desks in his classroom when he heard the voice from the far wall. He scampered to the sound the way his students were launched by the dismissal bell that rang every day at three o'clock.

"*Pwofesè?*" was all the voice said, but it was enough to send an unexpected adolescent thrill through Simeon's heart. He felt the same emotions as did the teens in the school who gathered between classes in the cool, shadowed stairwells, posing for the opposite sex.

In the months since he first encountered his covert class member, he had become increasingly intrigued by her presence. More than intrigued, attached. Whether it was her voice, her ingenuity, or her passion for learning, he didn't know, but Simeon found himself drawn to the woman on the other side of the wall.

The instructor's enthusiasm traveled through the narrow crack as clearly as his voice when he responded, "More questions?" It was as much a statement of desire as it was a query.

"No," Fania replied, "A favor. I was hoping you might have another workbook I could use. I've finished with the first one."

A gasp left Simeon's lips. His class would be using the current books for another six to eight weeks. "How..." was all he good manage to say before he retreated to stunned silence.

Fania anticipated the rest of his question, "I've been working ahead. I have a lot of free time to study."

After walking across the room in a fog, Simeon opened the briefcase on his desk. "I'm impressed. Too bad I can't take credit for your progress. You're way ahead of me." He fumbled through the briefcase and pulled out a workbook before returning to the hole. "This is the next book. It's an extra copy." The truth was that he had enough books for his class and no more. He would have to pay for another copy to replace that one, but it was worth it to him. Whether his professional concern for her progress outweighed his personal interests was a question he avoided.

"*Mèsi, pwofesè*," Fania said as the book scraped through the crevice with no room to spare.

"You can call me Simeon."

"*Mèsi, Pwofesè* Simeon."

He smiled at her shy decorum, so consistent with her confidentiality. "Just Simeon will be fine."

Fania stuffed her scrap of cement sack into the gap, prompting Simeon, sounding more desperate than he intended, to call out, "Wait!" He knelt at the plugged hole and asked, "Won't you tell me your name?"

The teacher endured a long silence on his knees before the paper receded from the hole.

"Fania."

"Fania," he repeated with satisfaction. "Nice to finally have a name for my mystery student. Maybe some day I'll have a face to go with it. It's a pleasure to work with you, Fania."

"*Mèsi.* I have to go. *Ovwa.*"

As the paper once more filled the breach, Simeon leaned against the wall and whispered to himself. "Fania."

After her shift in the kitchen that day, Fania waited in the courtyard for the bell that would release Rose and her classmates. In her mind, a lovely young woman with an armful of books came toward her. It was Rose as she wished to see her in a dozen or so years. Her fantasies were violently interrupted as a cinder block crashed on the concrete ground, no more than an arm's length in front of where she stood. She vaulted back. When Renaud slid down a rope from the second floor, landing where the block had struck, she jumped farther back.

"I am so sorry, miss." His mock remorse sickened her. "It would be a shame to spoil the smallest patch of that lovely skin." She recoiled when he reached out to brush his hand across her face.

"Get away from her," shouted Simeon, rushing to her aid.

Renaud looked with disdain on the teacher in his spotless white shirt. "Go back to your books, teacher."

Simeon didn't flinch, but shouted off, returning Renaud's glare all the while, "Lamosier!"

Renaud's cocky facade dropped at the sound of the Boss Man's name. "Wait. There's no need to drag him into this. I was just having some fun."

Simeon responded to the man's sudden discomfort with an old proverb, "The dew dries quickly when the sun appears, eh?" Lamosier was on the scene before Renaud could figure out its meaning.

"Boss Lamosier, dropping blocks near people in the courtyard is this man's idea of fun. He could have hit this woman," Simeon informed him.

"Renaud, I've had it with you. You're fired."

"But I wasn't..."

"No more excuses. See Boss Remy for your last day's pay."

Renaud glowered at Simeon and Fania before he trudged

off, with Lamosier calling after him. "And I don't want to see you hanging around here!" He turned back to Fania. "I'm sorry, *madmwazèl*. That fellow has been nothing but trouble since he started working here. You won't see him again." He added a hint of a bow to affirm his regret at the incident.

Fania was still frozen. Simeon gave voice to her unspoken feelings. "*Mèsi anpil*, Boss Lamosier."

As he strode back to his work, the Boss Man called out to all his workers within hearing distance, "Let that be a lesson to all of you. This is a working school. Accidents and unsafe behavior will not be tolerated."

While most everyone in the area was captivated by Lamosier's voice of authority, Simeon was captivated by the quiet girl before him. "You're the girl from the kitchen, aren't you?" Fania nodded but remained silent. "You shouldn't have to deal with such recklessness. I'm Simeon, by the way. I teach a Creole class." He extended his hand. Fania shook it, but not without hesitancy. She dipped her head toward him but still didn't speak. Simeon held her hand for a few seconds waiting in vain for a response. None came.

Simeon finally walked away. As he went, he glanced back at Fania, stunning in her stillness.

Recent events had left Fania uncertain and numb. Her run-in with Marta could have cost both her job and Rose's education. Still reeling from that near disaster, the skirmish with Renaud had come close to unhinging her. In search of consolation, she sat in her doorway that night and opened the book she'd found in the box Granmè had left her. Knowing her protector had once held that book and written in it brought a calm to Fania she couldn't summon on her own.

By the dim light of the full moon, Fania could see the words in the notebook. Her comprehension had increased considerably as the result of her studies.

When she read this night, she recognized the format of a date at the top of each page. At last it occurred to her that this was a diary kept by Granmè. Out of curiosity, she flipped the pages to the day they had met at the seaside. (One month ago, before Simeon had taught his class numbers and dates, none of this would have been possible.)

Tears blurred Fania's vision as she read, *I buried all my children but now God has sent a miracle. Like Sarah, I've been blessed with a child in my old age. Mèsi, Lord, for sending Fania to me. I pray she stays.* Fania clutched the book to her chest as the tears began to run freely down her cheeks.

The words on the page beckoned Fania on, but she looked up, thinking she'd heard a noise. Before she could react, Renaud had her by the throat. She would need more than Granmè's words now.

"I've caught you without a defender." He kicked her back into the house then dived in after her like a *lougawou* hungry for fresh blood.

Renaud leaned over Fania's petrified body and shone a flashlight in her face, blinding her.

"Renaud doesn't forget. Now you'll pay for my finger and my job." With one hand pressing Fania to the ground, he swept his light around the room. Rose's sleeping form became illuminated. A vile expression contorted his face. "Maybe I'll take the little girl, too."

His ill-advised threat transformed Fania's fear into fury. Her scream echoed the tortured cries of nearby Fort Dimanche as she slammed her feet into the intruder's chest, sending him flying through the air and out of the house, his flashlight knocked free and left behind. He sprawled on his back in the street, stunned, the wind knocked out of him. By the time he was aware of what was happening, Fania was coming for him with her knife, looking rabid in her rage.

Renaud tried to regain his advantage by lunging at the frenzied girl.

Maybe it was anger that moved her, but later, when she reflected on the events, she was certain Granmè's words had empowered her. Without thinking, Fania ducked out of the way and swung the knife at him. Two fingers went flying. He screamed and grabbed his hand.

"Bitch! I'll kill you both now."

Still moving on instinct, Fania leapt at him, an inhuman growl issuing from her throat. The sound frightened Renaud more than the knife did. But before she had a chance to attack him, he crumpled to the ground. Standing over him was Lamosier, holding a hefty length of lumber.

Ever attentive to his project, the Boss Man had decided to

stay on site for the evening to watch for Renaud, whom he'd correctly appraised as a scoundrel of the first order.

Fania seemed not to notice that her attacker had already been dispatched. She still went after the unconscious figure, knife flashing. Lamosier seized her arm. "No, no, no. This isn't the way to deal with him. You're safe now."

Fania continued to strain for Renaud. Only Lamosier's strength saved the unconscious man from being shredded. She struggled until her will was exhausted, then fell to her knees in tears. That's when she became aware of her daughter's cries, which had begun at the moment Fania screamed.

"*Manman*! Where are you, *Manman*?"

Fania scrambled back into her home and gripped Rose as though Renaud were still there, trying with all his strength to wrest the child away.

Lamosier leaned in after her. "Everything is all right. Calm down. It's okay. I've been watching for him. I knew he'd be back. His kind never learns. I think I saved him more than you." Despite the seriousness of the situation, he couldn't help but snicker at his accurate assessment of his actions.

"He threatened Rose." Fania's eyes were wild and her breath still labored.

The Boss Man reached out his hand to comfort her, but she cringed. He pulled back and spoke softly but with firm reassurance, "He won't bother you again. I'll see to that." Rose could barely breath, Fania's grip was so tight. Lamosier continued to watch her until her breathing finally started returning to normal. "Will you be okay?"

There was no response to his concern.

"Your Granmè and I had our differences, but I respected her strength. There's a lot of her in you, *madmwazèl*. Get some sleep. Morning will bring a new sun." The Boss Man, who never left a job incomplete, watched her for several more minutes. When he was sure she could be left alone, he stepped outside the house.

When he did so, Lamosier was unnerved to find Renaud missing from the place where he'd fallen unconscious. He looked around but couldn't see where Fania's assailant had disappeared to. The only traces of him were two detached digits. He kicked them far out of the area and walked back to the school, knowing he would need to maintain his vigilance for some time to come.

Back in her house, Fania was unaware her attacker had escaped. Rose sobbed in her arms, not even knowing why. Fania tried to comfort her with a calm she herself lacked. "It's okay. Everything is fine."

"What... was that... noise?" Rose sputtered between weepy gasps.

"Nothing for little girls to worry about. Go back to sleep. I love you."

"Love you, too," the child responded as Fania rocked her more vigorously than she ought. Was she trying to rock her daughter to sleep or herself? Or was it merely nervous movement? She hardly knew. She began to sing a lullaby her mother had sung to her and that she in turn had sung to Marie-Fleur at the orphanage in their many times of distress.

Rose's lips kept moving, sighing mostly incoherent syllables. Occasionally, real words came together: *Manman*, sunshine, play, *bonbon*, chickens. Fania couldn't tell if Rose was asleep and dreaming or trying to communicate some strange story.

As Fania's rocking slowed and Rose's muttering quieted, the child slipped into a deep slumber.

Fania gently laid the girl down and sought solace in Granmè's words once more, reading the diary by the flashlight Renaud had dropped.

Young Fania has brought laughter to my life as Isaac did for aged Sarah. There is joy where there was none. My soul is joined with hers. I will lay down my life for this child. God has been good to me.

The next night, by the light of the moon, Fania, still jittery from the previous night's attack, soothed Rose and herself by braiding the little girl's hair, decorating it with barrettes and ribbons. Rose savored the touch of her mother's firm and gentle hands on her scalp. She was lulled into a state of purity and innocence partial only to little children. Her question was as natural as her mother's caress. "*Manman*, why don't I have a father?"

Fania dropped the barrette she was holding. Were it not for the love in Rose's voice, she might have cried.

"Sometimes fathers go away. Like mine did."

"Did my father die, too?"

"I don't know what happened to your father." Fania cleared her throat before struggling to continue, "Do you wish you had a father?"

"Sometimes," said the serene girl without a hint of sorrow. "I'm happy I have a *manman*."

At that, Fania turned Rose around and fell under the spell of the deep brown eyes that gazed back at her. "As I am happy to have you." She kissed Rose on the forehead. "You're thinking big thoughts for a little girl, *ti flè-m*. You need an adventure. There's no school tomorrow. Shall we go to the beach?"

Rose leapt up, unraveling the braid Fania had been working on, leaving a long, bouncing spring dangling from her head. "Yeah!"

Their *tap-tap* rumbled down a tree-lined paved road that skirted the coastline traveling northwest away from Port-au-Prince. They rode for hours, trying to leave the polluted waters of the capital city as far behind as possible. Above the cab of the *tap-tap*, a sign was painted with the words, "*Bondye bon*", God is good. The sentiment, so true to the words in Granmè's diary (and a concept Fania was finally growing comfortable with herself), felt to her like a good omen.

Rose hung out the back of the converted pickup like an excited puppy. Fania's arm held her firmly around the waist as each pothole and speed bump threatened to toss the girl from her seat.

Fania hid her excitement, but it was every bit as genuine as Rose's. Neither had ever been this far from home. Fania's parents had always promised to take her to a real beach, but they never had the opportunity and money at the same time. Fania was able to afford the trip by dipping into the tiny inheritance Granmè had left her. In her mind, the investment was worthwhile and overdue.

The landscape was foreign to both mother and child. The mountains, scarred by decades of unchecked erosion, felt closer, the houses farther. They'd never seen such wide open space. It bewildered them with its expansiveness. Cacti, growing where once there had been a dense forest, were a revelation to Rose who thought they must be monsters with their strange shapes and appalling spiked skin.

A wizened corn field isolated between villages reminded Fania of the Bible story Pastor Henri had told about Joseph's dream of withered grain that portended famine. Predicting the future of such growth in Haiti didn't take spiritual insight. Every year seemed to be famine.

Although other passengers boarded occasionally, carrying articles that ranged from chickens to chairs, they usually got off at the next town or marketplace. All the while, Rose clung to her place at the back, where she could watch asphalt pass underneath them and structures of all shapes and colors whiz by.

Official looking vehicles filled with armed men passed them in both directions. Whenever the *tap-tap* approached a slower vehicle, the driver zipped around it paying little heed to oncoming traffic. At times, he completed his maneuver with less than a meter to spare.

Whenever they passed through one of the humble towns along the way, the progress of the *tap-tap* was impeded either by local traffic or by the towering speed bumps that fit in so well with Haiti's mountainous landscape. It often took the fully laden vehicle two or three tries to get over the colossal obstacles.

Each time the *tap-tap* slowed, vendors flocked to it like mosquitoes to a solitary light. Rose would have loved to accept one of the treats they offered—peanut brittle, watermelons, bags of water, or plastic bottles of colorful sugary drinks, among other delights—but a discouraging glance from her mother quickly quelled her desires.

Rose and Fania were amazed at the trucks laden with stacks of charcoal or sacks of fresh fruit piled higher than the trucks were wide. It was a wonder to them that they didn't topple over at the slightest bump, and the bumps were anything but slight. The trucks reminded Rose of the children in her school whose weighty backpacks made even their shortest walks an adventure in balance.

More amazing still were the men who rode atop those tall piles of goods. With the most placid expressions imaginable, they looked completely oblivious to their precarious positions. It was a common state for many Haitians, Fania among them.

When they arrived at the beach, Rose's mouth fell open upon seeing the wide expanse of sea, uninterrupted by the wrecked ships or floating trash she was accustomed to back home. Through a palisade of waving palm trees, she drank in the most pristine sight she had ever seen, one unprecedented in her limited memory.

Children played in the clear shallow water at the shore while older swimmers ventured out to where the limits of the beach had been marked with floating orange and white plastic balls linked by a matching colored rope. The colors reminded Rose of her school uniform.

The beach itself was a collection of rocks, pebbles, and shells. As such it wasn't a comfortable surface to sit or lie on but it was irresistible to the little family for whom everything in sight was unfamiliar and breathtaking.

Haitian teens danced to some *kompa* tunes blaring from a beat-up old boombox whose volume was set so high the music was distorted. From all appearances, none of them minded.

The most amazing sight to Rose, though, was a group of people, young and old, whose skin was almost as white as the shirts teachers at her school wore. In her short life, she had never seen a white person. As her path brought her nearer to the group than she felt comfortable with, she clung fearfully to Fania's leg. Fania had little more experience with *blans* herself, but she tried to comfort Rose as best she could.

As repelled as Rose was by the *blans*, they were magnetic to the vendors who wandered around the beach hawking their handmade craft items. Few, if any, Haitians at the beach had means or reason to purchase their paintings, carved boxes and plaques, jewelry, icons, and vases, but the white visitors swarmed over the souvenirs like bees attacking the last flower of the season. It would be an exceptional payday for the men who usually got nothing more for their efforts at the beach than sore feet and headaches.

When she was finally comfortable with the setting, Fania sat down at the water's edge and let the gentle surf lap at her feet as she read Granmè's diary and looked out to where a fishing boat bobbed on the rocking surf. A fisherman dangled a hopeful line over its edge.

Rose, naked for want of a bathing suit, splashed close by. Still wary of the white-skinned group who played so raucously down the shoreline, she never strayed more than a meter from her mother. She watched as the *blans* threw an oddly shaped ball around and occasionally shoved each other under the water like savages warring among themselves. Yet each victim of a dunking emerged laughing every time. These were a strange people indeed.

Granmè's words filled Fania with both joy and sadness.

What a blessing to welcome a new life into my home as my life winds down. My heart is so full today. I pray for only a few more years with them both, then I could leave this world in peace.

Drops of water moistened the page Fania read. When she looked up, Rose was looking at her with an impish grin. "Don't you ever stop reading, *Manman*? Get wet." She splashed more water at her mother.

"So you want to get wet, do you *Ti Malice*?" Fully dressed, she leapt for Rose who squealed and tried (or pretended to try) to escape. Fania wrapped her arms around the giggling child and dunked her into the surf. Their uninhibited frolic drew the attention of all the others on the beach, but mother and daughter felt alone in the universe in their joy.

Exhausted from sun, surf, and sport, Rose curled up to nap on one of the wood slatted lounge chairs spread across the rocky beach. Fania sat at the foot of the chair with more contentment than she had ever dared dream could be hers.

Above the endless murmuring of the surf, she heard the babble of the *blans* and, not knowing for sure, assumed they were from the US and were speaking English. Fania knew little more than Rose did about America or Americans. The stories others told her were wildly inconsistent, painting them alternately as angels and demons. All Fania knew for certain was that she was grateful they had started the school she and Rose shared walls with.

Not far down the beach, in the direction where the sun was beginning its descent toward the mountainous backdrop, the fisherman pulled ashore and stepped out of his boat. He unloaded a bright orange crab whose shelled body, its legs still flailing, was as large as Fania's head. Next, he pulled from his boat a silver-scaled fish longer than Rose was tall.

The Americans, if in fact the *blans* were American, flocked to the fisherman's catch the same way the dogs in La Saline attacked a piece of meat thrown on the street. Before long, the catch was fried up and picked clean by the voracious *blans*. If Rose weren't dozing, their ravenous hunger might have heightened her fear of the foreigners.

One of Granmè's proverbs came to mind: "*Staying too long at the market puts you in debt.*" Fania knew it was time to go. She lifted Rose's limp figure and carried her to where the *tap-tap* would pick them up to transport them back to La Saline.

Rose slept for most of the ride home, dreaming of infinite oceans and sunny beaches with cool breezes where children fed on fresh fish and played without a single care.

Chapter 14

THE NEXT DAY at *Lekòl Lespwa*, Simeon watched impatiently, his eyes darting periodically to the far end of the room as his students seemed to exit more slowly than he could ever remember them having done before. Once he was alone, he dashed to the crack in the wall.

"Fania? Are you there?"

"*Wi.*"

Simeon settled to the floor with his back propped against the wall. In her home, Fania rested against her side of the wall. If no cinder block barrier were there, they would have been resting against one another. Indeed, Simeon imagined he felt the warmth of Fania's back against his.

With unmistakable relief, the teacher said, "Good. I wouldn't want to lose my prize student. We're so close to the end of the year."

"That would explain why the class was so restless today," Fania declared.

"Were they?" Simeon would have been embarrassed to admit what had distracted him from his class's behavior.

"Where have you been? Schneider almost broke into a rap."

Simeon laughed aloud before acknowledging, "He can be wild, but he's a smart kid."

"I like him. I'm sorry I took his book." Simeon and Fania simultaneously smiled at her remark. Fania grew serious. "Did he lose his leg in the earthquake?"

"He did."

"We all lost something."

Both sat for a long time thinking about how the earthquake had changed everything in their lives and their country, how its emotional aftershocks still shook their souls occasionally. It was the quake that had resolved Simeon to become a teacher of the poor. It was the quake that brought the pair back-to-back at that moment.

Respect for Fania's obvious desire for privacy barely held in check Simeon's intense desire to rush to her house, to hold her, to know her. He knew the longer he sat there resisting, the further his self-control would crumble like buildings had during the quake, some of which still remained in random heaps around the city.

Simeon at last interrupted their reflections. "It's a good class. I wish you were part of it."

"I am."

"You know what I mean."

"It's a privilege to be able to get an education here in La Saline. Especially with such a wonderful teacher." Simeon was surprised at the warmth her compliment brought to his heart. He basked in it for too long.

Thinking she'd lost her teacher (though she actually had him spellbound) she asked, "Are you still there?"

"*Wi*. I didn't know what to say. I don't get many compliments from my students."

"Why are you teaching here? You could teach at a better school and make more money than this school can afford to pay you."

"That would be the easy way, I suppose, but not the best for what I want to do." His words lifted Fania as she heard someone else give voice to one of Granmè's most precious principles. "There are plenty of more wealthy schools, but none needier. I believe La Saline can be a better place if its children are given a chance. I want to give them that chance."

His voice conveyed a passion that gripped Fania, but all she could manage to say in return was, "I'm grateful you're here for us."

"And I'm grateful you're here," he responded with a sincerity equal to hers.

A vacuum in the conversation hung in the air waiting for either party to fill it. Neither was ready to risk full truth. "I should go," Fania finally said.

"Where do you rush off to every day after class?"

Fania hesitated, not sure what she should answer, if anything. She relished her anonymity and didn't care to lose it at this point. She compromised by saying, "I have a job."

"Really? That's great," Simeon said, genuinely surprised. "A job and school? Each is a rarity here. Having both is a miracle. What do you do?"

Fania wasn't ready to go further. "I work hard."

If it's possible for a grin to share lips with a grimace, that's what Simeon's face showed. "I understand. Will you be here tomorrow?"

"God willing. *Ovwa*, Simeon," said Fania, before leaving her home.

Her voice echoed in Simeon's heart long after it had ceased in his ears. He'd never enjoyed the sound of his name as much as he did when it came from her unseen lips. "*Ovwa*, Fania," he said to no one. It was with great effort he finally dragged himself off.

As usual, Marta and mayhem reigned in the kitchen. The tail end of the student line was still visible when she barked, "More rice in here! The teachers are on their way."

Sure enough, the line of white shirted teachers was already formed and awaiting lunch. Fania slaved away, fearful of Marta's wrath as always. Suddenly, she looked up to see Simeon standing directly in front of her, talking to a fellow teacher who looked to be many years his elder.

"I've never even met her. We've only talked."

The other teacher couldn't help but tease the younger man. "How? By phone? Skype?"

"Much more low-tech than that. Her voice, I swear I'd know it anywhere." He looked up to see Fania transfixed before him, a bowl of rice held in her quivering hand. "*Bonswa*. How are you doing today, silent one?"

Fania only nodded. Afraid her tongue would speak of its own free will were she to loose it, she closed her lips so tightly they hurt.

"What's wrong? Does Marta fine you for talking to customers?"

Marta rarely missed anything in her kitchen. It was no wonder then that Simeon's comment caught her attention. She treated her patrons with the same ruthlessness she exercised on her workers. "Take your lunch and move along, mister. There are plenty of others here who would take it without all the mouthing."

Simeon, not missing a chance to flirt with the kitchen worker he found so alluring, leaned over the counter and whispered to Fania loud enough for her co-workers to hear, "Is it true you all call her 'Mama Doc' behind her back?" While the workers choked back laughter at his joke, the teachers on either side of him showed no such restraint, laughing out loud and drawing Marta's unwanted attention. Fearing her, they bit their tongues and moved on.

Fania smiled, her lips still pursed, but couldn't resist staring after Simeon as he approached the exit. Marta noticed the girl's distraction and bellowed at her, "Keep your mind on your work, Fania!"

At the sound of the name, Simeon wheeled, causing the bowl to slide off his tray and crash on the floor. The racket echoed off the concrete walls. Everyone in the kitchen and many in farther areas looked to see the source of the ruckus, surprised that it all centered on one of the teachers.

Simeon and Fania locked eyes for no more than an instant before Marta came rushing to the scene to seize control. "Teachers! Do you think we have food to waste? Get out. You can go hungry for the afternoon for all I care. Go!" A ladle swat to Simeon's backside drove home her point.

Fania was beyond distracted, but somehow she continued her duties. She could practically feel Marta's eyes boring into the back of her head, ladle poised to strike. She was extra vigilant for the rest of the day, but her thoughts never drifted far from wondering where Simeon's thoughts were drifting.

As troubled as Fania was in the kitchen, Simeon was feeling even more unsettled sitting with his colleagues in the cafeteria.

Even if he'd had food before him, he would have been hard-pressed to have the presence of mind and body to eat it. His lack of attentiveness to their conversation wasn't lost on the other teachers, who had to continually prod him back to his senses.

Simeon's state was understandable. He tried to reconcile the fact that the woman who had attracted his eye for the entire school year was the same woman who so appealed to his heart all along. On the one hand, it was a dream come true. Yet, was it too good to be true? How could a female so bright and determined be so lovely? (He was ashamed to contemplate such a thought, but he did so anyway.) Worse, what was the chance that same woman didn't already have at least one man (one *other* man) desperately in love with her?

As if all that weren't enough—and it was plenty by Simeon's account—he found himself in the peculiar dilemma of feeling guilt at being unfaithful to a woman he didn't know, by being attracted to the same woman. His head ached at the thought of it.

Unable to resist confronting the mystery woman who, although her identity was now known to him, was an even greater riddle than before, Simeon waited at the kitchen exit for Fania to appear. When she emerged at last, after a delay Simeon found agonizing, he stood alongside the passage and whispered to her, "The mystery is solved."

Partially blinded by the transition from the dark kitchen to the bright sunlit courtyard, the young woman couldn't see the speaker beside her, but she was used to hearing that voice without seeing its source. It was as familiar to her as the tiny whistling sound Rose often made in her sleep or as the sound of her own heart beating. Aware of what was unfolding, she didn't turn toward him, but stopped in her place. She didn't quite know why, but she was embarrassed to have been discovered against her will.

Simeon walked around to face her. "To Marta's many other offenses, add the fact that she exposed you."

"I wasn't trying to hide," the shaken girl protested.

"Then you weren't doing a very good job of not trying."

Fania appreciated her language teacher's ability to verbalize her behavior so uniquely. She confessed, "Maybe I was."

"But why?"

"I'm more comfortable being invisible."

"That's a shame. You're a lovely vision. I looked forward to lunch every day."

Fania's embarrassment doubled at his compliment, but she was composed enough to challenge him. "While you were flirting with the woman on the other side of your wall?"

"Guilty as charged," he confessed. "Are you jealous of yourself?"

Though nervous, Fania couldn't help smiling, as baffling as the idea was. Her smile came also from the relief of finally being able to speak to Simeon without concealment.

"Where are you off to now?" he inquired, "Another secret

meeting?"

"I have to pick up my daughter." She searched Simeon's eyes as she said this, seeing in them what she feared, yet expected.

Surprise and disappointment were equally apparent in his face and voice. "Oh. You have a child?"

"*Wi*." She wilted as she watched her long anticipated meeting with her teacher turning disastrous.

"Does her father work at the school, too?"

Fania looked down at her feet as she tugged the kerchief from her hair. "Well, I don't..."

It was Simeon's turn to be embarrassed. "I'm sorry. That was rude of me. Please forgive me." Trying to spare herself and her teacher further discomfort, she started to walk away.

Simeon didn't perceive Fania's disappointment at his failure to call after her, but it couldn't have been greater than his disappointment in himself. He couldn't imagine a more perfect woman than Fania, but a child altered the picture entirely. He wasn't afraid of children; he rather liked them. No, he was afraid of what a child said about this woman about whom he otherwise knew little. Several scenarios that would explain the presence of a child in her life came to his mind. None of them comforted him.

Fania met Rose at her classroom and brought her home. The little girl was always attuned to her mother's mood. Today she knew something was wrong. Fania's pace was slower than usual and she didn't respond to the child's customary after-school chatter. When at last she couldn't resist, she asked directly, "*Manman*, your face is droopy. Are you okay?"

The question surprised Fania for two reasons. First, her mind was elsewhere. Second, she didn't realize how much of an open book her mood was to Rose. She responded with as much cheer as she could muster, "Of course, my little rosebud." She leaned over, lifted Rose to her face, and kissed the end of her nose. "We have each other. What could be wrong?" She meant it and Rose knew it.

On their way home, a light sprinkle started to fall. Dark clouds sometimes hovered over the city but they usually continued on their way without dropping precipitation. Mother and daughter scurried back to their home as the drizzle rapidly grew into a steady, heavy rain.

Once in the house, they pulled everything away from the walls. When rain fell, it ran down the walls of the school and into their crudely constructed dwelling. Neither of them minded. They had a good home and they always found ways to pass the time when the weather discouraged outdoor activities.

Today, the activity of choice was Rose's favorite: story time. Fania initiated the traditional Haitian exchange to begin a story. She looked at Rose intently and asked, "*Krik*?"

Rose knew her part well. With an excited voice, she responded, "*Krak*!" and story time was underway.

Fania had a gift for storytelling. Sometimes she read from a book. They owned two books and only one of those was for children, the one she'd bought at the market during Christmas break. Recognizing the mother's and daughter's love of learning, Rose's teachers were also quick to loan them books.

Other times, Fania told stories she'd heard from the Bible at church. Noah and the ark and Daniel in the lion's den were among her favorites. Occasionally she made up a story on the spot, powered by the imagination that had kept her company during the many lonely times of her life.

She always made the characters and worlds come alive to Rose. The little girl could close her eyes and hear the lions growling with hunger as they stared at Daniel. She thought she could feel the breeze as she read a book about sailing on the sea.

That was the story they read today, the one children's book they possessed. The title was, "The Little Red Boat Came Back." The boat in the pictures closely resembled the one Granmè had bought for Rose at the Mache Fè for her third birthday. It was Rose's favorite toy and was the one thing that helped her remember her beloved Granmè. She always clutched it in her fist as she listened to her mother read the book.

With her reading skills improving rapidly, Fania was able to glide through the story with little or no stumbling. The fact that she'd read it about twenty times helped more than a little. She didn't use the resulting efficiency to make the story go faster. Rather, her familiarity gave her the freedom to enhance it with more emotion and drama. Rose couldn't have been any more absorbed in the tale if she were living the events herself.

* * *

The Little Red Boat Came Back

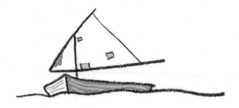

"We have no food," said Manman to Wilda. "Our house has been sold. We cannot live here anymore."

Wilda was sad. "What will we do?" she asked.

Manman said, "There is a place I have heard of where there is food and there are homes to live in."

Wilda asked her, "Where is it?"

"It is far up the coast from here," Manman said.

Wilda wanted to go to the new place. "When will we go?"

Manman said, "I must go alone to see if the story is true."

Wilda started to cry.

Manman held Wilda. She told her, "Do not worry. I will come back for you."

Wilda tried not to worry, but she could not stop. "How will you get there?"

Manman smiled. "I will take the little red boat."

Wilda still worried. "What if the little red boat sinks?"

Manman said, "Your Papa made the little red boat strong. It will not sink."

Manman got the little red boat ready. She put the sail up so that the wind would move the boat.

Wilda cried again. Manman hugged her. "I promise I will come back for you. Wait here for me."

Manman got in the boat and waved to Wilda.

Wilda waved as Manman sailed away. She watched the little red boat get smaller and smaller. At last, she could not see the little red boat at all. She began to cry.

"Why are you crying?" said a voice.

Wilda did not know who was talking. She looked and saw a big fish in the waves.

Wilda told the fish, "I am crying because my Manman has gone away. I am waiting for her to come back."

The fish said, "Your Manman will not come back. There was a big storm. Many boats were lost. You should come live with me in the sea."

"No!" Wilda shouted at the fish. "I cannot live in the sea. Manman promised she would come back."

"Silly girl," said the fish. Then he swam away.

Wilda looked out to sea until night came. She was tired. She lay down on the beach and went to sleep.

The sun came up. Wilda woke up and looked for the little red boat. She could not see it.

A group of wild boars walked down the beach. One of them spoke to Wilda, "Why are you looking out to sea?"

Wilda said, "I am waiting for my Manman. She has gone to a place where there is food to eat."

The boar said, "You should come with us. We know where we can steal food."

"No!" Wilda shouted at the boar. "Stealing is wrong. Manman promised she would come back."

"Silly girl," said the boar. Then all the boars ran away.

Wilda looked out to sea again, but all she saw were waves. She did not see the little red boat or her Manman.

The sun went down. Wilda sat on the sand and fell asleep.

When the sun rose, Wilda woke up. Ti Malice was sitting beside her. Wilda was afraid of Ti Malice.

"Come with me," Ti Malice said. "I will help you look for your Manman on the mountain."

"No!" Wilda shouted at Ti Malice. "I must stay here. Manman promised she would come back."

Ti Malice did not go away. He said, "You are a smart girl. Did your Manman promise she would come back to the beach?"

Wilda did not like Ti Malice. "Manman told me to wait here. I will wait here until she comes back. Go away, Ti Malice."

Ti Malice went away. Wilda looked out to sea again. She saw a little red dot far away.

She looked and looked. The dot grew bigger and bigger. It was the little red boat! Manman had come back just as she promised.

She took Wilda to a new home where they had lots of food to eat.

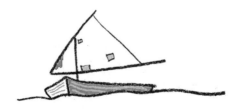

* * *

Rose always interrupted at the same points in the story. When the little girl watched her *Manman* sail away, she'd knit her brows and ask, "Will she come back, *Manman*?" Fania never sounded sure that the woman would return to her daughter but, much to Rose's relief, she always did.

Another reading game they played had Fania occasionally altering a word in the story. When she referred to the boat as the little blue boat, Rose would interrupt indignantly, "No, it was a red boat!" Fania always apologized and they shared an intimate laugh.

The rain fell all the while as the two talked and laughed. They weren't aware that another listener was eagerly sharing their story time. On the other side of the wall, Simeon had settled near the fissure that was his lifeline to Fania. Although the hole was plugged up with paper, he could hear most of what was going on in the house. He was enchanted.

The woman he knew as a clever and astute learner as well as a disciplined and hard-working laborer was also a loving and compassionate mother.

Over the next week, he made it a practice to listen in on them from time to time. He listened as Fania read story books. He could always tell when she was reading as opposed to improvising. In unfamiliar books, she still hesitated on some words and read slowly. She breezed threw her imagined tales.

At bedtime, she sang Rose to sleep with a hymn or a

children's song. More than once, Simeon dozed off during one of those tunes. When he awoke, he never knew how much time had passed. Nor did he care.

One night, Fania read "The Little Red Boat Came Back" for the second time in a week. When it was done, she paused and asked Rose, "Do you like this book?" The little girl let out a yawn as she nodded yes. "Me, too, but it's time for something new. How would you like to go to the market tomorrow morning? We can pick out a new book."

"Yeah!" Rose cried out, stirring a half dozing Simeon, who sat only centimeters—but a cement wall—away.

Simeon overheard their plan to leave first thing in the morning and decided it was time to enact a plan of his own. What he heard during those times he spent eavesdropping conquered any reluctance he had about accepting the child in Fania's life. He wanted to be part of their lives with no wall of separation.

Chapter 15

Simeon arrived at the school early the next day, a Saturday, before there was much activity in the village. He went to his classroom and waited by the blocked hole for the sounds of movement that would indicate Fania and Rose were on their way out.

Soon after waking up, Fania dressed herself and Rose in preparation for their trip. When they were ready, they headed out to find a *tap-tap* to take them to the Mache Fè. At the same time, Simeon made his way to a point of ambush, though he preferred to think of it as a rendezvous. He loitered at the school's entrance gate, which had a clear view of the road out of La Saline.

Other than curt greetings in the food line or obligatory classwork related exchanges through the wall, Fania hadn't spoken to Simeon since she'd been exposed as mystery student and mother. She was perceptive enough to know why her teacher had kept his distance, but she didn't know about his eavesdropping or his change of heart. She certainly didn't suspect he was lurking at the entryway, awaiting their approach.

He heard their voices as they grew nearer. They were arguing about how many books they should buy, Rose insisting that two books were better than one. Fania, however, knew their financial limitations and held her ground at one.

Without warning, Simeon sprang into their path, causing them to skip back a step.

Although he had already grown attached to the little girl, it was the first time Simeon had laid eyes on Rose. Yet if he'd seen her in a crowd without her mother, he could have picked her out as Fania's daughter. As young as she was, a few months shy of her fourth birthday, Rose's innocent and carefree beauty transcended her surroundings. She was a spark to Fania's fire, a tiny bud that would one day blossom into the ravishing vision Fania was. Like her mother, Rose made everything around her look more appealing. Standing in a slum in ragged clothes, she might as well have been in a flower draped meadow. Simeon even thought he caught the scent of gardenias as a breeze swept by the two of them.

Also like her mother, she had captured Simeon's heart long before he first saw her.

Trying and failing to appear casual when their eyes met, he affected an expression of astonishment. "Fania! What a surprise." He stumbled through an explanation for why he was at the school on the weekend. He threw out random phrases he thought might distract her from suspicion of his motives. "Some papers... My classroom... Late, grades... Deadlines..." His ploy was unraveling so he ceased his rambling.

Fania guessed his game but played along, pretending she wasn't thrilled to see him. She introduced him to Rose, who was completely unaware of the double deception being played out before her. "Rose, this is *Pwofesè* Simeon. He's my teacher."

Rose screwed up her face, then looked from her mother to the stranger and back again. Then back again. After a few more seconds in this muddle, she gave up and asked, "You have a teacher?"

"*Wi*. Is that so strange? You have one."

"But you're old."

Fania and Simeon burst out laughing, further confusing the little girl. "Nice to meet you, Rose," he said as he knelt down to the little girl's eye level. Continuing his ruse, he asked, "Where are you two headed today?"

Rose jumped in before Fania could answer. "We're going to the market to buy a bunch of new books!" Rose's face took on a guilty look even before her mother glared at her. "To buy one new book." She lightened up when she asked, "Do you want to come with us, *pwofesè*?"

Once again, Rose had anticipated what was already on her mother's mind, what Fania herself was barely able to suppress. As glad as she was about Rose's invitation, she couldn't help offering Simeon a convenient way out. "Rose, you heard the *pwofesè*. He's busy with many things already."

Simeon wasn't looking for a way out, he was looking for a way in. He wasted no time in asserting, "Actually, there are a few things I could use at the market, too. Do you mind?"

Fania's smile was all the answer he needed, but she affirmed, "What can I say? Rose has already included you."

With that, the three started off down the road together. Rose held Fania's hand on one side and took Simeon's on the other. She thought to herself that this made a fine picture and grinned widely as they strolled along.

A busy *tap-tap* is a crowded affair. The drivers take as many passengers as are willing to squeeze in. On the day the trio made their trip to the market, everyone seemed to be going somewhere and carrying something.

For a while, there was a man precariously holding a hand-carved headboard out the back of the vehicle. Once, when the *tap-tap* bounced through one of Port-au-Prince's many gigantic potholes, which more reminiscent of craters, his burden scraped the ground and he nearly lost his handiwork and grip at once. Others on board reached out and helped him, saving both.

A man with a huge woven basket full of mangoes plopped in next to Simeon, shoving him up against Fania, who held Rose on her lap. There were no complaints.

Once inside the market, Fania's mood sank. With Rose ahead investigating every colorful booth, overflowing with what were to her exotic goods, Simeon was left to notice the change. "I shouldn't have come, should I?"

It took a while for Fania to respond, lost as she was in her thoughts. "What? No, it's fine."

"Then what's wrong?"

Fania swallowed back her sadness, but it caught in her throat and cramped her voice. "I haven't been here since we lost Granmè."

"Who was Granmè?"

"My friend, adoptive grandmother, and guardian angel."

Seeing her despair, Simeon instinctively took her hand. "I'm sorry."

"Rose and I wouldn't be alive today if it weren't for her." Suddenly assaulted with bitter memories, she looked all around, half panicked. "Rose!"

Rose ran back to her distressed mother. She had three books in her arms. Each was so appealing, she was unable to decide among them. All had colorful illustrations. One was covered with miraculous animals, another had three children on the cover, the smallest of whom, Rose thought, resembled one of her classmates. The third had a picture of a *tap-tap*. Rose adored *tap-taps*.

"Rose, we talked about this. We can only buy one."

The little girl had one last idea. "But you read so fast now, we need more." Rose followed her flattery with her most winning juvenile smile.

"She's good," Simeon acknowledged.

"She's too good for her own good," Fania countered, adding, "or for mine."

When Rose's hopeful facade began to crumble and she felt she might break down under the stress of choosing, Simeon came to her rescue. He offered to pay for the other two as long as she promised to let Fania read it to him, too.

"He's your teacher, *Manman*," Rose said confidently with her new ally looking on. "You have to do what he says."

Fania knew she was outnumbered and had no chance of wriggling out of the arrangement, but she tried. "This isn't fair. You two are ganging up on me."

Simeon threw Rose a wink as he reinforced their shared stance, "I'm just trying to get you to do more reading homework."

Fania gave up the nominal resistance she'd offered as Simeon and Rose celebrated with a high five behind her back.

With Fania savoring her surrender as much as Rose was her victory, they all walked out of the market into the crowds that swirled perpetually around the place. Among the masses of people who flashed by her field of vision, Fania thought she caught a glimpse of a man who looked like Renaud. She froze in place, unaware of how hard she was squeezing Rose's hand.

"*Manman*, you're hurting me."

In the brief time it took Fania to release Rose and say, "Oh! I'm sorry, *ti cheri*.", the man was gone, if in fact he'd ever been there. Would his face haunt her forever?

Once more, Simeon noted that her mood had darkened. "What happened? Are you okay?"

She forced a smile and said, "I'm fine." Remarkably, her mood turned suddenly flirtatious as she challenged Simeon, "I thought you needed some things at the market. You didn't buy anything."

He was up to her challenge, however. "I got everything I wanted."

No further looks or words were exchanged, but both felt amazingly warm as they walked. It had nothing to do with the temperature.

For some unknown reason, the *tap-tap*'s load was surprisingly sparse for the trip back to La Saline. The explanation for why Fania was still pressed up against Simeon was left unspoken. Rose didn't care. She was already engrossed in the latest additions to her tiny library, flipping through the pages, scanning the illustrations to come up with her own storylines, some of which were more creative than what were in the books themselves.

The group had a wonderful ride home, talking about subjects as varied as school, *futbol*, and the possible destinations of the ships in Port-au-Prince harbor.

The subject of travel led Simeon to tell the Dieusel girls about an exciting event coming up in his life. "The group that runs the school is sending some of the teachers to America for training this summer. I was chosen as one of the candidates to attend their school in New York."

Rose was entranced. She couldn't have been more impressed if the *pwofesè* had said he was going to the moon. Fania wouldn't have been more depressed if that were the case. She politely asked questions, but Simeon saw she was far less enthused about his adventure than he was. As a result, he curtailed his excitement. The truth was, while he was excited about furthering his teaching skills and seeing America, now that he had finally made a solid connection with Fania, he wasn't at all happy about leaving her for the two months involved.

They all hopped out of the *tap-tap* at the end of the road leading into La Saline. Rose was still in a welcoming mood as she asked Simeon, "Do you want to come to our house? *Manman* built it."

On hearing Rose's proclamation, the thought came to Simeon, *Is there anything this woman can't do?* He was also ill at ease about going to the house under false pretenses. He spoke to Rose, but with a side glance at Fania, "I have to confess that I've been to your house before." He couldn't decide whether Fania's expression was one of curiosity or displeasure, so he turned to her, "I tried to respect your privacy as long as I could. Then one time after we talked, I walked off the distance from where the hole in my wall is." Trying to justify himself in her eyes, he continued. "I wanted so badly to know who you were."

"And?"

"I decided your desire for privacy was more important than my curiosity."

"Guess I'm not the only one keeping secrets."

He dared not imagine her reaction if he told her he'd eavesdropped on her quiet evenings with Rose. Some day he'd confess that, too. At least, he hoped he'd get that chance.

Before they reached it, the three could see unusual activity at the house. Two men were putting long pieces of wood across Fania's door as Wilmina stood by with a look of merciless delight.

"What are you doing to my home?" Fania demanded.

Without otherwise acknowledging her, a gruff-looking, middle-aged man named Evens, one of countless Haitian government bureaucrats who did little beyond accepting graft, held out a sheaf of papers in her direction. "According to these papers, it's not your house... unless you died last year." With that, he finally looked up at Fania. "You look pretty good for a *zonbi*."

Ignoring the man's lecherous gaze at Fania, Simeon grabbed the papers and flipped through them.

Fania turned to Rose and said, "Please wait in the house, *cheri*." Rose went inside, ducking under the boards that barred much of the doorway. She didn't know what was happening but it was clear even to her that it was not good.

Simeon told Fania, "The papers say that this property was granted by the government to a squatter named Mimose Estimable. When she died without an heir, ownership was supposed to have transferred back to the government."

"That was Granmè. This was her home, but it's mine now. I've lived here for over four years."

Evens was unimpressed. "I don't know anything about that. I'm here to tear the place down. If you have anything you need in there, get it now."

"*Wi*, I have a few things that are important." In an act that characterized her outrage at the sight of her home being violated, she ripped the boards away from the door. Evens had to duck to avoid being struck by one of the flying timbers as she leapt in. A few seconds later, she reappeared with several sheets of paper. Thrusting them into Evens's face, she snapped, "Read these."

The suddenly uncertain hack scanned the papers studiously, occasionally glancing up at the people surrounding him.

Fania noted the confusion in his eyes and challenged him further. "Read it out loud."

Evens dropped the papers to his side while his eyes dropped toward the ground. "I can't read," the embarrassed civic drudge confessed.

With no desire to give the humbled man a chance to recover, Fania attacked, "Then let me explain them to you. Slowly. According to these papers, Mimose Estimable legally transferred ownership to me before she died."

Simeon took the papers from Evens, whose head hung as low as his pride as he said, "If you say so. I'm only doing what I was told."

Fania was gaining strength each moment. "Go back to whoever told you and tell them I'm not going anywhere."

Simeon confirmed, "This is all quite clear. The property still belongs to her."

Wilmina stood and grunted, "How did you learn to read?"

"I have an excellent teacher." Fania and Simeon smiled at each other while Wilmina fumed.

"The squatter has a boyfriend. Does he know where your bastard came from? Do you even know?"

Fania lunged for Wilmina but Simeon restrained her. "Ignore her, Fania. What's on the ground is for the dogs. You're better than that."

Wilmina stormed off as Evens mumbled, "I'll have to check into this some more," and followed her.

"I'm sorry," Fania said, "You shouldn't have been dragged into this."

"Don't be sorry. I can't believe how quickly you've learned to read." He held out the papers to her. "And such complicated legal language." Simeon became fascinated as a sly smile came over Fania's face. "What?"

"I didn't read those papers. Not entirely. The words were too hard. I had a feeling that man couldn't read."

Simeon's fascination turned to amazement. "Then how did

you know what was in them?"

"I wasn't sure. There were enough words in there that I recognized and there are those fancy gold seals. I was pretty sure they'd help."

Simeon lit up, bursting with elation. "You bluffed?"

"Was that wrong?" she asked in complete innocence, naively uncertain about the morality of her actions.

Simeon extended his hands out toward her. He was shaking with excitement. "No! It was brilliant." The flustered teacher was unable to put a complete thought together. "You are... I'm so..."

Simeon was a demonstrative person by nature. Anyone who knew him well wouldn't be overly surprised by his reaction to Fania's successful ploy. Yet he himself was shocked when he grabbed Fania, hugged her, and, caught up in his own emotions, held her head in his hands and kissed her unprepared lips.

Fania's arms shot out straight from her sides, her lips tightened, and her entire body went stiff. Suddenly mindful of his impulsive actions, Simeon pulled back. He'd never felt more embarrassed.

"I'm so sorry. I don't know what I was thinking. No. I wasn't thinking. It's just that I've never known anyone as amazing as you. Can you forgive me?"

As he rambled, Fania tried to collect herself, folding her arms around her body in a defensive posture. "No, I mean, yes. I... You shocked me." There was a long, embarrassed delay while Fania decided how much she was willing to risk. Knowing she was inviting more speculation, she continued, "No one has ever kissed me before."

Simeon was mystified and it showed on his face and in his voice as he began to ask, "But Rose..." When Fania's eyes dropped to the ground, his previous embarrassment was forgotten in the pain he felt for her sake. "Oh, Fania." He hugged her again, but tenderly. This time she returned his embrace.

Tears filled Fania's eyes and heart. She was sure she would have burst into uncontrollable sobbing had Rose not poked her head out of the house at that moment.

"*Manman,* stop playing with the *pwofesè.*" The couple quickly released one another. Fania rubbed her eyes. "When are we going to read my new books?"

Simeon was at a loss for what to think, never mind what to say. In his heart, leaving gracefully was the best he could do. "I should be going. It's been a long day. I'll see you... or hear you, at school." Crouching down to Rose's level, he looked in her cheerful eyes and said, "*Ovwa,* Rose. It was a pleasure meeting you. You're a very lucky girl." He took her hand and kissed it before dragging himself from the scene.

Rose smiled at her mother. "I like the *pwofes*è. Is he a good teacher?"

"*Wi.* He's a wonderful teacher."

There were times when Fania thought her life could not be more difficult, more punishing. The earthquake and the orphanage would forever lay siege to her thoughts and feelings. Now, as if her life insisted on an intolerable level of uncertainty, she had a vision of Renaud following her.

She knew she would never be completely free of those ghosts, but standing there in front of *her* home, holding Rose's hand, and thinking about Simeon, she was tempted to believe that her life might be more than something to be endured. Maybe, she thought, forcing aside the fear and apprehension that were forever close neighbors, it could be a life worth celebrating, one blessed of God.

Chapter 16

THE SCENE IN the kitchen was chaotic as usual as the final days of the school year approached. Fania's mood, however, was bright and unshakable. She worked with the power and efficiency of a well-maintained machine but with the joy of a child at play. Not even the ever-threatening Marta could rattle her. Marta was none too pleased that she couldn't erase the smile from the girl's face. In her mind, workers didn't earn their wages unless they were miserable in their drudgery.

The women behind the counter shoveled noodles into

plastic bowls and handed them to the passing children. The flow was interrupted when someone about twice as tall as the average student took a place in line. It was Theodore, Marta's immediate supervisor, who addressed the group, "Fania Dieusel?"

Fania looked up from her task and said, "*Wi?*"

"Basile wants to see you in the school office."

Seeing a chance to test the limits of her authority, Marta complained, "Can't she go after lunch? These children won't feed themselves."

Theodore was insistent and ominous, "It can't wait."

Marta grumbled under her breath, but she knew where she stood in the school hierarchy and it was well below the level of headmaster Basile. Being Marta, though, she couldn't resist pushing her point. "And I suppose feeding children can wait?"

Knowing how this battle of wills would end, Fania wiped her hands on her apron and followed Theodore as he headed for the exit.

Marta's parting shot was, "Come back as soon as you're done! You won't be paid for work you don't do."

Basile's office was impressive only by La Saline standards. It was about as large as a classroom, but was filled with beat up file cabinets and chairs. He sat at a well worn steel desk, which like everything else in the room was a castoff from some defunct business, most likely from the United States. Americans were fond of unloading unwanted leftovers of all kinds on Haiti. While well-intentioned, such generosity eliminated the need for (and possibility of) Haitian entrepreneurs. Haitian businesses had learned the hard way: It's not easy to compete with free.

As Theodore ushered Fania in, she tried to assess the encounter she was being led into. Basile sat at the far end of the room. Against the wall to her right sat Claude, Wilmina, and an imposing man in a suit. Fania shuddered at the sight of them.

Theodore gestured to an empty chair on the other side of the room then left. When she sat down, Fania sensed her adversarial position no less than she felt the concrete floor beneath her feet.

Although she feared the answer, Fania asked, "What's going on here?"

Basile's concern etched deep lines on his brow. "Fania, these people have brought some disturbing charges against you. I want to give you a chance to respond. I must tell you, however, if they are true, the consequences will be severe."

Fania was more defensive than she knew would be helpful. "What are they saying? What do they know about me?"

Claude, the *houngan,* stepped forward and spoke to Basile with the detached calm of a serpent slithering toward its victim. "Wilmina came to me for," here he paused and lowered his voice to increase the gravity of his statement, "spiritual counsel. She was concerned for her daughter's welfare. I have discerned that what she told me is the truth. It proves that this girl is neither fit to work in a school nor to raise a child."

At his words, Fania grew enraged. "You have 'discerned'? How? With chicken blood? You're a madman and a fraud."

The *houngan* responded to Fania's frenzy with a stillness that felt like death. "See for yourself. Confronted with the truth, she lashes out." Shaking his head, he continued, "She should be completely removed from the vicinity of this school. This man is from the Victory Orphanage. He will take her daughter to where she can be raised properly."

"How dare you!" Fania screamed like a trapped animal being brought to slaughter.

Wilmina added her thoughts, "Marie-Fleur told me about the way you behaved at the orphanage."

Basile explained, "They say you mistreated the children there."

"She abused the children and beat them for her own amusement." Turning to Fania, the *houngan* finally directed his malice directly at her. "You treated them like your slaves, doing your bidding at all times."

Fania stepped toward her accuser, but he stood firm. Their exchange grew in intensity and ferocity with each utterance.

"You're a liar!"

"She assumed that, being the oldest child in the orphanage, she could oppress the others."

"It's all untrue, but why are these accusations coming up now?"

"Even here in La Saline she has continued her domineering ways. Do you deny that you forced Wilmina's daughter to help you when you were constructing that hovel you're squatting in?"

"I only asked her to play with Rose while I..."

"And can you deny that you were dismissed from the orphanage because of your promiscuous behavior that resulted in the birth of your impure child?"

Fania pleaded with Basile, "It was nothing like that. I..."

Claude turned back to Basile, an icy calm returning to his voice as quickly and coldly as a knife cuts through flesh. "Promiscuous, abusive, and unrepentant. Do you approve of a woman like that being in the proximity of your students? Or raising another profligate like herself? The child should be removed to the orphanage immediately."

The *houngan* went so far as to prompt the man from the orphanage to take a step toward Fania. When the mountainous man turned, Fania recognized him from the scar running down the side of his face.

Not yet persuaded by the accusations, Basile held up his hand to check the suited man. "No decisions have been made, although it does appear that some action will have to be taken."

Fania turned to Wilmina in desperation. "Why are you doing this? What have I ever done to you?"

"You can stop the sweet act. You think you're so special, a little princess. You aren't, you know. You're just another orphan and a squatter."

Fania stiffened at the disparaging labels she'd so often endured from Nadine during her days at the orphanage. "Where did you hear that? Those aren't your words."

Wilmina suddenly looked nervous and turned away. "I don't know what you're talking about."

Fania gave up on her and turned to Basile. "These are all lies. I loved the children at the orphanage and treated them well. I was like a mother to little Marie-Fleur. She was..." Fania froze and slid her gaze to Wilmina. "Is that what this is about? Is that why you've tried to keep her away from Rose and me?"

"It's because you're an evil example to her. I don't want her ruined by your wickedness."

Fania took two long steps in her direction. Unlike the steel-willed sorcerer, Wilmina backed off. Fania pressed, "Who put you up to this?" Wilmina looked away from her cutting gaze. Fania's expression took on an unyielding resolve as she demanded of Basile, "I want to face my accuser."

The *houngan* responded, "We stand before you. Make your defense."

"You know nothing, witch doctor. I want him to hear from Marie-Fleur." The room exploded with an outburst of objections and derision.

"I won't let that whore near my daughter!" shouted Wilmina, her fear magnifying her anger.

The witch doctor added his complaint, "She's going to terrorize the child again."

Basile said nothing, but raised his hands until a relative calm settled on the room. "In all fairness, I think I should hear the girl's story directly."

Wilmina began to panic. "But, sir, the poor wretch can barely talk. She can't help with..."

"Wretch?" Fania challenged. "Is that what you think of

her? She's a sweet, delicate little girl. You are the wretch."

A reprise of the uproar continued until Basile shouted, "Enough!" He called out, "Monite." The woman appeared promptly at the entrance to the office. "Would you bring Marie-Fleur Paul-Louis here? She's in..." He searched through a pad of papers on his desk. "...*Madmwazèl* Emirene's class." The woman went off on her errand.

"She'll try to frighten her," objected Wilmina, who was feeling more and more uneasy with the way the hearing was proceeding.

Basile motioned to a chair in the corner of the room behind his desk and said, "To prevent any coercion, Fania, please sit in this corner, away from the girl." Fania complied while the atmosphere in the room grew so tense the air seemed to convulse.

Monite reappeared with Marie-Fleur at her side just as the occupants of the room had reached the limits of their patience and gave the impression that they were on the verge of attacking each other physically. The little girl, who sensed the hostility, wore the expression of one being led to her own execution. When she saw Fania, she immediately lit up. "*Bonswa*, Fania! Is Rose..."

Wilmina stood and shrieked at her. "Quiet, girl!" She grabbed her daughter's arm, tightened her grip, and scowled into her eyes. Marie-Fleur looked afraid for her life.

Basile brought matters to order. "We want to ask you some questions, Marie-Fleur."

In her fear, her stutter grew unbearable. "W-w-wha..." She stopped, gulped, and tried to continue, "W-w-what q-q-q-q-questions?"

Wilmina loomed over the quivering child and spoke with an intimidation that was so transparent, everyone in the room recognized it. Claude hoped in vain that Basile didn't catch on. "Remember what we talked about this morning, child? About the way Fania treated you at the orphanage? It's very important that you remember."

The child remained silent and looked as though she might explode in tears at any moment. "Do you see how afraid she is? We shouldn't make her remember how horrible it was."

"Send the pathetic creature away," urged the *houngan*, less confident than he was when the inquisition began.

"I can see she's afraid. I want to know why."

"Isn't it obvious?" Claude asked.

"I'm beginning to believe so." He turned to Marie-Fleur and spoke in a gentle voice. "Little girl, was Fania mean to you and the other children at the orphanage?"

Eyes wide and filled with fear, Marie-Fleur looked from Basile to Fania to Wilmina. Fania smiled. Wilmina glared at her and squeezed her arm tighter, causing the child to wince.

Basile came out from behind his desk and beckoned the petrified girl to himself. Wilmina let her loose and shoved her in his direction. "Go to him." Marie-Fleur approached Basile with tiny, scuffling steps.

"Marie-Fleur, there's no need to be afraid. Nothing bad will happen to you. You can tell us the truth." The child looked around the room once more. Wilmina's eyes continued to bore into her daughter's face while Fania maintained her smile. The *houngan* stared into a vacant corner of the room, as if expecting to be advised by some spirit being who might be hidden there. No such help was forthcoming.

Marie-Fleur was the one who needed supernatural intervention. "I... I... I..." was all she could manage to say.

"It's all right," Basile tried to soothe her. "Stop and take a deep breath. We want to help. The truth is all that matters."

Marie-Fleur inhaled and exhaled to the point where she began to hyperventilate. When she finally managed to calm herself, she blurted out, for the first time without a single stammer, "It's not true! Fania was always kind to all of us. We all loved her. She's the nicest lady I know. I wish..."

A slap from her infuriated mother stopped Marie-Fleur. "You lying little dog. Of all the ungrateful..." Basile grabbed her arm before she could strike again. Marie-Fleur ran to Fania who clasped her in her arms.

Basile confronted Wilmina and Claude. "I want the two of you out of my office while I decide what to do with the girl."

Wilmina futilely attempted to maintain the deception. "She should be tossed out of the school and have her daughter taken away, of course."

Basile had had enough. "Not Fania, fool. Your daughter. You two will be dealt with later." He shouted his last command so that it echoed throughout the school and out into the streets.

"Get out!"

Wilmina and the *houngan* limped out of the office, whispering together in confidence. Basile turned to Fania and Marie-Fleur. "I'm terribly sorry to have put you two through that. Fania, you may return to your work. We'll try to comfort this little one." As Fania left the office, she turned and blew Marie-Fleur a kiss. Marie-Fleur returned the gesture with a smile from tear-touched lips.

That afternoon was a fretful one for Fania. Although she knew she had survived the trial and been vindicated, she couldn't shake the feeling that, in the same way threatening clouds gathered over the mountains most afternoons, there were more troubles darkening her horizon. When her shift was over, she raced to Rose's classroom to wait with the other parents.

As each child emerged, Fania grew more anxious. Finally, there were no more children and Rose was nowhere to be seen. Fania ran to the teacher. "Where's Rose?"

"Didn't you pick her up already?"

"If I had I wouldn't still be waiting here." Her tone was getting harsher.

The teacher called behind her. "Yvonne? Is Rose back there with you?"

A younger woman came out from a back room Fania recognized as the play area. "I haven't seen her since she was playing with that little stuttering girl and her mother."

"Wilmina? What was she doing here??"

Yvonne sounded as confused as she looked. "She said she wanted to check out the class for her younger child."

Fania erupted. "She has no other child."

"Let me get Basile, he'll know what to do."

"I know what to do." Fania fumed as she wheeled and flew off.

All Haitians who had experienced the hurricanes that annually battered the island knew they were powerless and vulnerable in their paths. The same feeling came over anyone who stood in the way as Fania charged down the dirt road from the school to Wilmina's house.

When she arrived there, Fania ripped the flap off the door. "Get out here, Wilmina." There was no immediate response. Wilmina sat curled up in a corner. "Where is Rose?"

"How would I know? She's your daughter."

Wilmina had drastically underestimated a devoted mother's rage. Fania dove through the doorway and grabbed her by the throat. "Neither of us wants to find out what I'm capable of. Where is she?"

On a couple of occasions, Wilmina had accompanied her *houngan* to one of his *vodou* ceremonies where the participants were mounted by whatever *loa* chose to visit their ritual. Fania's countenance brought to the frightened woman's mind the time she watched a woman become possessed with Ogun, the warrior deity.

Fania squeezed tighter as Wilmina struggled. Wilmina's

full voice could no more escape Fania's grip than she herself could. She croaked out, "It wasn't my idea. Claude set it up. He took both girls. He was the one who forged the papers to have you thrown out of your house."

"Why is your witch doctor doing all this?" demanded Fania who slightly eased her grasp on the terrified woman for the sole purpose of hastening her confession.

"He needed the money." Wilmina answered.

"Money? Is someone paying him?"

"He wants Rose. She's with him now."

None of the woman's statements made any sense to Fania. To her ears, they sounded like the random and disconnected ramblings of a madwoman. She loosened her grip once more. "The *houngan* wants Rose? Why?" Wilmina hesitated, paralyzed, caught between her fear of the priest and Fania's more imminent threat. Fania was not about to let up. She squeezed tighter and demanded again, "What does your witch doctor want with my daughter?"

"Not him. Eli."

An explosion went off in Fania's skull when Wilmina uttered the name she found so repulsive. As confusion and anguish spun in her mind, she felt dizzy and disoriented. She released Wilmina without thinking. "Pastor Eli?"

"He said he'd take Marie-Fleur back if I helped him put Rose in the orphanage. They're both there by now."

"Why do you want your daughter in that horrid place?"

Wilmina came unnerved. Her voice trembled as she

screamed in frustration, "I don't know what else to do with her. I'm not like you. I'm not a mother. I can't even care for myself in this place."

Wilmina broke down, her eyes filled with tears. For the first time in the four years Fania had known the woman, Wilmina stirred up compassion in her heart. The woman's anger and spite, she now saw clearly, were mere masks for intense pain and fear. There was a history behind those tears that Fania had never sought to understand and it moved her.

Pity removed the edge from Fania's voice as she warned Wilmina, "Trust me, woman. You don't want her anywhere near that man." She turned to leave.

Wilmina, no less distraught, called after her. "Where are you going?"

"To see Eli and get my daughter back."

Wilmina shivered at the thought and spoke to Fania in a frozen whisper, "You can't see him. He's dying. They say he has *vodou* disease. I didn't think a man of God could get *vodou* disease."

The edge returned to Fania's voice in full force. "He's no man of God." She stormed off.

Fania sprinted forward, reversing the path she had stumbled along after being thrown out of the orphanage. The entire experience of her exile was rewinding within her. As each faltering step she took over four years ago had increased her despair, so now her resolve strengthened as she strode forward.

Each step was also threatened by fear. Fear that Rose might already be gone forever. Fear that Eli would win in the end. Fear even of the consequences of success. Most of all, she feared not having the emotional and physical strength to do what she knew had to be done. Was her will up to the task that her heart set before her? If she'd had the presence of mind to recollect what she'd already accomplished in her life, that doubt would have been dispelled. At the moment, however, she was acting on impulse alone.

The gate to the orphanage was closed, as Fania knew it would be. The place appeared to be abandoned, so quiet were the building and yard. She beat on the gate with her fists, screaming, "Open the gate. I'm taking my daughter back. God help anyone who tries to stop me."

Frustrated but not disheartened, she paused long enough to look around and consider her next step. A few thoughtful seconds later she dashed off toward the house next door. It must have been built after she had left the neighborhood. She remembered that spot being occupied by a shapeless pile of debris during her time at the orphanage. When no one was looking, kids would climb all over it, treating it as a play area, not a remnant of disaster.

She barged through the front door of the house without the slightest hesitation. She scurried by a woman preparing rice over a coal fire in the kitchen.

Seeing a set of wrought iron steps on the far side of the room, she crossed toward them. "I need to use your roof," she told the woman as she passed without slowing. Fania knew the roof would be accessible. Residents would dry laundry, collect rain, and even, if the evenings were stifling enough, sleep up there. Although the home was a single level, she hoped it would get her the height she needed.

Surprised but not shocked, the woman in the kitchen stared after her without moving. This was Haiti.

If she'd had the time and inclination on that rooftop, Fania could have looked across the skyline of Port-au-Prince to see the man-made jungle that had displaced the rain forests of its ancient days. From almost every roof in sight, including the one she was on, fingers of rebar reached far into the sky, each waiting for more floors that would likely never be built. They proclaimed an optimism that eluded most of the capital's citizens.

Instead of such musings, when she reached the top of the stairs and emerged onto the concrete span of the roof, Fania remained focused on her mission. Racing across the roof, she ducked under the laundry that hung from cords strung between the rebar towers, all the while avoiding several mostly empty rain barrels. (It had been a dry spring and summer didn't hold much promise of relief. Potable water would be hard to come by.)

She reached the corner of the house and swiftly thought through her options. A gap of no more than a couple of meters separated the roof she stood on from the orphanage wall, but the one story height difference would have been insurmountable to all but the most desperate. No desperation rivals that of a mother facing the loss of her child. Fania would have scaled the walls of Citadelle Laferrière to recover Rose if she needed to.

When she spied a four sided cage of rebar reaching from the corner of the roof five meters into the air, she saw her best hope.

The woman Fania had passed in the kitchen didn't own the house. She was renting it from a relative who had emigrated to Miami. She had turned down a chance to move as well. Even if Haiti wasn't always kind to her, it was the only home she knew. It was also where the husband and children she'd lost in the earthquake were buried, though she would never know precisely where. She had no claim of ownership to the property, but she was still concerned about a fierce-looking woman invading the place. She followed Fania up the stairs. When she poked her head through the hole in the roof, she didn't know what to make of the sight before her.

Fania was climbing up the rebar as if it were a ladder set there for no other purpose. Her hands gripped the pieces of steel that protruded vertically from the corner of the roof, forming the beam cage. Her feet climbed on the thin, reinforcing metal cross wires woven onto the rebar structure. With each step, the wires slipped a couple of centimeters, impeding her already arduous progress.

When she reached a height above the level of the orphanage roof, she began to sway the metal rods back and forth. To an outside observer, her rhythmic movement might have looked like a daredevil dance routine. With each beat of her bizarre ballet, she drew closer to her goal. She reached out each time until she was at last able to catch hold of the other roof.

With one hand firmly clutching the rebar and the other clinging precariously to the edge of the orphanage roof, she spanned the chasm between the buildings. A few meters below was the orphanage's barricading wall, ready to consume her with its hungry teeth of razor wire and glass shards. She knew she would have to release either her future or her past.

Anyone seeing Fania in that position would have advised her to take the safe route, keeping hold of the rebar. That choice never held serious consideration for her. She let go of the rebar column (it wobbled back and forth through the sky as if waving to passing aircraft) and slapped her other hand on the orphanage roof. Her feet scraped the wall and her arms were badly scratched as she scrambled up and over the edge of the roof.

Fania wasn't conscious of the danger she had evaded by the slimmest of margins, but her body felt it. She rested on her back panting for several seconds before returning to her quest.

The woman from the house, who had witnessed the entire maneuver, shook her head and ducked back into the house. The invader's puzzling behavior could be ignored. Her rice couldn't.

A ladder extended out of a hole in the cement roof of the stronghold she assumed held her daughter. It was a familiar sight to Fania who had often escaped to the solitude of the roof while she lived in the orphanage. Staring into the hazy sky at night was one of the few retreats she enjoyed in those days. She would put Nadine and her other woes beneath her, lie on her back, and watch the airplanes as they climbed from Toussaint Louverture Airport on their way to places so foreign she couldn't even imagine them. Each plane's landing lights formed a beam through the dusty sky above her that looked so solid she swore she could have walked on it. She always wished she could.

Her intentions were more down-to-earth on this occasion. She slid down the ladder without touching a single rung. Once inside, she shuddered as she took in her surroundings. Even after more than four years, the place made her legs unsteady. She had to lean against the wall for fear of collapsing. That familiarity had its positive side, though. She knew every hallway, room, and corner of the building. She would search each and every one of them until she found Rose.

To avoid drawing any attention to herself, Fania slipped off her shabby sandals that insisted on slapping noisily on the floor with each step. The tiles under her feet felt cool in spite of the warm air. They also felt as grimy as the last day she'd walked on them. She paced noiselessly along the hallway, peeking in each door she passed.

In each room, from small nurseries containing a few cribs to larger dorm rooms filled with cots and flimsy mattresses on the floor, children were either sleeping, playing silently on the floor, or huddling in corners. No one was in the halls or outside the building. The whole house was in lockdown.

*   *   *

Rose and Marie-Fleur were cowering together on a cot when they saw Fania's head lean into the doorway. Rose shrieked, "*Manman*!" before her mother could hush her. They clung to each other so fervently, the other children in the room, of which there were several, became invisible to them.

Soon all the children in the room crowded around Fania waiting for a chance to embrace her. Most of the kids in the house had arrived since Fania left, but her legacy lived on. The older children spoke in reverent tones about the angel who had made their existence in the orphanage tolerable during the year she was there.

As much as they tried to keep the noise level down, their excitement conquered their caution, drawing children of all ages from other rooms on the floor. It took some effort, but Fania was finally able to calm them all down. She told Rose they were going home. Marie-Fleur looked disconsolate at the news, but Fania comforted her, saying, "Don't worry, *ti sè*. I'll come back for you as soon as I can."

With a series of hugs and a near monsoon of tears, Fania left the room with Rose in her arms and a long train of children in her wake.

Down in the dining area, Nadine and Claude stared anxiously out the barred windows toward the front gate of the compound. From their fidgety movements to the frantic edge on their voices, they reacted more like the victims of a siege by a vast army rather than the object of an encounter with a lone young woman. There was no sign of Eli anywhere.

"She's probably halfway back to La Saline by now," Nadine hoped more than believed. "How could she even know the girl is here?"

"Let's get on with it. I can't wait here all day," urged an agitated Claude. Nadine handed him a slip of paper. The witch doctor didn't look at all happy as he inspected the scrap with disdain. "What the hell is this?"

"That's the hospital and room number where they admitted him yesterday."

"Where's the damn money? I need that cash, woman. There are people..." his voice failed him as he recalled the threats those "people" had made after a foolish wager he'd placed on a cock fight.

"Calm down, priest. He has the money with him at the hospital. You bring the girl, you'll get it."

Claude choked back his frustration, trying to will himself to relax. "Where is she?"

His last trace of composure vanished when he heard a voice that was serene yet as uncompromising as stone. As the unwanted answer bounced off the concrete walls, it surrounded and temporarily immobilized him.

"Where she belongs. With her mother," Fania said from the top of the stairs where she stood holding Rose. Marie-Fleur hovered behind her while several other children peeked from around the corner. "And she's staying with me," Fania continued resolutely as she stepped down to their level and walked up to them. Every child in the orphanage had formed a procession behind her. They expected an explosive confrontation and they weren't disappointed.

Nadine grabbed Fania's arm. "What do you think you're doing, little princess?"

Fania easily shook free, twisting Nadine's arm until she winced in pain. "No more, woman. You have no power over me anymore." Then she yanked the paper from Claude's hand.

"Give me that," grunted the *houngan* as he reached out to try to wrench the paper from Fania's grasp. Before he was able to get his hand on it, a dozen children, none of whom had any trouble evaluating the dispute and its combatants even if they lacked the specifics, rushed in and mobbed the man, grabbing, biting, and kicking him. He bellowed in pain before falling unceremoniously on his bottom. A ten-year-old boy who wore an oversized Boston Celtics tank top sat on Claude's chest. He alternately twisted the beleaguered man's nose and poked his eyes. Another pair of kids sang a song in unison as each pinned one of Claude's arms.

At the same time, three kids grabbed each of Nadine's legs. She was unable to move or shake them off. Another boy took advantage of her immobility by dropping a bucket over her head. It dripped an unknown but unpleasant smelling substance over her body.

Marie-Fleur separated herself from the fracas and shouted, "*Ale*, Fania! Run!" She was grateful to see Fania and Rose escape whatever cruel fate the conspirators had planned for them. It also occurred to her that her cry of warning to her two friends had been loud and firm, with no trace of a stutter. Her elation about those two blessings was short-lived. She soon came to the realization that her condition had not improved. She was still trapped in Victory Orphanage and she would likely soon feel the wrath of a humiliated and vindictive Nadine.

Chapter 17

MEDICAL CARE WAS a luxury few Haitians could afford. One night of intensive care required more money than most would earn in a lifetime of labor. A prolonged hospital stay would be out of the question for all except a privileged few. Fortunately for Eli, he was a member of that class. By virtue (or lack thereof) of his various enterprises, he had amassed a small fortune—an exorbitant one by Haitian standards. He had plenty of money. What he was running out of was time.

* * *

The hospital room reeked of death. Eli felt it himself. He inhaled it with each of his increasingly shallow breaths. In spite of his countless sermons on the blessings of heaven, he received no consolation. It was the hellfire messages that rang in his ears today.

His wife Paulette had left him, no longer able to tolerate his many indiscretions. He had tried to convince his flock that a false teacher had led her astray, but most everyone knew the truth. The congregation was much more open-minded when it came to their minister's lifestyle. Few had deserted him.

Soon, against his will, he was going to desert them.

The tiny room contained few medical instruments and even those were idle. It was barely distinguishable from a typical bedroom. Eli was dwarfed in the bed, covered with rumpled blankets. He was a shadow of the dynamic presence he had once been. His cheeks were sunken, his hair thin, and his eyes gray and empty. Every one of his bones could have been counted, his body was so wasted away.

His labored breathing was the only sound inside the room. Outside the room was quite a different story. Shouts of an argument echoed around the tiled corridors, disturbing the sickly silence.

"You can't go in there," came the nurse's emphatic warning from the hall as Fania strode through Eli's doorway. "He's too sick for visitors."

"I'm not a visitor," Fania said to the nurse, although her

gaze was fixed on Eli's pathetic form.

He was just strong enough to force out a few words at a time. "It's all right, nurse." He paused to catch his breath. "Leave us."

The truth was, the nurse didn't care much for Eli either. He treated her with the same dismissive arrogance he had practiced so well with most of the people he had ever known. Her attempt to stop Fania wasn't meant to protect the sick man, only to preserve hospital protocol. She turned and walked away with no delay. As she retreated down the hall, her footsteps faded as quickly and completely as her interest in her patient.

Fania let loose her fury, heedless of the man's weakened condition. "Ruining my childhood wasn't enough for you?"

"I'm sorry." He continued in the third person, trying to somehow distance himself from his own behavior. "This old man knows now he was wrong."

"As penance you get a witch doctor to steal my daughter?"

"I have no one left. Paulette left me. My only son is gone. I wanted the child with me. I didn't think you'd bring her on your own."

Fania laughed bitterly. "You have something right at last. But you've failed. I wanted to tell you to your face. You won't destroy her as you tried to do to me."

As she took a step toward the exit, Eli called after her with all his waning strength, breaking into a thick, painful cough as he finished.

"Fania, wait. I have to know. Why did you never tell

anyone?"

"Who was there to tell? Who would believe the word of an orphan against the mighty man of God? You held all the power then."

"If you had let me help you, the problem would have gone away."

"There is no problem; there never was. She's my daughter. If you'd helped me, as you call it, she'd be dead. Isn't there enough death around to satisfy you?"

Once more, she moved to leave. Once more, weaker still, Eli tried to stop her. "Wait! Can you bring her here so I can at least see her? So she can see me?"

"Never." Fania's response couldn't have been more final had it been carved on a gravestone. "She's waiting in the hallway, right outside that door, not ten meters away." She pointed and paused to watch his already dimming light fade even further. That brought to her face a smile so vengeful, she almost felt guilty. Almost. "She has no idea who you are and she never will." Her statement cut him deeper than any surgeon's blade. "Now I'm in love with a good man and I'm happy. Your ugly story is over."

"At least let me help you." His request was punctuated with a cough that brought up a wad of blood that hung on his chin and stained his sheets. With what might have been the last vestige of strength left in his failing body, he leaned over to a teetering nightstand by the bed and lifted a thick envelope. He could scarcely keep his arm up as he held it out to her and said,

"Take it."

She accepted it, being careful not to make contact with Eli's withered hand. Inside the envelope was a bundle of bills, more money than she had ever seen, more than she had ever imagined. She pulled the cash out and turned it in her hands distastefully as Eli fell back onto his pillow. "You were going to buy my daughter with this. Do you think I want your blood money?" She paused before telling him, in a tone more vicious than she thought herself capable of, "Take it with you to hell."

With that final exclamation, she tossed the bills at him. She watched them flutter onto the bed, scattering all over his body. It would have reminded her of a gentle snowfall, had she ever seen snow. She turned and left, closing the door behind her with all her strength. Eli never heard the final echo of the slam.

Unaware that her tormentor's heart, if he had one, had already ceased to beat, Fania took Rose's hand and left the hospital. The memory of the man who had raped her then shamed and rejected her would pollute her mind long after he had left this world. Of that, she was aware. She also knew, however, she would never look back. That chapter of her story was closed forever.

Rose never did find out why they went to the hospital that day. All she understood was her mother was shaken to the core. That explained why, instead of going home, the two of them hopped on a bus and took the long mountainous road over Massif de la Selle to Jacmel on the southern coast of Haiti. Fania didn't give

Eli the satisfaction of knowing it, but she had palmed a handful of his "blood money." Now she would use it to fund a time of recovery she badly needed but could never have afforded otherwise.

As hard as she tried, she couldn't banish the traumatic visions her confrontation with Eli had revived. She hoped that, with time, those memories would erode like the mountains through which they passed, but she also prayed for the possibility of better memories rising to take their place.

Fania and Rose spent three wondrous days at a little inn that, while it wasn't on the beach, was close enough to the sea that the sounds of surf lulled them to sleep each night. Their room had a massive carved mahogany door she thought must be as heavy as the iron gate that guarded the orphanage. Its intricately carved decorations reminded her of Granmè's treasure box. She wondered if the same craftsman had created both.

Jacmel showed signs of life since the time when the earthquake had all but flattened the former resort village. The beach was busier than it had been in years. The artisans in the village were once more churning out colorful crafts and artwork. There was even new construction portending the possibility of an influx of tourist dollars. All this united to lift Fania's spirits and dispel, or at least temper, her painful reflections.

Rose played in the dirty sand, leaving Fania free to recline against a wall bordering the beach and look out over the sea. The view restored to her mind a message she had recently read in Granmè's diary.

"The tide leaves dead fish on the beach. Then the waves wash them away. Each day brings new trials but also new help. I pray Fania will see a time of peace and love. She has endured enough discord and fear."

Those times came sporadically and never lasted long, but as she watched her daughter play and thought of her future, Fania dared to dream Granmè's prayer would be answered soon.

Their respite was memorable and Jacmel was filled with hopeful progress, but eventually Fania and Rose had to return home. On the bus ride back over the mountains, they saw a rainbow so sweeping, it appeared to arch from the beaches on the southern coast all the way to Port-au-Prince. They cherished this promising sign as they drew closer to home.

Back home the following day while Rose was in her class and she waited for hers to begin, Fania reviewed the current state of her life. She was finally free of Eli. She had faced an agonizing inquisition and turned back the accusations of her adversaries. She had every reason to believe Simeon loved her and had no doubt about her love for him. She should have felt free and without a care. Instead, a sense of dread hung over her that was as real as the steel roof above her head.

Maybe it was the thought of soon having to face Marta after an unexcused three day absence from work. Possibly it was that Rose had acted lethargic when she dropped her off. Or it could have been the old sense of doom that was always close at hand whenever her prospects began to look up.

Whatever it was, the dark feelings vanished when she heard Simeon's voice.

"Fania?"

Fania pulled the paper plug from the opening and replied, "*Bonjou*, Simeon."

"I'm so relieved you're there. Where have you been the past few days?" His voice was strained with the distress he'd experienced during her absence.

"Rose and I needed a break. Did I miss a test?"

"No, nothing like that. I've wanted so much to talk to you. Ever since I met you through this wall..." He tapped the cinder blocks for emphasis. The sound of shuffling feet and scraping benches interrupted him before he could continue.

A voice rang out from the classroom, "*Pwofesè*, what are you doing on the floor?" Fania recognized the voice as belonging to Emmanuel, the oldest and smartest boy in the class. They had never met, but she felt a special kinship with him. Whenever she had a question about the classwork, Emmanuel usually verbalized it. She had thanked him a hundred times in her thoughts for helping her solve problems she might never have otherwise found the answers to. That was why she found it impossible to be upset with him now for interrupting what she hoped was a life-changing declaration from Simeon.

Caught, Simeon jumped up. "Nothing. I..." He gave up trying to concoct an excuse for his improbable pose and went on the offensive to keep the students' minds off his strange behavior. "I hope you're all ready because there's a quiz today."

A collective groan signaled that the *pwofesè* had regained the upper hand.

When the class began, Fania dove back into her studies as though she'd never missed a day. She was well ahead of the rest of the class, so the few days she missed wouldn't matter in the long term. She was distracted, though, by the prospect of facing Marta. She dreaded the fate that awaited her when they clashed in the next hour. She wondered whether her educational pursuits would soon end.

The time came and Fania could no longer delay it. She had no idea what she would say when Marta attacked, and attack she would. Though probably unwise, she decided not to plan anything ahead of time but rather to, as one of Granmè's proverbs advised, let the river flow according to its own course. She was glad the school year was nearly over, but it was the prospect of more intimate tutoring from her teacher that gave her a sense of liberation and was mostly responsible for what happened next.

Fania sauntered in, tying her apron. She didn't have to wait long. Marta accosted her the instant she entered. "Where have you been?" she bellowed loudly enough to be heard throughout the kitchen and the cafeteria as well as much of the school. She raised her ladle, poised to pound it on her prodigal employee's head.

The mood in the kitchen tensed as the entire staff waited to see what would follow. They had listened to Marta curse her truant charge for three days. They had imagined all manner of sadistic disciplinary techniques their tormentor would dole out on their co-worker. None of them predicted even a remote approximation of the scene they witnessed.

Fania reached up and grabbed Marta's ladle from her hand. She wagged it in the woman's stunned face as she growled, "Don't mess with me, Marta. I'm not in the mood for it. I've had enough trouble lately." She stuffed the ladle into Marta's apron and went about her labors as if it were just another day in the kitchen.

The other women stared in shock and fear. Relief came upon them when Marta's catatonic silence was mercifully interrupted by Simeon's appearance. Marta took her frustration out on him. He leaned over the counter to speak to Fania but couldn't get a single word out before the tyrannical kitchen boss drove him away with shouts of, "Get out! Go on, get out of here!" She returned to her work, shaking her head and muttering, "Teachers."

Fania smiled and continued to fill bowls of noodles. It was then that she and all the other workers realized that, although Marta had scared away many a worker, she had never fired one. That wasn't her style. Her tactic was to terrorize them until they surrendered and left on their own. She hadn't expected to ever come up against someone like Fania. In her days and nights of study over the past school year, Fania had learned a lot of new words. "Quit" wasn't among them.

* * *

Fania was encouraged by her victory but, as she watched child after child pass by to collect their meager bowls of noodles, she couldn't keep her mind off Rose. The previous night, the little girl was more tired than usual. She went right to sleep when the sun went down, uncharacteristically skipping story time for the night. Fania dismissed it as exhaustion after their Jacmel adventure.

When her shift ended, her pace to Rose's classroom was more hurried and harried than usual. When she arrived, the child was leaning listlessly in the doorway waiting for her. Instead of her usual dash into Fania's arms, she put her arms up, the implied signal that she wanted to be carried. Fania complied, but asked her, "Are you feeling all right, *ti cheri*?"

Rose's voice was weak when she replied, "My tummy hurts." As they turned to leave the schoolyard, Simeon rushed up to them.

"Fania! May I walk you ladies home?"

Fania looked at Rose, who flashed a weak smile to make it clear that the *pwofesè* was more than welcome. Fania was once more grateful that Rose had expressed what was in her mother's heart when she was hesitant to do so herself.

"You've been approved."

"I'm honored," he responded as he lifted Rose's languishing head with a finger under her chin.

They walked in silence until they reached the house.

Not wanting to make himself too vulnerable in front of Rose, Simeon whispered to Fania, "May I talk to you alone?"

The hopeful mother told her daughter, "Rose, you go inside and rest. I'll be in soon to check up on you."

Rose did as she was told while Simeon scuffled for a while.

His voice cracked as he began speaking. He had to clear his throat to continue, "Every time I've tried to talk with you lately, something interrupts us. Should I take that as a hint?"

"No," Fania replied without hesitation.

"I teach the language, but I'm still at a loss for words."

Fania had waited too long to let this moment pass or even be delayed. "Let me help. I..."

With that prompt, Simeon was able to finally express his feelings. They finished the statement in unison,"...love you."

"*Wi!*" Simeon smiled before going on with more confidence, "I love you, Fania. I think I've loved you since the first day I heard your voice through that hole. Thoughts of you occupy my entire day. When I teach, all I can think about is you on the other side of the wall. I want nothing—no wall, no person, nothing—to separate us anymore." He paused over a deep breath, dreading a negative response from Fania. None came. He took her hand. "Classes end tomorrow and I'll be leaving for my training in America a few days after that. I'll be back the week before school starts. Will you wait for me?"

"Do you want Rose to wait for you, too?"

"Oh, Fania, do you need to ask? I want you both in my life. Forever."

"God willing, I'll be here when you return."

Simeon kissed her. She was still uncomfortable and

Simeon sensed it.

Nervously, she told him, "You'll have to wait for me, too. It's hard for me to express myself that way."

"Don't worry," he replied as he embraced her again. "There will be plenty of time for more lessons."

"Will I see you before you leave?"

Simeon rubbed the back of his neck and shook his head. "I won't be around much, if at all. I just got word that my father died. I'll have a lot to take care of before my trip."

"I'm so sorry for your loss, Simeon."

"We weren't close. In fact, we haven't spoken in years. He threw me out of the house when I told him I wanted to teach rather than follow him into the ministry. He always thought I'd take over his church, but I..."

For the first time, Fania saw it in his face, heard it in his voice, and recognized it in his mannerisms. She went completely rigid and her eyes locked on his. She was frozen. She was petrified. She might as well have been dead.

"What's wrong?" Simeon asked.

A mortal struggle took place in her soul before she was able to force out her question, one agonizing word at a time. "Who is your father?"

"His name was Eli. He was the pastor of the Victory Baptist Church in..."

She couldn't look anymore. She turned her back on him and began to cry.

Simeon had no idea where her reaction came from.

"What's wrong?"

Slowly as a sunset, Fania turned back to face him. "I was in his orphanage." She saw her entire destiny crumble like the bakery she watched disappear before her eyes during the earthquake. This was even more devastating. Against every instinct, she tried to continued, "He was... It was him..." She couldn't go on. She didn't have to.

Rose peeked her head out. "*Manman*?" she asked, her eyes sagging more deeply than before.

Fania moved her gaze from Simeon to Rose and back. Simeon glanced at Rose. Suddenly his face contorted in pain. "No," he said softly, shaking his head in disbelief. Silence. Now he screamed, "No!"

Fania couldn't speak. Her voice was taken from her, as was her heart, her future, maybe her life. She nodded.

"Oh, God," Simeon wailed as he ran off.

Rose had no clue what had transpired. "Is the *pwofesè* sick, too?"

Tears in her eyes, Fania answered, "*Wi*, Rose, I think he is." Through those tears, Fania took a good look at her daughter. She was holding her stomach and couldn't keep her eyes fully open. She was whimpering but no tears were falling. A second later, she threw up.

"My precious girl!" Fania ripped down the flap that covered her doorway and wrapped it around Rose. She ran off, carrying Rose like a bundle of rags.

Chapter 18

Since the day *Doktè* Georges delivered baby Rose, he was the only medical professional she had ever seen. Not that Rose or her mother would have noticed or cared, but he'd recently completed medical school and been pronounced a "real" doctor. He was the first person Fania thought of when it came to her daughter's care, so she rushed the child to the hospital where he worked.

She tried to board buses and *tap-tap*s but no one wanted to share space with the little girl who was so obviously and seriously ill. As a result, she ran until she was exhausted then slowed to a rapid walk. When she sufficiently recovered her strength, she ran again.

By the time they reached the hospital a couple of hours later, their journey slowed by some sort of protest in the streets marked by overturned vehicles and burning tires, Rose reeked of the diarrhea that was seeping from the vinyl wrap enfolding her. They were a sorry sight standing in the entryway to the emergency room, but no one at the hospital was shocked or surprised. In the years since the earthquake, they'd seen enough victims of cholera to know what to expect.

Unsure what to do, Fania asked for Georges. The staff, however, was already working on Rose, who was now unconscious. After cleaning her up, a nurse brought her to a large ward of cots filled with other cholera victims. After several attempts to find a vein, the nurse succeeded in putting an IV into her arm. Fania was glad Rose wasn't awake to feel the repeated stabs of the needle in her tiny arm.

The cholera ward was a disaster in itself. Buckets of liquid stool and vomit were everywhere. Some had spilled. The place was swarming with flies. Every patient had someone there with them. Fania knew she would never leave Rose's side.

Simeon was suffering from his own malady—an emotional one. After leaving Fania at the school, he walked back to his home in Dèlma 31. The long hike, made longer still by his burdened pace, gave him time to think over his dilemma.

He adored Fania, of that he was sure. He was equally certain of his attachment to Rose. The question he struggled with was how to balance those affections with his intense desire to distance himself from his father and that man's detestable legacy. The more he thought about his father's character and measured it against what he knew of Fania, the clearer the situation became. He couldn't conceive of a single scenario in which Fania would bear any responsibility for her plight as a single mother.

Furthermore, Simeon long ago grew weary of his father trying to squeeze him into an Eli-shaped mold. It didn't fit and he still wore the psychic scars of his father's attempts to force him into it. By refusing to allow his father to come between him and the woman he so loved and admired, he would be making a final stand against the man.

As for being a father to a child who was also his half-sister, Simeon still struggled in his mind, if not his heart. He determined to seek out Fania the next day and try to work it out. He owed her that much, no matter how it was all resolved.

Georges eventually made it to Rose's bedside, where he tried to relieve Fania's anxiety. "If you'd been another few hours, we might not have been able to help her. She's not out of danger yet but she should recover." Fania's distress decreased only marginally.

Rose wasn't vomiting anymore, so the nurses wanted to use a special drink to help her regain her lost fluids.

Unfortunately, the hospital had run out of the medicine and was waiting for more. It could be days before the supplies came. Rose would have to stay in the hospital for observation in the interim.

Fania's mind reeled. She couldn't afford what had already been done for Rose. The expense of a longer stay was out of the question.

"I pay for her school by working there. Is there something I can do here to cover the costs?"

No one was more aware than Georges of the hospital's need for help. They had the same problem as Fania: no money. At Fania's request, Georges discussed her bartering arrangement with hospital administration. Between their need and their desire to save a girl's life, they agreed to her proposal.

As Fania paced the halls awaiting their decision, praying constantly, she panicked as she saw someone who resembled Renaud walk by the ward. She prayed with that much more fervor.

Every effort Simeon made to contact Fania ended in frustration. He went to the house but it was empty, the door flap missing. The paper she always used to plug the little gap in the wall was intact, still filling the hole from the last time she had finished listening in on his class.

He stepped inside and sensed her presence, leaving him with a feeling of homesickness. Her scent was alive in her home. Scanning the tiny living space for remembrances of Fania or clues to her whereabouts, he happened upon Granmè's diary. It was open to a page that began with one of her many proverbs.

"A mosquito without a stinger can buzz, but can do no harm. I sense the buzz of death near, but the sting is gone. The last three years of my life have been a treasure. I wouldn't trade them for a hundred years without my girls. *Mèsi anpil, Jezi*."

With those words as clear as a whisper in his ear, Simeon felt not only Fania's presence but, though he'd never met her, Granmè's as well. He also felt their absence in the deepest part of his heart. He fully understood Granmè's love for the girl and wanted the chance to express his love to her once again, without reservations and without limits.

Simeon dreaded the next obvious step in his search but finally forced himself to go to the kitchen to ask Marta.

She never looked up from her tasks. "I don't know and I don't care. All I know is where she isn't. She won't be here in the new school year, either. I'm through with her."

Desperation pushed Simeon on, "Do you know how I could get a message to her?"

Marta finally stopped working and glared at him. "What do I look like, Digicel? We're shorthanded because your friend left without notice. I have work to do and it's not babysitting or message-taking." She went back to work while Simeon dragged himself from the room. He returned to his classroom and closed out the school year for his students but his heart and mind were elsewhere. It wasn't unusual for the kids to have to rouse him when they caught him staring blankly at the back wall.

*   *   *

Fania became convinced that the man she had seen was Renaud. She'd caught sight of him on three different occasions. *It makes no sense. What would he be doing here?* she reasoned, although her more urgent thoughts all revolved around Rose.

It was two days before the medicinal fluids arrived and Rose could be removed from the IV. By then she was improved but far from herself. They remained in the ward for another day, Rose drinking the precious fluid and feeling stronger by the hour.

Meanwhile, Simeon was absorbed with Eli's funeral. Thanks to the efforts of various members of the congregation—mostly women—the arrangements were already in order. A long line of people wound through the building leading to the sanctuary where an ornate casket displayed his emaciated remains. Many wept. Simeon was not among their number. He stood by and mechanically greeted the mourners.

Before his arrival, people had wondered aloud whether Simeon would make an appearance. Now they still had questions and, though whispered, they echoed throughout the church.

"Where has he been?"

"Will he be the new pastor?"

"Can the church survive without Eli?"

"I'm going to have to find a new church."

At times, Simeon was tempted to cry, but not at the loss of his father.

*　*　*

Rose had completely recovered when she suddenly spiked a fever. Georges came back and examined the girl.

"I was afraid this might happen. She's picked up an infection around the site of the IV. She'll need antibiotics."

There was a rushed conference between Georges and some of the other staff. Fania couldn't hear what was being said, but she knew there were more problems.

Georges came back to her. "We can't do any more for her here. We're overcrowded, short-staffed, and our pharmacy is depleted." Fania's spirit had reached its breaking point. She didn't think she could handle another life-threatening crisis, all while the specter of Renaud hung over her. Georges tried to steady her, saying, "We're going to send you to a facility in Croix-des-Bouquets. It's quieter and they'll take good care of her."

"How will I get to Croix-des-Bouquets? I have no..."

Georges eased her concern, "Don't worry. We have a driver who can bring you there."

Fania was relieved to be able to get as far away as possible from the hospital and the threat it posed in the form of her attacker.

While Rose was being cared for and Fania remained steadfastly at her side, Simeon found himself on an airplane bound for New York City. Until the flight left the tarmac of Toussaint Louverture Airport, he wasn't certain he would ever actually leave. He'd reluctantly dragged himself through the packing process, delayed until the last possible moment finding a *tap-tap* for the airport, and, once there, plodded through the terminal like a man condemned to the old Dimanche prison back in La Saline.

Leaving Fania and Rose behind in such an uncertain state was no easier than leaving his luggage or one of his arms behind. That his heart would not be accompanying him on the flight was never in doubt.

His heartache was compounded by the guilt he felt knowing he should be excited about the American adventure he was privileged to experience. His emotions were entirely outside of his power. No matter how hard he tried to distract himself throughout the flight, his thoughts never drifted far from the little hole in his classroom wall and how the woman on the other side had changed his life. And how she might change it yet.

Fania held Rose in her arms as Georges walked her to the truck that would take them to the clinic in Croix-des-Bouquets. Still nervous about her daughter's condition, she climbed in while Rose slept.

"Don't worry, Fania. I've already called a friend of mine at the clinic. They're ready to help you." With a smile, he added, "Do you think I'd let anything happen to a child I brought into this world?" He walked away, leaving her alone in the truck's passenger seat.

While she watched after Georges, the driver's door opened and a man jumped in. Before Fania could react, a hand with two and a half fingers gripped the steering wheel. Its possessor drove the truck swiftly away from the hospital, offering a cheery greeting, "Nice day for a ride, *madmwazèl*." By the time Fania gathered her wits sufficiently to consider jumping out, the vehicle was already speeding down the road.

The atmosphere in the truck was impossibly tense. Fania's teeth were clenched so tightly her head ached. In an effort not to draw attention to herself, she refrained from making even the slightest sound or gesture; she scarcely breathed. She attempted to will herself to disappear. The dozing child was virtually clamped in her arms.

For his part, the driver was enjoying himself, singing and drumming on the steering wheel along with a *kompa* tune on the truck's staticky radio. He paid little heed to his passengers.

The traffic along Boulevard Jean-Jacques Dessalines was typically dense, vehicles bare millimeters from scraping sides and touching bumpers, weaving in and out of gaps that didn't look large enough to fit a goat, never mind a moving vehicle. Even if she wanted to escape, Fania wouldn't have been able to open her door wide enough to get out. Once in a while a daring motorcycle rider would zip between cars. Nothing spoiled the driver's sunny mood.

Sensing Fania's distress, he spoke up, "Don't be alarmed, *madmwazèl*. The traffic is always this bad. We'll get you and your little girl there in plenty of time." He went back to singing, occasionally waving to another driver. "Same people in the same traffic jams," he joked.

Fania was still terrified, but somehow she stuttered, "Wh-where are you taking me?"

"To the clinic in Croix-des-Bouquets. Isn't that where you're headed?" With his mutilated hand, he grabbed a piece of paper stuck in the visor that hung down, partially obscuring the windshield. As he looked the paper over, he let out a sigh of relief and said, "*Wi*, that's it. You had me worried."

His casual air did nothing to ease Fania's fears. He noticed. "You look nervous, *madmwazèl*. Don't worry. You're in good hands with me..." Here he paused, glanced at his deformed hand, and added with a tragic laugh, "...even if one of them isn't much good." For the first time since their ride began, the driver took a good look at Fania. "You look familiar. Do I know you?"

Fania shook her head almost imperceptibly. With that little encouragement, the man proceeded to tell Fania, in great detail because there was plenty of spare time in the gridlock, the story of his life as far as he could remember it.

Somehow, several months earlier, he had found himself half conscious in the street in a slum with a throbbing headache and a lump larger than a *kenèp* fruit. Two of his fingers were cut off and bleeding while another fingertip was missing. He'd stumbled around in the dark until a passerby saw him and brought him to the hospital.

He remembered nothing about his life before that night, not even his name. He'd been working at the hospital ever since, partially to help pay off his medical bill, but also because he had nowhere else to go.

It took the entire trip to Croix-des-Bouquets for Fania to reconcile herself with the possibility that she and Rose were not in imminent mortal danger. Even then, the image of the now benign driver invading her home and threatening Rose wouldn't release her entirely. When the truck pulled up to the front entrance of the clinic, she opened her door even before it came to a stop.

As she began to exit, Renaud took hold of her wrist with his maimed hand and said, "*Madmwazèl*, do you recognize me? You look very familiar. I'd hate to think I once knew such a lovely woman and forgot about her." Fania could do no more than shrug, wishing all the while he would let go of her hand voluntarily and immediately.

With that, he let her out and, with a friendly wave and a call of "*Ovwa. Bondye beni-w,*" he headed back to Port-au-Prince.

Fania was still shaking and Rose was still sleeping when they were ushered into the clinic. They remained there for three restless days.

Chapter 19

Rose recovered fully from the infection as well as from cholera. She was more fortunate than most. After a brief stay in the clinic in Croix-des-Bouquets, she was well enough to leave. She and Fania stayed for another week at the home of *Doktè* Georges' friend, Jonas. He was the doctor who had mentored Georges through medical school and given him his medical bag. After a few hours with Jonas, the model for Georges' skillful and gentle care became apparent.

* * *

Jonas's home was situated at the edge of the sprawling metalworking community in the village. Rose would fall asleep to the rhythmic "tink, tink, tink" sound of hammers as artisans worked sheets of recycled steel into furniture, jewelry, souvenirs, and other wondrous creations. The sounds were comforting and Jonas and his wife were exceptionally hospitable, but she longed to be back in her little home clinging to the side of her beloved school. Her school friends were there. So was everything else she held dear in this world.

Fania was less excited about the prospect of returning. After being gone so long, she dreaded what would be awaiting her. Certainly Simeon would *not* be.

Jonas extended his hospitality to drive them back to La Saline, although he offered to let them stay for as long as they wanted. He and his wife lost their only child in the earthquake. Dyane was a vivacious young woman studying to be a nurse. Along with about 400 classmates, she perished when their nursing school collapsed during the earthquake, wiping out an entire generation of Haitian medical professionals. The older couple savored the presence of young people in their home once more. Fania promised to visit them again, but returning home couldn't be delayed any longer, regardless of what misfortune it might bring.

On the drive home, the car's occupants were quiet to the point of being solemn. Rose napped. Jonas was preoccupied with thoughts of his daughter, wondering what her life would have been like had it been allowed to continue. Would she have a child like Rose? Where would her nursing career have taken her? She'd talked about bringing medical care to the countryside where it was scarce, more often left to local *houngans* and *mambos* who tended to be as unethical as they were unskilled. It wasn't only *his* world that suffered as a result of her loss, he brooded, but the world as a whole.

In the silence, Fania stared out the window watching Haiti fly (or, depending on the traffic, crawl) by. Not wanting her thoughts to dwell on her past trials or advance to her uncertain future, she concentrated on the narrow perspective her ride afforded her. The landscape was no different than the one she passed on her trip out to Croix-des-Bouquets, but Renaud's presence had blinded her view on that trip.

That was when the words struck her. They were everywhere—on billboards looming over the roadway, *tap-taps* whizzing by, and banners strung overhead. They marked clothes, buildings, and abandoned walls. Colorfully painted, carefully printed, or carelessly scrawled, they all reached out to her. It was the first time she was truly aware of their omnipresence. Each had a purpose, each had something to say.

Talk talk with Digicel. Barber shop. Long live Titid. Don't Hate, Appreciate. Just Do It. Nautica. Stop. Seventh Day Adventist School. Daihatsu. Eternal Father Lottery. Drink Prestige Beer. Stop AIDS. Texaco. Doctors Without Borders. Beware. A Huggies baby is a happy baby. Police. Martelly: victory for the people. Barbancourt. Spain 3, Haiti 1.

She was jolted to her marrow, a feeling not unlike what she

felt when the earthquake shook her world, when she realized they weren't simply words. They were messages—messages aimed at her. She wanted to know those messages. She wanted to understand their intent. It was suddenly critical to her to know which pronouncements were true and which were not, which directives were important and which could be discarded as soon as they were deciphered, which led to life and which to destruction.

It was even more important for her to pass that discernment on to Rose. Thanks to all her strenuous studies (and to Simeon), she could read every word, though she didn't always know their precise pronunciation or meaning. She was hungry again. Not for food but for knowledge. The level of understanding she craved would require more persistence and more hard work than she had ever undertaken, but she knew the effort would be worthwhile. Her education, she now realized, had only begun.

Jonas would have driven Fania and Rose right to their front door, but for some reason they wanted to travel the last quarter kilometer to their home on foot. With no belongings to slow them down except for one of Dyane's childhood picture books Jonas's wife had given to Rose, they raced most of the way, Rose with great anticipation, Fania with trepidation.

Arriving before their home, Fania's pessimism appeared to have been groundless. Mother and daughter were relieved to see the place, shabby though it was, intact except for the door flap in which Fania had wrapped Rose. Their relief was short-lived.

With the crash of steel against stone, the walls of the hovel crumbled before their eyes. Rose was confused and devastated. Fania was immediately transported back to the earthquake. Where their home had been, two men with sledgehammers stood with idiotic smiles on their faces. Thinking it would bring more enjoyment to the menial task, the two workmen had demolished the house from the inside. What they hadn't considered was the roof. A moment after their triumphant bashing, the metal sheet plunged onto their heads. Amazingly, they laughed all the more.

Baffled by what she'd witnessed, Fania roared at the clueless pair, "What are you doing to our house?"

The men looked at each other with no more indication of awareness than their sledgehammers showed. One guffawed to the other, "What house? I don't see any house. Do you see a house, Serge?" That induced more mindless mirth.

Judging from their expressions that the two workers would miss any message more subtle, she yelled, "You two destroyed our house."

With much work still to be done, the worker addressed as Serge saw no need for further amusement. He switched immediately to a brusque business-like tone. "Got a problem? See the headmaster." The men returned to their work with an enthusiasm fed by Fania's frustration.

Gone. The house, the (few) furnishings, the books, Granmè's chest—everything was gone. The tears Rose couldn't shed because the cholera had dried them up came back in that much greater volume now. Homelessness was not new to Fania.

The pain she felt was for Rose, not herself. *How can this be happening to my little girl?*

Her own experience and Granmè's example had conferred upon Fania a genius for translating her grief into anger and anger into action. She took Rose's hand and strode into the schoolyard like an invading force. Following Serge's advice, she carried her crusade for justice to Basile's office.

Basile was sitting with a group of white men at a conference table in his office when Fania appeared in the doorway with Rose. Basile saw a gathering storm, but the other men saw a gorgeous woman from whom they could not avert their gaze. Each of the men was momentarily stunned, but Basile jumped at the chance to head off a potentially embarrassing confrontation. "Fania..." was all he was able to utter before the woman's indignation gave her the advantage.

"Where is our home?"

"You disappeared. It's been over two weeks."

"That gives you the right to destroy my home and take my belongings?"

Basile sounded as gracious as he could, but no tone could soften his message. "The Americans," he said as he gestured to the other men in the room, "saw an abandoned house and wondered why we weren't using the space for the school."

"The *blan* gives, the *blan* takes away. Is that it?"

Being ignorant of the Creole language, the Americans were equally ignorant of the content of the conversation. Not knowing how to react in the face of her beauty and passion, as one they affected dull grins. She glared at them in return, a look they found somehow agreeable.

Basile explained their lack of perception, "They don't understand Creole."

"They don't understand a lot of things. Where are my daughter and I supposed to live now?"

The headmaster explained one possible alternative he'd been holding onto for this contingency. Folks in the village had been spreading the word that Claude, the witch doctor, had vanished. His house was abandoned and no one had seen him for over a month, not an unheard of occurrence, especially for those who were unable to pay their gambling debts. Although it was the largest house in La Saline and was vacant, everyone was afraid to use it. Based on what she'd overheard when she took Rose from the orphanage, Fania had an idea he wouldn't be back. Living in his house, however, was out of the question.

"I didn't think you could possibly come up with something worse than homelessness." Fania considered her options for a moment. Nothing came to mind, but she felt the need to move ahead, even if she didn't know where ahead was. "Where are my things?"

"I set them aside in case you came back."

"You should have set my house aside in case I came back. Get them."

Basile knew what she said was true. Like so many before him, he'd buckled under pressure from his American superiors.

With remorse from that moral failure making his voice falter, he explained Fania's dilemma to the men in English. All listened to him with rapt attention using his speech as an excuse to stare at Fania, which they were all anxious to do anyway. Rose was still wary of the white people but was struck with the thought that they resembled chickens, regularly bobbing their heads up and down and speaking with a prattling that was lost on her.

After Basile went off to collect her belongings, Fania sat in a chair opposite the *blans* with Rose cowering on her lap. Fania hadn't been this uncomfortable since her ride with Renaud. In some ways, this setting was more threatening to her. Rose gawked at the white faces with such fear and intensity, the men felt even more awkward than Fania. They looked away, sparing Fania further discomfort.

Fania's relief was palpable when Basile returned carrying Granmè's box. When he handed it to her, she jumped up and was out the door without another word or glance. Her swift exit left the American men speechless but thoughtful.

Baking in the La Saline heat away from the admiring stares of the smitten *blans*, Fania was struck by an urgent awareness of her insecure position. It was shakier than the ground during the aftershocks that rattled the capital for weeks after the earthquake, shocks that regularly came back in one form or another ever since. She placed her box on the ground and inspected its contents as her daughter watched. Rose was thrilled when the books were uncovered, Fania equally so when she caught a glimpse of Granmè's diary. The knife couldn't be missed. It extended well above the lid of the box.

Satisfied that the few items they possessed in this world were intact, Fania knelt beside Rose. Looking in her eyes, she was moved to ask her a life-sized question that she knew would be unfair for anyone in such straits, least of all a little girl, but Rose had surprised her more than once before.

"Rose, what do we do now?"

"I don't know. I'm a kid. Why don't you ask God?"

Fania marveled at the profound simplicity of her answer. "That's what I'll do."

A few minutes later, the two found themselves sitting on one of the rustic pews in the La Saline church. (She still didn't know its name.) They weren't actively praying; they were waiting, knowing that the greater part of prayer is waiting.

Unexpectedly, Pastor Henri, the man most responsible for restoring Fania's faith, ambled in carrying a cardboard box filled with worn and tattered Bibles. When he saw the two, he paused, put the box down, and sat alongside them.

He sat with them for several minutes, saying nothing. Knowing all they'd been through and were continuing to endure, he couldn't bear to disturb their meditation prematurely. When at last he felt the freedom to speak, he did so with a gentleness that opened their hearts to old questions and new possibilities. "You must be thinking God has turned His back on you."

"He *has* been quiet," Fania answered with a hint of a smile.

The pastor gave Fania a compassionate look, one that might have looked practiced coming from another man. From Henri, it couldn't have been more sincere. "I understand." Here, he picked up Rose and gave her a tight squeeze. The girl, to whom the minister had always been a favorite, returned his embrace. "Do you always tell Rose your plans? In silence, there is still love."

"Maybe so, but silence is of no use to one who is lost. Granmè always seemed to have the ability to know His way. I wish she were here now." Fania's eyes lit like torches on a beach at sunset. "She *is* still here." She pulled Granmè's diary from her box. "I remember something I read here." She flipped through the well worn pages until she came to a proverb that had once moved her deeply but she'd since forgotten. "Giving your sandals to a neighbor lets you both walk easier. Life will always be hard in La Saline but when I help another we're both lifted up."

Henri shook his head in agreement. "I'd prefer you find solace in scripture, but you could do a lot worse than following Granmè's wisdom."

Fania wasn't paying attention to the man. She was already collecting her things. "Come, Rose," she said, her hand extended to the girl.

Rose gave Henri a hug before taking Fania's hand. Henri asked, "Where are you going?"

"Home," was the woman's puzzling response.

"But where?"

"Sometimes, we don't know where home is until we arrive there."

Henri couldn't help but laugh as he told her, "You sound more like Granmè every day."

"*Mèsi*, Pastor," she said with a thoughtful look in her eyes. "That's one of the nicest things anyone has ever said to me." Without another word, she and Rose strode off as if they knew where they were going and what the future held for them.

Henri watched hoping that were the case and went back to his Bibles.

Fania was following her instincts... and Granmè's advice. She'd been thinking of herself while others still suffered. She remembered promises she'd made to herself and to others but failed to keep. The first stop on her journey of redemption was Wilmina's house.

Crouched in her familiar corner, the woman was as alone as a cactus on a naked Haitian hillside. Marie-Fleur was in the orphanage. Her *houngan* had disappeared and, like the countless anonymous victims of the earthquake, would never be seen again. Because of her toxic personality, she had no friends in La Saline. Her headaches had increased in frequency and severity to the point where they kept her inside most of the time. They had become her lone companionship, their constancy her consolation.

When Fania shouted Wilmina's name into the doorway, it

sounded foreign to the paralyzed woman inside. No one had spoken to her for a week and she hadn't heard her name spoken in longer still. When her mind cleared to the extent she knew who was calling her, her defensive reflex kicked in. "What do you want, squatter?" Her heart wasn't in it.

Fania had no patience for tired old attitudes. She was moving forward. "Enough of that," she responded. "Come out. We have to talk."

Wilmina poked her face out into the daylight looking as meek as a mouse stumbling on a room full of starving snakes.

Seeing her so insecure and vulnerable, Fania could easily have punished the woman for all her cruelty, but mercy was her motivation now. She asked as pointed a question as Wilmina had ever heard: "Do you love your daughter?"

If she were honest with herself, Wilmina couldn't remember feeling or expressing such an emotion toward Marie-Fleur. The wall of resentment Wilmina had built on the day the girl's father abandoned them was beginning to show cracks lately, though. A combination of the child's unconditional love and her own loneliness was transforming her from the inside out. Until Fania's question, she'd never verbalized it. She worried she'd never have the chance. She took that chance. "Of course I love her, but I can't..."

Fania was in no mood to hear what couldn't be done. "Then come with us. Maybe we can rescue both of you." She didn't wait for Wilmina's reply. She'd presented her offer and was continuing her mission. She walked off with Rose and didn't look back. She did, however, hear distant scuffling feet trying to keep up with her purposeful pace.

Fania and Rose shared similar misgivings as they stood before the open gate of Victory Orphanage. While Rose's incarceration there was short-lived, it was no less disturbing for its lack of duration. She gazed up with anxious eyes at the inappropriately cheerful images on the wall as she said, "I don't like this place, *Manman*."

Fania's response was tainted with a heaviness accentuated by her daughter's fears. "Neither do I, *cheri*, but I promised Marie-Fleur I'd come back for her."

Rose smiled at her mother's words. In less than four years, she'd absorbed more about justice from her mother than most adults could conceive in a lifetime of study. Though neither Rose nor Fania saw it, a vaguely perceptible smile emerged on Wilmina's face as well.

In the empty dining room of the orphanage, a familiar scene was playing out. Evens, the man who had tried to evict Fania from her home, was plying his unscrupulous trade with Nadine. The woman was not as naturally skilled at such disputes as Fania had grown to be. The man brandished his obligatory stack of paperwork like a machete ready to cut a swath through a field of sugarcane. Nadine was not much of an obstacle.

"What am I supposed to do?" she whined.

That question was the last thing Evens was concerned with.

"I don't care what you do. All I know is, these papers say you have to be out of here before Monday." His look of insidious anticipation was immediately wiped from his face by the voice and words he heard from behind.

"How would you know what they say?" Even if her words were missed, the slamming of Granmè's box onto one of the tables would have gotten the pair's attention. Fania stood in the doorway with Rose at her side and Wilmina hovering behind. "The donkey never strays from its crooked path."

Evens shouted, "Damn!" Nadine spoke in unison with him as he continued, groaning, "What the hell are you doing here?"

Sensing a rare benevolent presence in the house, the children, who had been sent to their rooms by Nadine when Evens arrived, appeared to ooze from the walls, drop from the ceiling, and rise from the floor. They all rushed to Fania and hung onto her like a bunch of *banane cochon* clinging to their stalk.

When she saw her mother, Marie-Fleur ran directly to her. The girl's eyes were red and a nasty welt marked her tear-streaked cheek.

Trying her best to restore order, Nadine cursed and barked and screeched at the excited throng. She threatened to use her stick and deny them meals. The kids were unimpressed. She might as well have been five kilometers out at sea for all the attention she got.

Fania spoke, not raising her voice above normal volume. "Children." With that single word, every face in the room turned toward her. "Would you please go up to your rooms for now? Rose and I will be up soon to visit with you. Everything is fine." The kids walked peacefully up the stairs in response to the one person who had earned their trust.

While this was going on, Wilmina inspected the mark on her daughter's face. Although she'd struck Marie-Fleur many times, somehow this abuse incensed her. When some quiet had descended on the room, she walked up to Nadine. "What have you done to my daughter?"

Never one to take much personal interest in the children in her care, Nadine wasn't sure who or what Wilmina was talking about. When she saw Marie-Fleur there, her irritation surfaced and she glared at the girl, who was cringing behind her mother. "She won't stop that annoying stutter. It's driving me crazy. If she'd try harder to..."

Her crass speech was cut short by a slap from Wilmina, who, besides being furious with the wretched woman, was uncomfortable with how much of herself she could see in her. It pained her to realize that, between the orphanage and their home, her daughter had no refuge except Fania and Rose.

When Nadine attempted to retaliate for her injury, her arm was stopped mid-swing by Fania. Nadine withered under her former charge's piercing glare. Fania pulled the woman close to her face and snarled, "Get. Out."

Nadine wavered between resentment and fear. She never had any credibility on her own; she was accustomed to having power behind her. Impotence was a new and uncomfortable footing. With the futility of one trying to hold back the tide, she blustered, "Who do you think you are? You can't barge in here and..."

Fania's patience, already worn thin as a mosquito's wing, dissolved entirely. She would be hesitant to admit it, but she enjoyed having the upper hand on her former bane. She spoke softly to spare Rose's fragile memories. "Unless you want me to go to the police and tell them how you kidnapped Rose, you'll go now."

Any pretense of swagger Nadine retained melted and pooled in the pit of her stomach, adding to the queasy feeling she already felt welling up within her. Speechless, she looked around the room but found no allies. Fania grabbed Evens's clipboard and pulled a pen from his shirt pocket. The pathetic man showed token resistance, but even that was shattered at a look from Fania, who was clearly in control.

"I'll do more for you than you did for me," Fania told the woman who, during the confrontation, seemed to have lost several centimeters of height and gained several years she couldn't afford. Fania scribbled a couple of lines on a piece of Evens's paper. "Here's somewhere you can go to find a job and a place to live." She tore off a shred of paper and handed it to the broken woman. Nadine stared at it blankly. As a final indignity, Fania added, "I'm sure you can find someone to read it to you."

Nadine made a move for the stairs, but Fania blocked her. "Where do you think you're going?"

"I have to get my things."

A painful image from the past, when the current roles were reversed, assaulted Fania's memory. She had to fight back a violent response. Instead she simply said, "I'll have them sent to you. You aren't going anywhere near those children. Ever."

There was a brief standoff as Nadine refused—or was unable—to move.

"Go!" Fania shouted, sending Nadine scuffling toward the exit.

Fania turned her attention to Evens who, in spite of himself, was impressed with the young woman's command of her environment. His admiration did nothing to abate Fania's exasperation. She tossed his clipboard back to him and said, "Your turn."

Sounding like a man quoting a memorized script, which in fact he was, Evens weakly began, "These papers say..." Resigned, he didn't wait for Fania to interrupt. That his speech would come to nothing was a foregone conclusion. He dropped the clipboard to his side and lamented, "What now?"

"This building legally belongs to the former owner's heir. He's temporarily in the US. When he comes back, he'll expect to take possession of his property. In the meantime we..." To Wilmina's astonishment, Fania indicated the two of them. "...will run the orphanage in his name." Even though she was improvising, the certainty in Fania's voice gave her statement a sense of ultimate authority to Evens.

Not wishing to provoke the wrath of his illegitimate superiors with news of what was doomed to be another failed swindle, he made his futile protest.

"What's that got to do with you?"

"He's my fiancé."

"What makes you think you can run a place like this?"

"Let's think about that. I've worked in an orphanage, a hospital, and a school. And I can read and write. I'd say that qualifies me more than you or any *vakabon* you work for."

"But..."

"Do you want me to write it out for you?" To close the discussion beyond question, Fania dumped the contents of Granmè's box on the nearest dining table. Through some accident of menacing grace, the knife stuck in the table and stood upright.

His defeat sealed by the unspoken threat of the Granmè's blade, Evens gathered his papers and pride and walked away, mumbling to himself, "I've got to find somewhere else to do my job."

Fania shouted after his receding steps, "Good idea. Port-au-Prince already has its share of crooks."

Wilmina had stood by during all this activity, holding Marie-Fleur's and Rose's hands. It wasn't a posture she had ever before been comfortable with, but it was beginning to feel more natural, more welcome. Still insecure, Wilmina was quick to question Fania's claim.

"Are you really engaged to the owner?"

"Not at the moment," said the woman for whom such ruses

had become effective survival techniques. Indicating the still warm trail of the bruised bureaucrat, she added, "...but he doesn't know that. The future is a bracelet whose beads are still unstrung. Who can say what will happen?"

Cynicism is a companion that is slow to release its stubborn grip. Wilmina wasn't quite ready to throw her lot in with Fania, though she was growing more intrigued by the possibilities of that bracelet. With more edge to her voice than she intended, Wilmina questioned her once more. "Are you planning to move in here?"

"We're squatters. That's what we do."

Rose released Wilmina's hand and skipped to her mother's side. "Yeah! We're squatters!" The little girl plopped herself down on the floor by Fania in what she assumed to be the fundamental squatter's attitude.

Fania and Marie-Fleur broke down in giggles. Wilmina even managed an approximation of a smile, something with which she had little experience. Maybe, she thought to herself in the midst of the satisfying scene, there will be more opportunities to practice the expression in that uncertain future.

"You're welcome to join us, Wilmina." Fania's invitation was as heartfelt as it was unexpected.

The emotions Wilmina felt upon hearing those words were were like nothing she could remember. She may have felt them as a child, but they'd long since abandoned her in favor of the bitterness, anger, and distrust she'd cherished in her soul for her entire adult life. To submit to those new feelings would take more faith than she thought she possessed. For reasons she could never name, she was ready to follow the younger woman's lead.

"What do we do now?" she asked, actually looking forward to what came next.

Fania gathered the other three close to her side, leaned them all into an intimate huddle and, looking as if she were going to whisper some secret intent, instead raised her voice and shouted, "Anything we want!"

Rose and Marie-Fleur cheered, "Yay!" and followed Fania as she tore up the stairs to where the waiting children would hear the best news in their short lives. Wilmina found herself close behind. Fania had become her new teacher and Wilmina was learning the meaning of the word "hope."

Chapter 20

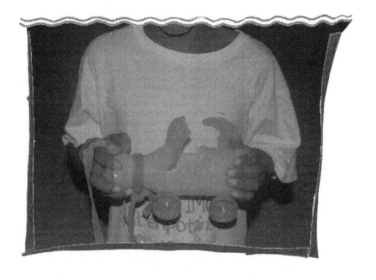

NEW YORK WAS every bit as exhilarating, exciting, and
exhausting as Simeon had hoped and feared it would be. He'd
often heard foreign visitors to Haiti comment on "the Haiti
odor", a pervasive smell they never became accustomed to. He
felt the same way about the constant din that filled the air of the
American city.

Port-au-Prince had an aural backdrop of cars revving, tires
screeching, roosters crowing, and an occasional gunshot. New
York appeared to be filled with at least one hundred times as

many cars, trucks, and motorcycles, all of which ran twenty-four hours a day based on what he heard. There was never a break of more than half an hour between the sirens that ran up and down every road.

People screamed and music played at all hours everywhere. What he took for the crack of gunfire resounded once in a while as well. The ground rumbled beneath him like a perpetual earthquake shaking the city, the tectonic plates never able to find a solid resting place. He wondered that the lofty buildings, which reached to the heavens and whose peaks were often cloaked in dark gray clouds, weren't felled by the constant tremors.

All in all, Simeon saw little difference between the two great cities. Yes, New York had more wealth and more people. As far as the humble *pwofesè* could tell, the latter were constantly consumed by the former. Everything he heard and saw revolved around the accumulation of money and goods. That the people didn't recognize this fact was to Simeon a form of short-sightedness, if not outright blindness.

Most of the people walked alone, consulting cell phones or other electronic devices. Their ears were plugged with wires and most stared at the ground at their feet as they walked. He thought of his neighborhood back in Dèlma where close-knit extended families supported one another through their difficult times and celebrated their occasional victories as a community.

Simeon reflected on his observations and came to the conclusion that poverty comes in many forms.

*   *   *

The teacher was as worn out by Americans' perceptions of his home as he was by his rigorous schedule. From their perspective, his nation ceased to be known as Haiti, becoming instead officially named, "the poorest country in the Western Hemisphere." No one appreciated the sad paradox that it was situated less than a thousand kilometers off the coast of "the wealthiest country in the Western Hemisphere."

People were also fond of repeating innuendos they'd heard but whose sources could never be identified. On learning that Simeon's late father was a minister, for example, a man told him he'd *heard* that, "Haiti is 80% Christian and 100% *vodou*." Simeon resisted the urge to comment on his own observation that the US was 80% Christian and 100% materialist. To each his own heresy, was Simeon's firmly held but unexpressed opinion.

By the end of his summer in what was considered by many to be one of the greatest cities in the world, Simeon was more than ready to go home to a city some considered among the worst.

Teaching had always been Simeon's life and calling. On his brief sabbatical to the States. he learned a great deal about his profession and for that he was grateful. He knew he would be a better, more effective teacher for the skills and knowledge he acquired. It was an invaluable experience. During his travels he heard another calling, too. A calling back to Haiti, to a young woman and her daughter.

His newly acquired American friends shared a couple of their proverbs with him, "Out of sight, out of mind," and, "Absence makes the heart grow fonder." They were complete opposites, but somehow these Americans attached equal credence to both.

Simeon learned the real truth. Fania's absence had established within him the desire to never leave her side again. The only thing "out of mind" was his former reluctance to unconditionally accept mother and daughter.

He literally counted the hours until he could see Fania and tell her all he had learned, not about his profession, but about his love for her and Rose. His fear was that she wouldn't accept him. He prayed—he had relearned his need for prayer, a need his father had driven from him—that Fania had also been able to overcome the daunting obstacles to welcoming him back into her life.

His flight landed at Toussaint Louverture Airport early enough in the morning that he knew he would have time to seek out Fania. There was little chance he would be able to sleep a single night without seeing her first.

Offering a sizable tip, he found a *tap-tap* at the airport that took him directly to the school. He carried a single soft-sided suitcase, but it was a behemoth held together by duct tape and wire. Toting his unwieldy load with him, he hurried as best he could to where Fania's home had been. It was gone and he was devastated. In its place was an expanded wall of the school. The larger building had swallowed up the house, not unlike a shark that grew tired of a remora clinging to its side, ridding itself of the pest by consuming it. Her home had been converted into a closet for school supplies.

His disappointment was no match for his determination. He would find Fania before the day was out. His search began with Basile, whom he knew was aware of everything that went on in and around the school.

Basile was excited to have his star teacher back. He dove right into his interrogation about the man's experiences in New York, hoping to confirm that the trip was worthwhile. "How was the training, Simeon?" he began.

That's where he ended, too. Simeon was on a quest that couldn't be delayed. He genuinely respected the headmaster, so it pained him to speak to him so brusquely. "That can wait. What happened to Fania?"

"The squatter?" Basile had no idea of his involvement with the girl.

"Fania. Where is she?"

"I don't know. Did you know her?" The headmaster's words washed Simeon's hopes away as a rainstorm washes masses of Haitian mountainside into the ocean. People in Haiti disappeared for any number of reasons, but if Fania was still alive, he would find her. He meant to do it without another day passing.

* * *

On a hunch, Simeon went to see Henri at the La Saline church. He knew Fania frequently went to the kindhearted pastor for advice and counsel when she faced trials. Certainly, losing her home would have been a reason to seek such help.

For some reason, Simeon had to overcome an invisible barrier to enter the little church. When he finally edged tentatively in, he found Henri repairing a bench that had shattered during one of the more raucous songs in the previous Sunday's service. Watching him perform such a humble task, Simeon wondered how it could be that this gentle man and Simeon's own father could serve the same God. In truth, they didn't. When Eli died, his god died with him. Simeon could see Henri's was still very much alive.

"Ah, Simeon. Nice to meet you at last. Fania has told me so much about you." The two shook hands, their shared affection for the Dieusel family making them feel like old friends.

"Have you seen her?"

"Yes. She moved out of La Saline, but she and Rose still come here for church occasionally."

Henri's words brought fresh hope to Simeon's heart and search.

"Where did she move?"

"She's in Cité Militaire, living at the old Victory Orphanage, but now it's..."

"That can't be!" The hope Simeon had felt turned to a shock that was visible in his traumatized expression and quivering limbs. "Are you sure?" he added.

"*Men wi*, I've visited her there myself. She's been doing a tremendous... Wait!"

Simeon was already gone, engrossed in his own bewilderment and walking away, muttering to himself, "Why there? Of all the places?" Henri heard no more as the teacher's voice trailed off down the road along with him.

Anyone who saw the teacher scurrying up Rue Paul Morale, by all appearances arguing with himself, oblivious to the people and vehicles with which he nearly collided, might have considered him deranged. They would not have been far off.

The developments that had taken place in Simeon's absence confounded him to the point where he questioned his own sanity. There was no way he could imagine Fania living at the orphanage where she had been raped by his father. All the assumptions, expectations, and strategies he had contemplated while away had been upended. Part of him hoped he wouldn't find her in that godforsaken place. The rest of him wanted her more than life itself, under any circumstances.

Walking down the alley toward the orphanage, his pace bogged down as if he were fighting the ocean tide. Waves of apprehension slowed his approach and eventually stopped him short of entering the yard where a band of about a dozen children romped inside the open gate. He leaned against the wall, fighting a losing battle with his anxiety.

He peeked into the yard. Something was different. In fact, the entire area felt unlike anything Simeon remembered from his last view of the place, when he surveyed his late father's estate days before traveling to New York. He'd intended to dispose of it all at the first opportunity. He wanted no vestige of the man's depravity to taint his life or his memory.

Yet this wasn't the old Victory Orphanage. Even the air tasted sweeter to him, less like the stench of the slums. It reminded Simeon of the fresh clean air he had once inhaled during a trip through the mountains on the way to Kenscoff. It was a resurrected space. On the wall behind him, a new name had been painted: *Lakay Lespwa*, House of Hope. The name summed up Simeon's sentiments, so much so that he made up his mind to take what was for him a heroic step through the gate.

As he was about to do so, a van careened down the alley and through the gate, missing Simeon by mere centimeters. He drew back behind the wall, heart pounding from his near miss with the wayward vehicle. He recovered in time to see Ben, the *tap-tap* driver from Fania's days at the orphanage, bring the vehicle to a skidding halt before the building's main entrance. Gone was his decaying tap-tap, in its place a smart new van whose horn, which he sounded every chance he got, played a few notes from *La Dessalinienne*, the Haitian national anthem.

At the call of that patriotic horn, Ben bounded out of the van. Fania, wearing her apron from her job in the school kitchen, stepped from the building to meet him. She had a baby settled on her hip and Rose at her side. Ben called to them, "Your limousine awaits, my beauties!"

As Simeon continued his snooping, the young man bowed

and kissed Fania's hand then hugged Rose and the baby. It was at that moment, when panic darkened Simeon's eyes as he watched Ben fawn over Fania, Rose caught a glimpse of Simeon skulking around the corner of the wall. Caught in the act, the teacher once more fell back against the wall with a sigh as heavy as the gate he dreaded passing.

"Pwofesè!" the little girl squealed, too naive to appreciate Simeon's ambivalence about being discovered. She rushed to the gate and peeked around it. Seeing the man cringing against the wall, she thought he was drawing her into a game. "Are you playing hide-and-seek?"

Rose had seen right through Simeon.

"I think I am," he replied truthfully.

"Well, I found you!" was her victorious cry.

He suddenly identified with the deception Fania had maintained over him for so many months. Now he, too, coveted his seclusion. Rose proved as irresistible as cool shade during a long, hot Haitian summer. She tugged on his hand and dragged him into the compound. Simeon didn't try to fight her efforts.

When they reached the entrance, Rose informed him, "We missed you..." Then, turning to Fania, she asked, "...didn't we, *Manman*?"

"It's true," Fania confirmed. The baby she carried appeared to offer a wiggle of agreement as its feet and hands thrust repeatedly out.

"How do... Who is... What did you... Why are you here?" Something about Fania often turned the well-educated Creole teacher into an stammering imbecile.

"We're watching the place for you." Fania spoke as articulately as Simeon was unable to.

"For me?"

"It's your inheritance, isn't it?"

Ben watched all these pleasantries with a wary eye. "Do you need any help with this guy, Fania?" The young man still felt a certain protective attachment to Fania.

"I think I can handle him. The girls will be out for you soon."

"Your words are sweeter than sugarcane to me." His ardor for the ladies hadn't waned; it had cast a wider net. Several young women burst out of the house, racing for Ben's van. Unlike Fania's former stance, these ladies showed no resistance to Ben's charms. They fought for the right to share the front bench with the driver.

Fania called after the group, "Enjoy class, ladies. Be good, Ben."

Simeon searched his brain for any question he could ask that might give him the faintest clue as to what was going on around him, but his thought process was interrupted when Wilmina stepped out of the building. She smiled at Simeon then turned to Fania.

"Do you have the key to the sewing closet?"

"*Wi*," Fania replied as she reached into a pocket in her apron while keeping the infant firmly in hand. She pulled out a ring of keys that appeared to be the size of a *tap-tap* wheel. She handed the whole set to Wilmina. "Do you mind finding it? I'm out of hands."

"*Pa gen pwoblem*," Wilmina said with a smile as she took the keys and ducked back into the building.

Mystery upon mystery. Simeon had heard about Wilmina, her infamous hostility, and her clashes with Fania. He was astonished to see her there at all, never mind seeing the two of them working together so amiably. It only added to his total disorientation. The world he'd left to visit the US had since been replaced by a new one that was, in its own way, more foreign to him than America had been.

Fania saw Simeon's bewilderment and assumed he was merely put off by her distraction.

"Sorry. This is a busy time for me."

Rose had a better understanding of the man's confusion. Beaming, she added, "*Manman* is the Boss Man."

She and Fania shared a laugh before the girl ran into the yard to join the other kids playing there. Fania remained with Simeon gawking at her. He juggled so many questions in his mind, he had no idea where to begin. He reacted first to Rose's proclamation of Fania's authority, which confirmed his own observations.

"You run the orphanage?"

Fania appeared slightly embarrassed; a look Simeon found appealing.

"Yes, but it's not an orphanage anymore. It never was. Most of the children who lived here had parents who simply couldn't afford to care for them. We made a few changes while you were away." Here she paused to gauge his reaction. There was none because he was too overwhelmed to know how to react. She continued, "I hope you don't mind."

"Mind? Oh, no. I didn't see myself in the orphanage business anyway."

"Good, because we're a day care facility and job training center now. The mothers bring their children here during the day, but they all live at their own homes. We still care for a few orphans like little Sonson here." She gave the infant in her arms a squeeze. In return, he drooled down her arm. She didn't notice and Simeon didn't think it lessened her allure.

"He's not yours?" Simeon didn't have the presence of mind to consider the plausibility of the scenario his question suggested.

Fania choked then laughed. "I haven't been *that* busy."

That loose end tied up, Simeon wanted to talk to Fania to settle the rest. Yes, he had questions about how the current state of affairs came to be, but more, he needed to know his place in her new life. Watching her in complete control of her surroundings, confident and independent, he felt inadequate and redundant, like an extra leg on a goat. The apparently romantic overtures from Ben didn't give him reason to be optimistic and Fania, enigmatic as ever, wasn't giving him any cues. The man was sweating through his white shirt, but it had nothing to do with the heat.

Before Simeon could seek any more information from

Fania, they were interrupted by a bundle of male energy in the form of a boy named André. Chased by another boy, he came to Fania holding a small toy in his grimy hand. It was a toy car he'd made out of trash he'd found in the alley. The body was an empty plastic bottle and its wheels were four bottle caps stuck on two axles made from straws. Before Fania had a chance to ask for an explanation, the other boy tried to grab it from André's hand. The crude toy was knocked to the ground, one of its wheels broken off in the attempted heist.

After listening to the two boys bicker, Fania handed the baby to a further bewildered Simeon, leaned over, picked up the car, swiftly repaired it, and took the baby back. Holding the toy above the boys' clutching hands, she told them to take turns playing with it. The rule they were to follow was: Each time they heard a car horn beep—a sound that was like clockwork in the neighborhood—they were to swap custody of the little car. If they continued to quarrel, she would take it away and let Simeon have it.

Neither went away completely satisfied, but a serious brawl was avoided. For his part, Simeon was embarrassed to have been dragged into the conflict but he was no less impressed by Fania's mediation skills. He'd thought his devotion couldn't become more intense, but the woman kept enticing him further with each act.

Alone with Fania again, Simeon once more tried to initiate a conversation he hoped would bring him some satisfaction. Once more, he was prevented. A clanging chime sounding from within the house drew every child in the yard toward them. Fania and Simeon were nearly trampled by hungry children dashing for the entrance in response to the lunch bell.

The man's frustration was beginning to undo him. He finally blurted out, "Can we talk alone somewhere?"

"*Dakò*. Melande is serving lunch so I won't be needed for a while. What were you thinking?"

"In my rush to find you, I left my bag back at the school. If you'd walk there with me, along the way you can tell me what I've missed." Simeon tried to disguise his desperation but it shook his voice just the same.

Fania agreed to go with him, something he considered a small victory. She called to Wilmina to take Sonson into the house for his nap. Relieved of her responsibility, Fania walked off with Simeon.

The couple strolled unhurriedly along the pockmarked streets of Cité Militaire for a couple of blocks in complete silence, neither ready to commit to the truth. Fania tried to sway the conversation toward a safe topic.

"How was your trip?"

Simeon was unable to respond. His head was spinning at what he could only imagine was a delusion. Try as he did to conceive of a series of events that would bring about the world he found himself in, he failed. Struggling to find words to introduce the subject, all he could stammer out was, "What - what happened?"

"What do you mean?"

The man finally allowed his frustration free rein. It was all he could do to keep from shouting. "I mean, what on earth happened here while I was away? Everything is backward and upside down. I've completely lost my bearings! Where am I? Who are you?"

Fania let out a sympathetic chuckle. "I suppose this isn't what you expected on your return. Believe me, I'm as surprised as you are."

With that introduction, she went on to bring him up to date on all that he'd missed. Consistent with her vivid storytelling skills, she brought each episode from the summer to life for her rapt listener. She reveled in reliving her invasion of the orphanage, but telling about her ride with Renaud sent the same crawling feeling over her skin. Simeon felt her pride as she talked of her work at the hospital and the second victorious ruse she pulled on Evens. More poignant, Rose's brush with death brought fresh tears to her eyes.

Simeon listened attentively, but was often grieved by the suffering the two endured in his absence. He wished he could have been with them, helping, comforting, and loving them in their need.

"I should never have left," he told her, more to console himself than her.

"You did what you had to do. Don't regret. Rose and I had to go through these things as a family. All that has happened has worked together for the best. I wouldn't change a thing."

In a nation known for its resilient populace, Simeon decided Fania must be the strongest of them all.

Cars, trucks, and *tap-taps* whizzed by the couple as they conferred on their way. Other than an occasional exchange of greetings with a passerby, they might as well have been walking along an abandoned beach isolated from all humanity, they talked with such intimacy. In spite of the range of topics they discussed, Simeon never got around to the question that was beating on the walls of his heart like a prisoner seeking his first taste of freedom.

Upon reaching the schoolyard, the couple found themselves in the midst of an uproar of activity as everyone, from teachers to construction workers, scrambled to get ready for the new school year, scheduled to commence the following week. Rising above all the other racket, they heard the sounds of war coming from the kitchen. Curious, they peeked inside the room. They watched as Marta ranted in the direction of a worker who was obscured from their view.

"I don't care how you did things in your last job. This is my kitchen and you'll follow my instructions!" She bellowed at the unseen unfortunate. Emphasizing her directive with a swing of the ever-present ladle, she concluded, "If you don't like it, you're welcome to go back to your last job, if they'll have you."

Fania and Simeon craned their necks to catch sight of Marta's nemesis. It was Nadine who was matching Marta taunt for taunt and gripe for gripe. "I'm surprised you get anything done, then. I've never seen such a badly run place in my life. I've got a good mind to walk out and leave you on your own." Not to be outdone, she beat on an old pot to make her point.

"Fine!" Marta shrieked turning her back on Nadine.

"Fine!" retorted Nadine turning her back on Marta.

Simeon and Fania fled the field of battle before they burst out laughing.

"Whose idea was it to put those two hens in the same ring?" Simeon wanted to know.

Fania was silent but wore a mischievous grin. Simeon gave her a playful shove, prompting her to admit, "They were made for each other, don't you think?"

They left the kitchen warriors and went directly to Basile's office, the last known location of Simeon's luggage. The headmaster was frantically preparing for the start of school. As usual, papers were everywhere.

Basile glimpsed up at Simeon, too engrossed to formally greet him. "If you want your bag, I put it in the new supply closet in your old classroom." He returned to his paperwork morass without another glance or word.

Fania effectively captured his attention with her brash response, "You mean, my home?"

At that, Basile looked up and truly saw them for the first time. He'd never seen his teacher and the squatter side by side, but they seemed to belong together, no less than a bougainvillea plant and its blossoms. He said nothing, but smiled slightly and dipped his head in her direction.

*   *   *

Standing there in Simeon's classroom, Fania's recollections of her stealthy education came rushing back to her mind, blocking out the present. It felt to her to have been ages ago, though it was a matter of months. All was not as it was, however. In the wall where she'd once carved a slim gap, a hefty steel door stood. Looking at it, she wondered how long it would have taken to pierce that barrier with Granmè's blade.

As Basile had promised, the baggage was stowed behind that door. Fania followed Simeon into the cramped closet. As she looked around, it was difficult for her to believe she had raised Rose in such a small space, even sharing it most of that time with Granmè. Yet she wouldn't have changed anything about the experience. She turned to share her sentiments with Simeon and found him staring at her.

"How did you do it?" he asked from his trance.

"Do what?" Fania was honestly baffled by his question and tone.

"Everything. Anything. How were you able to get over your..." He stumbled searching for words that wouldn't prompt painful memories. "Over your history at that place?"

Fania's shy smile reminded Simeon of the gorgeous, silent woman in the cafeteria line, before what he now viewed as her transformation. Or was he the transformed one?

"I have some experience at breaking through walls," she said with a light tap on the door.

"It takes more than a knife to get through some walls."

"You'd be surprised what can be accomplished with a two-edged blade of love and necessity. Besides, I was never alone."

"I came back with every intention of finding you and asking for your forgiveness for running off as I did. It was pure fear, but there was nothing to be afraid of, was there? While I was away I realized that."

The compassion in Fania's face comforted the grieving man. "Don't think about it. Fear is something I understand. I've had my share."

Head shaking, not looking at her, Simeon whispered, "I intended to ask you to marry me, but you don't need me."

"You're right, I don't need you."

Her response cut deeper into his heart than Granmè's knife ever could have. That wound healed instantly when she took his hand in hers.

"There was a time when I did and you were there for me. *Mèsi.*"

She made her gratitude more tangible by pulling the unprepared man to herself and kissing him in a way that belied her lack of experience. It took several seconds after the embrace for Simeon's senses to recover to the point where he could speak.

"You're still a mystery to me."

"Maybe it's time I sent you to school, *pwofesè.*"

Epilogue

FANIA MARRIED SIMEON on Sunday, January 10, 2016, two days before the sixth anniversary of the earthquake that changed Fania's life forever. In all her trials since that painful day, she sometimes dared to believe she could one day have a tolerable life. She could never have imagined the life of contentment and joy that was being celebrated on this day.

The wedding, officiated by Pastor Henri, took place in a magnificent church in Pétionville, one whose towering walls had somehow survived the quake. Its cavernous sanctuary was topped by countless sheets of corrugated steel, each of which resembled the one that had for a while been the roof of Fania's home.

By this time, Fania had become a favorite to all she came in contact with. Whoever she didn't know, Simeon or Rose did. As a result, it seemed that anyone who had ever been connected to the school or the orphanage was at the wedding.

Forty girls, ages six through ten, dressed in sparkling white dresses and brilliant red shoes preceded the wedding party down the center aisle. Leading them all was four-year-old Rose, beaming with a smile that outshone the sun that day.

It could have been her imagination, but Fania thought such angelic music had never been heard in all the world as was sung by the congregation that day. She didn't notice the photographers and well-wishers who wandered haphazardly around her and Simeon as they spoke their vows.

Her regrets were few. Certainly she wished her parents were rejoicing with her. She also ached to have Granmè there. More than anyone besides her parents, Granmè was the person most responsible for the woman Fania had become and the good fortune that had come her way. In that all three of them were part of who she was, Fania felt their presence.

During the entire service, Fania's eyes were locked on Simeon's, but they also looked into the future, a future that took the form of two divergent roads.

One road was dark, bleak, and frightening. It was overgrown with despair as menacing as the thorn bushes that choked the alleyways of La Saline and it was paved by inertia, envy, and self-interest. She looked away.

Down the other road, she saw a Haiti that never again had the need for "mud pies." No children gnawed on stalks of sugarcane for their meals. There were no organizations from America or anywhere else starting schools or feeding people. The Haitians fed their own and had enough remaining to export to other countries because their agricultural industry was no longer flooded with subsidized foreign food.

The people living there loved and supported one another. They rejoiced in one another's successes and helped in their suffering. Where once were hillsides stripped of vegetation, replanted forests grew lush down the sides of the mountains, meeting the sea along an unspoiled shoreline.

There were no orphanages along that road, and no vicious criminals terrorizing women. She saw no vast territories covered with tents stretching to the horizon. Instead, there were humble homes of wood or concrete, close by one another but with sufficient room for children to play freely and safely.

The light on that road was bright as the sun and clear as the Caribbean waters. It was lit with hope and built on a solid foundation of faith and peace.

Fania knew that road could be created and she would do everything in her power to make it a reality. She would travel the road with Simeon and Rose at her side for as long as she had breath within her.

Photographs

Chapter 1: A view of Massif de la Selle from a Cité Militaire rooftop

Chapter 2: One of the more conservative *tap-taps* sits waiting to be loaded

Chapter 3: Makeshift tent city built after the earthquake along a major road in Port-au-Prince

Chapter 4: USAID tarp tent home next to crumbled building

Chapter 5: Sunset from a road over Massif de la Selle

Chapter 6: Mud pies drying in La Saline

Chapter 7: Construction workers passing freshly mixed cement up a ladder

Chapter 8: Haitian cemetery

Chapter 9: School cafeteria in Village Solidarité

Chapter 10: Preschoolers waiting to be dismissed

Chapter 11: Students study illustrated history of Haitian revolution

Chapter 12: A typical classroom in a Village Solidarité school

Chapter 13: Boy fishing off a pier at President's Beach, northwest of Port-au-Prince

Chapter 14: US supplied and subsidized rice waiting to be used in Haiti

Photograph Credits:
All others: Rick Conti

Glossary

Creole words

ale – go

banane cochon – small bananas

blan – white person or foreigners in general (literally, white)

bonbon – candy

Bondye – God

Bondye beni-w – God bless you

bonjou – hello, good day (used before noon)

bonswa – hello, good afternoon/evening

boulanjri – bakery

cheri – term of endearment: dear

dakò – okay

doktè – doctor

futbol – football (i.e. American soccer)

gourde – unit of Haitian currency worth about 2.5 cents American

granmè – grandmother

gwo – big

gwo sè – big sister

houngan – a *vodou* priest

kompa – national music genre of Haiti, also heard in other areas of the Caribbean, similar to méringue

Krik? Krak! – traditional way to introduce a storytelling session: leader says "*Krik*?", if listeners want a story, they reply "*Krak*!"

Glossary

La Dessalinienne – the Haitian national anthem – literally, The Dessalines Song, named for Jean-Jacques Dessalines, the first ruler of the independent nation

lakay – house or home

lekòl – school

lespwa – hope

loa – demons and gods of Haitian *vodou*

lòt bò dlo – literally, "the other side of the water"; often refers to Africa, but can refer to any land overseas or, metaphorically, a place where people go after death

lougawou – in *vodou* mythology, a werewolf

Madanm – ma'am, lady, wife

madmwazèl – miss (to address a young unmarried woman)

mambo – *vodou* priestess

manman – mother

men wi – of course (literally, but yes)

mèsi (anpil) – thank you (very much)

mèsi Jezi – thank you, Jesus

ovwa – goodbye

pa gen pwoblem – no problem

pwofesè – professor, teacher

souple – please

tap-tap – ubiquitous taxis in Port-au-Prince; usually a pickup truck with a colorfully decorated cap

ti – little

ti flè-m – my little flower

ti manman – little mother

Glossary

ti moun – child (literally, little person)

ti sè – little sister

tonton macoutes – literally, "uncle knapsack"; from *vodou* mythology, a character who stole away and punished disobedient children; the Duvaliers (q.v.) used the name for their vicious paramilitary force, which openly practiced human rights abuses to suppress political opposition

vakabon – villain, scoundrel

vodou – often spelled "voodoo", primitive religion of Haiti, based on African ancestral practices

wi – yes

zonbi – zombie, in *vodou* lore, a corpse raised from the dead to do the will of the one who raised him

Glossary

Places

Baie de Port-au-Prince – bay on which Haiti's capital sits

Boulevard Jean-Jacques Dessalines – main road through Port-au-Prince

Citadelle Laferrière – massive fortress in Cap-Haïtien built by Henri Christophe in 1820 to defend against possible French attacks

Cité Militaire – neighborhood in Port-au-Prince, adjacent to Village Solidarité

Cité Soleil – poorest, most dangerous slum in Port-au-Prince

Croix-des-Bouquets – suburb about 13 kilometers northeast of Port-au-Prince, location of metalworking community

Dèlma – street leading from downtown Port-au-Prince to more affluent community of Pétionville; neighborhoods are identified by numerical crossing roads, e.g. Dèlma 31

Fort Dimanche – a building in La Saline once used as a prison and torture chamber during the Duvalier (q.v.) dictatorships, now abandoned and serving as home for some families

Gonaïves – a coastal city in northern Haiti that has been battered by storms and flooding over the years

Île de la Gonâve – large island in the gulf of Haiti

Jacmel – formerly popular tourist city on Haiti's south coast, home to craftsmen and huge *Kanaval* (Carnival) celebration

Kenscoff – city located high in the mountains south of Port-au-Prince

La Saline – slum neighborhood on the harbor in Port-au-Prince

Glossary

Latòti – Tortuga; island off northern coast of Haiti, famed as a pirate haven

Mache Fè – Iron Market, a large open air marketplace filled with individual vendors; structure was completely rebuilt after it was destroyed in the 2010 earthquake

Massif de la Selle – the mountain range south of Port-au-Prince (literally, mountains of the south)

Pétionville – a relatively upscale community adjacent to Port-au-Prince

Port-au-Prince – capital city of Haiti with a population of about two million, situated on the west coast, in the crook of Haiti's two "arms"

Rue Paul Morale – road leading from La Saline to Cité Militaire

Toussaint Louverture Airport – the main international airport of Haiti, named after a hero of the Haitian revolution (q.v.)

Village Solidarité – neighborhood in Port-au-Prince

Glossary

Names

François "Papa Doc" Duvalier – self-proclaimed president for life, tyrant who ruled Haiti from 1957-1971

Jean-Claude "Baby Doc" Duvalier – son of François, ruled as president of Haiti from 1971-1986 in the same ruthless manner as his father

Jezi – Jesus

Michel Martelly – president elected in 2011

Ogun – Vodou warrior loa (aka Ogoun or Ogou)

Ti Malice – trickster loa from Haitian *vodou* mythology

Titid – nickname for former Haitian president Jean-Bertrand Aristide

Toussaint Louverture – Haitian revolutionary general and hero

Brand names

Barbancourt – brand of rum

Digicel – Haitian cell phone company

Prestige – Haitian beer brand

Sogebank – a Haitian bank

Disclaimer

This is a *blan* book about Haiti. Although I've spent significant time there, talked to many Haitians, and read everything I can about the nation, its history, and its current events, I'm still just a visitor from the US. I can't provide the perspective of a native Haitian. For that, I commend to your attention the brilliant writer, Edwidge Danticat. I hope, however, that I've given you some small insight into that beautiful yet all too often tragic and slippery land.

I've done my best not to misrepresent anything in Fania's world. If I've failed in even the slightest detail, I ask your and Haiti's forgiveness.

Acknowledgments

This book was truly a labor of love. That's far from an original sentiment, but to know the truth of it is enlivening like little else. My love for the nation of Haiti and its people inspired it, the love of my family made it possible, and the love of God gives it meaning. Fania, Rose, Simeon, and Granmè are more real to me than many people I know. They have a home in my heart forever.

My Haitian friends are a constant inspiration to me, not only in fiction, but in life. Their persistence, resilience, and good cheer in the face of unrelenting difficulties humbles and challenges me. While there are too many to name individually, let me thank a few by name.

Thank you Guito Jean for your friendship and prayers.

Thank you Monite Metelus-Louis for all you do to create opportunities for Haitian women like Fania.

Thank you Pastor Rigaud Antoine for your hospitality while I've stayed at your home, visited your orphanage, and worked at your school. This book would not be possible without those experiences. (I want to make it abundantly clear that Pastor Rigaud is in *no way* an inspiration for Pastor Eli and no negative representation of people or places in this book is intended as a reflection on Rigaud's church or orphanage. The inspiration found there was *entirely positive*.)

Some of the Haitian proverbs used in this novel were drawn from Wally Turnbull's excellent book, "Hidden Meanings", and used with his permission.

Although writing is a lonely business, a finished work involves a community. Thank you to my first readers: Laurie Barker, Andrew Davenport, Nancy Feehrer, Laurae Richards, and Linda Sheeks. Their feedback and encouragement were a large part of any good found on the pages today. The flaws are mine alone.

I'm indebted to my friend and fellow writer, Bruce Fottler, who guided me through the independent publishing maze.

Thank you Kate at Cafe 12 and Candy at the Java Room for providing wonderful and welcoming environments for writing.

My *extreme* gratitude goes to Taylor Dueker for sharing his extraordinary talent in designing the cover and inside graphics. Visit his web site to learn more about his work and services: http://www.taylordueker.com/. More than that, my thanks to him for his long time and long distance friendship. "...there is a friend who sticks closer than a brother."

To paraphrase the old philosophical question: If a story is told and no one hears it... The question needn't be asked because *you* have read the story. If you're more aware of Haiti, if you feel more compassion for its people, and have more understanding of their plight, the story has truly been heard. Thank you, dear reader, for participating in Fania's story. Now it's yours, too.

What writer, indeed what person, can accomplish anything of value without the love and support of family? Thank you Josh and Molly, Leah and Adam, and Emmaline for adding so much to my life. Although they have no idea what's going on, life is sweeter since the birth of my adorable grandchildren, Malachi and Jenna.

There is no way to sufficiently express my appreciation to the most important person in my life, but I'll try. Jane is the love of my life, my best friend, my favorite and most honest critic, and my life's greatest blessing. MFEO.

Soli Deo Gloria.

About the Author

Rick Conti has written a dozen screenplays, a hundred or so sketches and short plays, and a handful of short stories. This is his first novel.

After barely surviving a career in software, a field populated by latent artists of all stripes, a series of misadventures and one tyrannical employer inadvertently gave him the chance to try his hand at writing full time. He's grateful for the opportunity.

Rick's love for Haiti began on a 10-day mission trip there in 2000. Suffering from a classic case of "reverse homesickness", he has returned several times. For eight years, he served as Director of Communications for a nonprofit that helps Haitian women like Fania create and maintain their own businesses.

Rick lives in Massachusetts with his wife and hundreds of photos of his children and grandchildren.

For more of his writing, visit his blog at http://www.rickconti.me

God bless Haiti.

Made in the USA
Middletown, DE
01 March 2016